Praise for

'Immensely gripping, ⸝ _____, thoughtful and very satisfying'

— SOPHIE HANNAH, NEW YORK TIMES
BESTSELLER, ON *BLOOD LIBEL*

'Lynes knows his history and tells the story with verve'

— HISTORICAL NOVEL SOCIETY

'I'm looking forward to reading the next Isaac Alvarez Mystery'

— VH MASTERS, AUTHOR OF *THE
CASTILIANS*

'Written with cinematic flair. The terror, danger, and suspicious atmosphere prevalent at the time is palpable'

— 5* AMAZON READER REVIEW

First published by Romaunce Books in 2023

Suite 2, Top Floor, 7 Dyer Street, Cirencester, Gloucestershire, GL7 2PF

Blood Libel
Paperback ISBN 978-1-7391173-9-9

Printed and bound in Great Britain

Blood Libel

1495 Seville, Andalusia.

As the Inquisition closes in can Isaac protect both his family and his faith?

The Inquisition is determined to execute heretics like Isaac - those who practice Judaism in secret. Friends and family are arrested and set against each other. Isaac's best friend is accused of heresy and he is forced to choose between him and his own family. King Ferdinand offers to help him - can Isaac trust him? As the mystery unravels what secrets will Isaac uncover about himself, his friends and his family?

Can Isaac discover the real killer and disprove the 'blood libel'?

If you enjoy reading Blood Libel please leave a review: Amazon UK or Amazon US

You can download a free short story and find out more about the Isaac Alvarez mysteries at www. michaellynes.com.

Michael Lynes

An Isaac Alvarez Mystery

the Heretic's daughter

✦ ✦ ✦

Can Isabel prevent her father from destroying their family?

THE HERETIC'S DAUGHTER

The second enthralling Isaac Alvarez Mystery.

Seville, 1498. As the Inquisition's grip tightens Isaac and Isabel must choose between family and faith. Will they survive the consequences?

Isaac seeks revenge on Torquemada for murdering his wife and best friend. He's not the only one who wants The Grand Inquisitor dead. The King commands Isaac to investigate. Should he save the man he hates? Fail and he loses the King's protection — the only thing keeping him alive. Feeling abandoned by her father and conflicted by his heresy, Isabel sets out to discover the truth. The trail leads to the darkest places in Seville. She's unnerved by a shocking revelation and a surprising discovery about her real feelings. **Can Isabel use what she unearths to save her father and their family?**

Discover what happens next:

Amazon US Amazon UK

BLOOD LIBEL

Michael Lynes

To Roger
Best wishes

Michael Lynes
Dubai, 2023

For Sadaf

Every heresy that rises against the holy, orthodox and Catholic faith we excommunicate and anathematize. All heretics we condemn under whatever names they may be known.

Third Canon of The Fourth Lateran Council of the Catholic Church, 1215

Iberian Peninsula at the end of the 15th Century

FRANCE

ASTORIAS
Bilbao
NAVARRE
Pamplona
ROUSILLION

GALICIA
León
Burgos
OLD CASTILE
Saragossa
CATALONIA
Barcelona

LEÓN
Valladolid
KINGDOM
ARAGON

Segovia
Ávila
Madrid
OF
TOLEDO

PORTUGAL
Toledo
CASTILE
VALENCIA
Valencia
MAJORCA

Lisbon

ANDALUSIA
JAEN
MURCIA

CÓRDOBA
Córdoba
Murcia
MEDITERRANEAN

SEVILLE
Seville
GRANADA
Granada
Almeria

Malaga
Cádiz
GIBRALTAR

ATLANTIC
OCEAN
Tarifa
Tangier
Ceuta

NORTH AFRICA

N

100 mls

Rabat
Fez

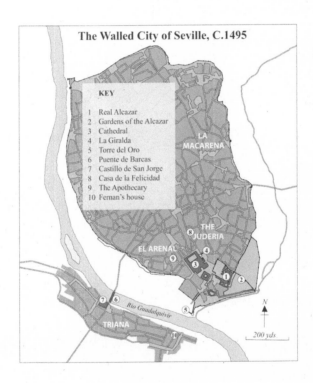

The Walled City of Seville, C.1495

KEY

1   Real Alcazar
2   Gardens of the Alcazar
3   Cathedral
4   La Giralda
5   Torre del Oro
6   Puente de Barcas
7   Castillo de San Jorge
8   Casa de la Felicidad
9   The Apothecary
10 Fernan's house

LA MACARENA

THE JUDERIA

EL ARENAL

TRIANA

Río Guadalquivir

N

200 yds

PROLOGUE
THE TESTIMONY OF FRIAR ALONSO

S eville, Torre del Oro, April 1495

DEEP in the heart of the night and I am alone in my cell. Sleep will not grace me with its balm. A single candle sputters, its light flickering across this parchment where I transcribe the secrets I dare not share with anyone, except you. I began this testimony two months ago having no one to confide in. The confession stall is far too dangerous. I must finish this entry before Lauds; it might be my last. I'll discover the verdict of my earthly masters in a few hours. Then I may not have much longer to wait for the heavenly father's judgment.

If this testimony is discovered whilst I live, I will burn on the cross. Once I depart this benighted world, I hope my testimony *is* found and that whoever reads it will not judge me harshly. Some might deem my actions sins. I fervently believe they were justified to further the faith. If absolution

1

is not granted me in this life it will come in the hereafter; from the Almighty or from the readers of this account. Perhaps from both Him and you.

Is there one of the seven cardinal sins I have not committed? Pride, greed and envy, surely - but gluttony, anger and sloth are not weaknesses of mine. A tendency to self-pity is. It might not be a sin, but perhaps it should be. To even think that is to put words into God's mouth. Another sin.

I have not spared myself in this account. I hope it will be viewed as an honest counterweight to the version of the story I fear will be propagated by those with most to lose from the real truth.

I look up at the only adornment on these walls and wonder whether Jesus on the cross looking down upon me forgives my thoughts, let alone my actions. I will get down on my knees and pray on my threadbare mat that he does. And that the Lord will guide me through whatever is to befall me when the sun rises.

BOOK 1

Two months earlier

February, 1495

CHAPTER
ONE

S *eville*

Isaac Camarino Alvarez stands alone in Bar Averno, thrumming the fingers of his right hand impatiently on the oak counter. At last, the barmaid brings salty rye bread, thinly sliced ham and the *mojama*, glistening in olive oil. He pushes the plate of ham to one side and places a slab of the salty tuna atop a hunk of the bread. His mouth full, he grunts at the barmaid as she returns with a glass of sherry. Hunger appeased, he is now relaxed enough to take in his surroundings.

Bar Averno is not somewhere you would find prostitutes and scoundrels; it is not in Triana after all. It is usually frequented by people who Isaac thinks of as similar to himself: intelligent, professional, interested in the day's politics. The dark wood, dim lighting and low ceilings allow

Isaac to keep to himself whilst eavesdropping. This is how he keeps up with what is going on *in* Seville, rather than far away in the Indies. Sugar contracts occupy far too much of his day at the Real Alcazar.

A tall man sits in the corner beneath the only window. A jagged scar disfigures the right side of his face. Isaac knows one of the two men he is sitting with: Cristobal Arias, night watchman at the cathedral, having a drink before he starts his shift. An oaf. Isaac ignores the suspicious looks they cast in his direction. Concentrating on his food, he listens discreetly to their conversation.

'Say what you like about them, they were damn good at what they knew,' states the large man sitting in the middle of the three. His companions grunt their agreement.

'I suppose the Jews were good people for the most part,' Cristobal Arias says, perhaps waiting for his companions to disagree. 'Aside from being Christ killers that is!' He bellows with laughter.

'Old Queen Isabella done the right thing getting rid of them three years ago. What do we need their like now for, anyway? Good accounters of money and such, but with good old Cristoforo Colombo bringing back those treasures from the Indies we shall all be rich,' says the large man.

Cristobal and the tall man bang their tankards on the table. 'Another round, another round,' they chorus.

Isaac cannot help but stare. As Jews by birth he, and Maria, were baptised as Catholics a year after their marriage. They did so before the growing violence against the Jews resulted in their expulsion from Spain. The men are too busy congratulating each other on their wit to notice Isaac's disapproval. He absent-mindedly strokes his greying, unkempt beard. Challenging their bigotry would be futile and as a *converso*, outright dangerous. Principles could get you killed.

HE SHOULD BE GOING HOME, back to Casa de la Felicidad. Maria will probably not have noticed that he is a little later than usual. She will be too busy overseeing the preparation of something delicious for dinner – he hopes for lamb, even though it causes him indigestion – whilst Isabel and Gabriel read or study. Of this he has more doubt.

The children are much on his mind. Isabel is fifteen and becoming more distant and difficult. Maria insists that Isabel acquire knowledge of the world. But what of her chances of finding a good match? A prospective bride should acquire a deep knowledge of household economy if she is to complete a successful union. Isabel does not spend enough time on domestic matters. Gabriel's chief assets are typical of any eleven-year-old boy: boundless energy and finely-honed selective hearing. What occupation will those attributes prepare him for? A royal courtier? He might have a word with King Ferdinand on the matter. They are, after all, connected by family history.

The conversation of the men has become more raucous, jarring Isaac out of his reverie. He finishes the sherry and slams coins down on the bar with such force that all three turn their heads in unison. He returns their stares and leaves.

Stumbling out onto the *calle*, feeling unsteady – Am I getting old? – he hears raised voices. It must be the trio of braying idiots in the bar. But the heavy wooden door has swung closed, so the noise must be from somewhere else. And it is getting closer. It sounds like, 'Stop! Murderer!'

coming from far down the *calle* on his left. He turns to see a white-shirted man, vaguely familiar, with long, black hair flowing wildly behind, running straight at him. Isaac catches a glint of light and sees the drawn rapier. The man stumbles, for a second it looks as though he might fall, but he steadies himself against a wall and picks up pace.

As the man closes in on him, Isaac shrinks back against the door. But then Isaac sees the wide-eyed stare of terror. Or is it recognition? The man draws even nearer, panting with exhaustion. The door hits Isaac in the small of the back and he is shoved into the middle of the street. He faces the running man, who is almost upon him. The three drinking companions mutter some apologies but stop when they see the chase. They shield themselves behind Isaac. Cowards, after all.

'For the love of God, please help,' the running man cries, coming to an abrupt halt in front of Isaac, 'they'll burn me.' Isaac looks around wildly, for what or whom, he is uncertain. The man casts a hurried glance behind him, turns back, clutches Isaac's arm and whispers, 'Please, hide me, help me, I beg of you.' It is Juan. Isaac feels his stomach lurch as he holds his friends' pitiful gaze. Then he sees the blurred red movement of two soldiers running towards them. Isaac shakes his head, almost imperceptibly, and mouths, 'Forgive me.'

The soldiers are almost upon them, shouting, 'Stop him. Child killer.'

The three idiots are muttering something. They push Isaac aside and grapple with the fleeing man, pushing him to the ground.

'Here he is officers, we've caught him for you,' the scarred man declares with a smile.

Isaac hurries away, and does not look back, not even when he hears Juan cry out, 'At least help my family, please.' He has walked straight into the pursuit and arrest of Juan de Mota, his closest childhood friend, and has done nothing. What is he to tell Maria?

CHAPTER
TWO

THE TESTIMONY OF FRIAR ALONSO

lcazar de los Reyes Cristianos, Cordoba

THIS IS AN IMPORTANT OCCASION: the first entry in my testimony. I intend to capture everything truthfully and in much detail. I hope to convince you this is the only authentic account of the events that will surely follow from tonight's momentous meeting. It is past Lauds and I have not slept for excitement. The sun will rise within the hour.

I am Friar Alonso de Hojeda and I was born in Toledo in the year of our Lord 1460. This is what the sisters in the convent led me to believe. I did not know my mother, my father, or any members of my family. When I was seven, Sister Manuela told me I was just a few days old when my mother left me at the convent. She claimed she did not know my mother. Perhaps she was a whore. I don't suppose that matters now. I can't recall the exact features of Sister Manuela's face. But I can summon the comfortable feeling of her holding me and singing to me. Sometimes, particularly after prayer, I recapture that deep sense of warmth and belonging. And her fragrance. It was the scent of blood orange from the soap manufactured by the brothers at the monastery.

Tonight may prove to be the single most important night of my life. Queen Isabella had granted me an audience at the Real Alcazar ...

... My footsteps reverberated along the stone walls of the passageway leading to her apartments. The torches crackled and flamed in their sconces. I watched my hooded figure become a distorted shadow, disappearing and reappearing, as it passed over each of the leaded glass windows. I was pleased by the drama of this.

Keeping my head bowed and ignoring the guards as they opened the immense oak doors, I entered Her Majesty's chamber. The coat of arms framed by a giant golden eagle dominated the stone walls. Emblazoned beneath was the Queen's motto, "Protect us in the shade of your wing". I wondered if I might need protection should this audience not go as I intended.

Her Majesty stood on a dais beside a small wooden table. She studied a chessboard, one finger tapping the black queen. Brother Tomás de Torquemada, the Queen's confessor and "Grand Inquisitor of All Spain" was slumped in a high-backed chair on the dais, apparently asleep. I approached, removed my cowl and bowed.

'Yes, yes, get up, we haven't all night,' she said.

Although I had met her before, two aspects of the Queen's appearance still surprised me: her shortness and her dark-blonde hair. Surely a woman who could induce such terror should be tall and dark-haired? I wonder if the shock of our first meeting six years ago had warped my memory.

'Why do you find it necessary to disturb us at such a late hour, Friar? It is almost midnight. Could this not have waited?' She picked up the black Queen and flicked the white bishop off the board. Brother Tomás shifted and grunted.

Fighting to keep my composure, I squinted into the shadows and wondered why the Queen could not afford to light more candles. 'My apologies Your Majesty,' I said, bowing again, 'but these are matters that cannot wait and are best discussed in the shadows of night. It is less likely that we will be overheard your majesty. I was informed today of ... the murder of a child.'

She sighed and glowered at me. Was she considering dismissing me, or worse?

'Explain yourself, I have other matters to attend to.' She glanced sideways at her bed. 'Why is the murder of a single child so important, and what is it you expect of me?' She cocked her left eyebrow.

I still recall with pride how, on the first occasion we met, I persuaded Her Majesty the continued existence of the crypto-Jews was an affront to The Almighty. If only she would listen to my entreaties this time. The stakes were even higher.

'Well?' she demanded.

I took a deep breath. 'Your Majesty, Fernan Rodrigo, a nine-year-old boy was viciously murdered in the Barrio Santa Cruz where, as Your Majesty knows, most of the Jews in Seville used to live.'

Another deep sigh from Her Majesty strained my nerves even further.

'The boy was decapitated and left to rot in a *calle*.'

She narrowed her eyes, sat down and gave me her full attention.

'Your Majesty is aware that the Jews have always murdered Christian babies to use their blood in pagan ceremonies.'

The Queen nodded.

'I believe Fernan's murder was for such a purpose. These *marranos* are plotting to murder as many of our babies as possible. One might call it an *un*holy crusade, Your Majesty.' I paused, expecting approbation, but receiving none, went hurriedly on. 'It has already happened to Simon of Trent.'

The Queen continued to glare at me, waiting for an explanation.

'You may recall, Your Majesty, he was the boy found dead in the cellar of a Jewish family's house in northern Italy. He was only two. The town magistrates arrested a gang of Jews who confessed they killed him to use his blood to make their bread. And this practice has spread like a plague to Spain. This is appalling and we – you – your government,' I nodded towards Brother Tomás , eyes still shut, 'should act to prevent this. I believe that – with Your Majesty's permission – we should institute a Holy Office for the Propagation of the Faith in Seville.' Her eyes widened. She was no doubt recalling King Ferdinand's long held opposition to the Holy Office being permitted to operate in his beloved Seville.

'The murder of the boy in this manner is a shock, but I have already spoken to Father Tomás about extending the Holy Office's sphere of influence. It will perhaps give further weight to our deliberations,' she replied.

At the mention of his name, Brother Tomás opened his

eyes, stood up, and stepped from the dais. He towered over me. His nose appeared broken, as though he had been in a street fight. His large forehead, separated from his bald, domed skull by an immaculately groomed tonsure, reinforced this thuggish look. The Queen smiled with admiration at her closest confidant. It was rumoured she had once told him, 'Confessor, I only feel that I am with an angel from heaven when I am with you.' I stepped back as my fellow Dominican Friar moved towards me. Brother Tomás stretched out a hand towards my shoulder as if to comfort me, but I flinched, and he was left patting air.

'I need my bed,' said the Queen.

We bowed our heads.

'We will talk further of this in the morning Father Tomás , but I think you already know my mind,' she said turning away.

Brother Tomás put an arm around me and pulled me close. I smelt something fetid on his breath, no doubt the remnant of yet another rich meal. This was reputedly the cause of his gout, which explained his irascible nature. 'Well, Brother Alonso, Lauds is an hour away, let us use the time wisely to further our discussions of *your* plan,' he said in his sonorous voice.

'Yes, Brother Tomás, why not?' I replied, trying to keep my voice steady. We bowed once more and retreated.

I STOOD IN BROTHER TOMÁS' chamber, awaiting further direction. It was the afternoon after we'd met Her Majesty. He sat at his desk, fingers steepled, apparently asleep. I was impatient to know if my request to open a Holy Office in Seville had been granted. The news of Fernan's murder would soon spread. Not even copious *maravedies* would stop tongues wagging for very long. We needed to act.

No doubt Brother Tomás was contemplating the most effective way to proceed. I admire his passion and his efficiency. These are useful qualities with so much to manage, so many heretics to discover, and a great deal I find unpleasant. He has many administrative concerns, the lands and money confiscated from the heretics require careful management. I believe I am helpful to him. He has such humility; he has often told me he is merely an instrument of the Almighty.

His eyes snapped open. 'What do you think our next step is, Brother?'

There was a challenge in his tone that was disconcerting.

I hesitated, then decided to be bold. 'We should immediately issue the Edict of Grace and establish the Holy Office in Seville, Brother Tomás.'

He raised his eyebrows. Was he surprised by my forthright views? 'Immediately? Why should I do that?'

'The news of the child's death will quickly become common knowledge. There will be justifiable outrage which may lead to civil disorder.'

'And? Why is that a problem?'

I was taken aback. I thought the answer was so obvious that I hesitated to reply.

'Well?' he pressed.

'There may be violence, other deaths ... of the innocent.'

'That could very well be. But wouldn't that just further our aims? Wouldn't that offer greater support to our claim to open the Holy Office in Seville?'

I looked down at the floor, surprised by his justification for the death of more innocents.

'For a long time, our cultured friends in Seville have resisted our help with reclaiming the heretics' souls. They claim they do not need direct intervention. The King has instructed us to occupy ourselves with matters in other cities. Why would a few more days, or weeks make a difference?'

I nodded.

'But perhaps you believe the boy's murder alters everything?' he continued.

'I do, we should act now. I believe it to be in everyone's best interests. Don't you, Brother?'

He narrowed his eyes at me and sighed. 'Her Majesty has discussed this with the King, at length. The murder has made it clear to him that Seville can no longer be an exception. He has graciously assented to open the Holy Office in the city.' He paused, eyebrows raised. 'Off you go.'

'To Seville?'

'Of course, to issue the Edict of Grace. What else did you think I meant?'

'Would you like to dictate it?'

'No, just use the same Edict we used in Granada, with the appropriate changes in dates, places and names. Then come back and we will talk with Señora Graciela about the accusations against her. I will complete the interview before we go to Seville. I agree with you that Castillo de San Jorge in Triana would make a suitable place for us to establish the office.' I awaited further instruction, but Brother Tomás closed his eyes. It was as though he believed he could make you cease to exist by the simple expedient of marrying his eyelids.

I hurried away to write the Edict of Grace. It would be nailed to the cathedral door and read out after mass in Seville before this coming Sunday's service. It stated: 'By order of the Grand Inquisitor of All Spain, Friar Tomás de Torquemada. In direct consequence of the murder of nine-year-old Fernan Rodriguez by the Jews the Holy Office for the Propagation of the Faith will be established in Seville. Citizens can relieve their consciences by attending the tribunals of the Inquisition and denouncing the heresies of their fellows. The Church, in its great benevolence, affords you thirty days' grace in which to offer information and reconcile yourself with the Church to avoid severe punishment. Whoever does not make use of this grace period, and is later accused of heresy, will suffer the just punishment of the Inquisition.'

CHAPTER
THREE

S *eville*

STRIDING home from Bar Averno past the church of San Pedro Isaac barely notices his surroundings. When he first moved to the city it had taken him a year to confidently walk the streets. It is easy to lose your bearings in Seville. The narrow winding *calles* take you off at gentle tangents. You end up staring at the nexus of four or five streets, turning this way and that, searching for a way home.

The memory of, "Help my family, please," inflames his mind. He had abandoned his oldest friend. What exactly *should* he have done in the circumstances? How could he have reacted differently with the soldiers bearing down on Juan? If he had vouched for him would the soldiers have simply let the matter drop? Although his employment by the King gives him influence, his status as a *converso* is well known. He might have bought some time for Juan, but at the cost of exposing himself and his family to great danger. That is too high a price to pay for friendship. He burns with shame.

Startled by the tangy scent of blood oranges, he realises he is already outside Casa de la Felicidad. The heavy door leading to the courtyard is open, anticipating his return. The clatter of pots and pans from the scullery greets him. He passes the babbling fountain in the centre of the courtyard, heading towards his study. On any other day he would stop to inhale the rich, calming smell of the jasmine and brush his fingers though the stems of the purple agapantha. But today he needs to be alone, to think. As if his ears are clogged with water after a swim in the river, he hears, 'Papa, papa.' He looks down, surprised to see Gabriel gazing up at him with a broad smile, golden hair framing his round face.

He picks up his son, clutches him tightly, and the boy cries out, 'Papa, you're hurting me.' Gabriel tugs his father's beard to make his point. Isaac puts him down, kneels and holds Gabriel's face, 'I'm so sorry, my boy.'

Gabriel just stares back, then smiles.

'Have you been good for Mama today?'

'Papa, I'm not a baby anymore.'

'Of course not. So, tell me about your studies with Mama, what did you learn?' Isaac pretends to listen intently as Gabriel tells him of the great Cristoforo Columbo. His recent return from the second voyage to the Indies, the wild stories and the exotic treasures he brought back with him. All Isaac wants to do is hold him and kiss his soft, golden hair. 'You have used your time well Gabriel, I'm impressed. Where is Mama?'

'Right behind you, my love.'

He turns to see the face he has seen every day for the past fifteen years. It is always her deep brown, almond shaped eyes that hold him. He feels like a foolish adolescent as his heart lurches for a second time that day.

'How are you?' Isaac asks in a monotone.

'Gabriel, find your sister and tell her to get ready for dinner.' Maria takes her husband's hand, leads him to the dining hall and closes the door. They sit facing each other in high backed wooden chairs. 'Well?' she asks.

'I saw Juan de Mota in the street,' he begins.

When he finishes recounting the incident Maria pauses. 'So, the soldiers have him. He is fortunate the Inquisition has not yet set up office in Seville, he might escape torture.'

'I felt powerless.'

'You were, we all are. What could you have done?'

'Defended him. Hidden him.'

'At what cost? Your children lose their father as well?'

'So, we just let this happen?'

'We are not idle. We do what is essential to protect our family, our children. Do you think Juan would give his life for yours?'

He is silent.

'My love,' Maria begins tentatively, 'we made a choice; we live that choice every day. I just wish ... that you would not attend the prayer meetings. They have Juan. You could be next. You should stop ... just for a while.'

'Let me give it some thought.' He rubs his palms over his eyes.

Maria looks at her hands in her lap, seeming to consider what to say. She stands up, takes a deep breath, smoothes her dress and as she leaves puts a hand on his shoulder. 'I must make sure that Catalina is not destroying dinner.'

. . .

AFTER THE SUCCULENT roast lamb that he will suffer for later, Isaac retires to his study, locking the door. He kneels before the wooden chest at the foot of the day bed. He caresses the smooth wood and the cool, inlaid ivory and admires the intricately carved design. The geometric patterns soothe him; he takes comfort in their order. He unlocks the chest, removes the false panel from its base and takes out a large, linen-shrouded bundle. He carefully lifts the cloth and brings the Torah to his lips. At moments like this, the description of Moses in the wilderness in the Bamidbar is profoundly reassuring. He reads one of his favourite verses that restates God's covenant with the Jewish people:

> *And I will espouse you forever*
> *I will espouse you with righteousness and*
> *   justice,*
> *And with goodness and mercy,*
> *And I will espouse you with faithfulness;*
> *Then you shall be devoted to the Lord.*

He hears a knock and Isabel calling, 'Papa?' He replaces the sacred book, spreads some legal papers across the desk and unlocks the door. Isaac notes that Isabel need not look up at him anymore – when had she grown so tall?

'I want to talk to you, Papa,' she holds out her hand and he leads her into the room.

'As you can see my dear, I'm a little busy.'

'You never have time for me,' she folds her arms across her chest and frowns.

'That's not true,' he says, even though he knows it is. He finds the company of his daughter frustrating. He loves her but is unsettled by the twists and turns of her moods. Maria counsels him to be patient, that it is just a phase. Isaac would like to reply that the moon has predictable, finite phases that do not result in volcanic eruptions. He keeps this thesis to himself.

'I have time for you now,' he says, rolling up the contracts and placing them to one side. 'Let's sit and talk.'

'Mama says we are to be careful. What does she mean?' Isabel begins, sitting down.

'Well, you are becoming a young lady now, wanting to be less dependent on us and, and, well ... there's no other way to put this my dear, attracting the attention of young gentlemen. You need to be careful.'

Isabel blushes but continues to look at him. 'No, that's not it. It's more than that,' she pauses. 'Go on father, I need to hear the truth.' She only calls him father when in serious, adult mood.

'I don't know what more I can say, Isabel.'

'You brought us up to be Catholics?' This is a dangerous non-sequitur. 'So why do we keep a ham in the front window but never eat the slices we cut from it every day?'

'Because we don't enjoy eating ham, it's just a tradition. And you know that Catalina takes them home for her family. It's our way of being charitable.'

'Why not just give her the whole ham for her to keep at home?'

Isaac takes a deep breath and says slowly, 'Isabel, not everything in the adult world will make complete sense to you, it often doesn't to me. Sometimes we do things just because they have become a habit. And that routine is comforting. Do you see?'

She cocks her head, a habit she developed as a very

young child. 'No, I don't see, Papa. If we know it's a meaningless routine, why continue to do it?'

'I don't have any other answer for you, Isabel.' Isaac tries to control his irritation. He waits.

'You and Mama were Jews by birth?'

'Yes, Isabel, you know that.'

'Do you miss being a Jew?'

This was the first time she has asked this. 'The truth is ... when I think about the rituals and the prayers, yes, but then I recall Jesus was a Jew. As Christians we follow his teachings, so the distinction is not as great as it sometimes appears. Do you see?'

She glances to one side, staring at the Persian carpet. 'But if that were true, why were the Jews expelled by the Catholics? Why do Catholics hate the Jews?'

He takes another deep breath. 'Because faith is often irrational, and belief sometimes causes men to commit unfortunate acts in the name of God. That has always been true, and I see no sign of it changing. We just have to learn to live with it. There's no other choice. Do you understand?'

'I will give it some thought,' she stands and turns to leave.

'Isabel, my dear. These are difficult, dangerous times. Please ensure that you only discuss these matters with Mama and me. And only in the confines of this house. Do you understand? Can you promise me, please?'

'Yes, I understand. Goodnight Papa.' She kisses him on the forehead and leaves.

Isaac is worried; it has been a difficult day. The shame he feels at his inaction during Juan's arrest and now his daughter's worrisome doubts. He wonders, not for the first time, if it had been inviting problems to name his daughter after the Queen, who married King Ferdinand in the same

year Isabel was born. If only children had the unques-
tioning faith in the benevolence of their parents, that God
expects of his worshippers. Despite Maria's comforting
rationalisation, he cannot help feeling that he must do
something to save Juan. He cannot stand by and let his best
friend die. But neither can he place his family in danger.

CHAPTER

FOUR

THE TESTIMONY OF FRIAR ALONSO

A lcázar de los Reyes Cristianos, Cordoba

AFTER ARRANGING for the Edict of Grace to be posted in Seville I accompanied Brother Tomás to his interview with Señora Graciela. It was approaching dusk and in times past the muezzin would have been calling the faithful to say the Maghrib prayers from the nearby – now derelict – Grand Mosque.

We left his office in the Alcázar de los Reyes Cristianos which had been our home for the past eight years. During this time the palace had undergone many changes under Brother Tomás' expert supervision. He had rid it of the many vestiges of the Moors' occupation and turned their bathhouses into cells and interrogation chambers. We headed to one of the latter.

The warden, a grotesque dwarf, stood on guard outside the entrance which was emblazoned with the royal insignia exhorting the faithful to, "prove their true loyalty to Isabella the Catholic". He bowed as we approached, clanked the keys in the lock, and opened the heavy iron door.

We stood on a small square of flagstones at the top of a flight of stairs. I caught the damp, fetid smell of sweat and excrement. We looked down into a large windowless room, lit by the torches positioned in sconces at an equal distance around the walls. The precision of their placement seemed to please Brother Tomás. The room was chilly as it no longer carried the hot water for the Moors' baths. As we descended, I could see that all the elements Brother Tomás prescribed for interrogation were in place: the clerk was at his table ready to record details of the session, the physician was present to monitor the health of the accused, and the black-hooded seeker of truth stood ready. I noted the exact arrangement of the eight earthenware jugs of water on a table. Brother Tomás had formulated these rules and procedures to ensure consistency and fairness. Due process must be followed. This was God's work, and much was taken on faith, but that was no excuse for disorganisation.

And now the last element was in place: The Grand Inquisitor of All Spain. These interrogations were unpleasant, but necessary. How were we to verify the truth otherwise? I took his silence to signal satisfaction and that we could begin.

Señora Graciella was tied to an *escalera*, in the centre of the room. She was extended to her full length, arms and legs tightly bound to the ladder, which was tipped so that her head was lower than her feet. Iron prongs held her jaws open and her nostrils were stopped with muslin rags so she could only breathe through her mouth. She thrashed her head from side to side as Brother Tomás advanced towards her. He picked up a white piece of linen and draped it, almost delicately, over her mouth. He took the charge sheet from the clerk and read in a slow, sonorous tone: 'Señora Graciella you are accused as follows: first, you were seen wearing clean, luxurious garments on a Saturday, and second, for several successive Saturdays no smoke was seen to come from your chimney. Judaism forbids manual work on a Saturday. We therefore believe you are a heretic and in fact are not a true Catholic, but a Jewess pretending to share our faith. Clerk how did she plead?'

The señora shook her head and tried to scream. All I could hear was a hoarse whisper. The clerk read the transcription of the accused's verbal statement: 'These things may be true, I do not remember, but I am a faithful Catholic, I am not a *marrano*. Even if true, it does not mean I am a Jew. My husband is a sailor, but has had no work for a long time and we could not afford kindling for the fire, so the house was cold. I don't recall any luxurious clothes. I have one silk shawl my husband brought back for me from his voyages almost ten years ago. I wear it sometimes just to feel something soft against my skin. These are wicked accusations, no doubt from one of my neighbours. I have two children and a husband. Please think of them. I do not know what else to say, what is it you want me to say? Oh God, please have mercy on me. Please, I beg of you for my children's sake.'

Brother Tomás nodded his thanks to the clerk. Señora Graciella writhed under his touch as he wiped the sweat away from her brow. He said with a warm smile, 'Do not worry, the Inquisition has taken every precaution to ensure that natural justice and God's mercy will prevail. You have my word.' He looked towards the physician, who opened his palm to the black hooded figure who ambled to the table and lifted the first jug.

The water slopped over the lip of the jug as he brought it back towards the señora. Her eyes widened and she tried to move her head again. The seeker of truth stood over her and poured the first jug into her mouth, the water washing the linen cloth to the back of her throat, preventing her from spitting the water out. Gasping for air only pulled the muslin cloth even further into her throat. Water filled her lungs, preventing the expansion of her chest to draw breath. She arched her back, straining, eyes wide, trying to scream. The physician, the clerk, and Brother Tomás looked on. I wondered whether all eight jugs would be necessary.

As the seeker of truth removed the cloth, I was reminded of the silk shawl that Señora Graciella liked to wear, just to feel its softness. She coughed as she strained to take in air, and I thought I heard her say, 'Listen, listen to me please.' Brother Tomás nodded at me and I bent my head close to the señora's mouth.

'Don't waste time on me ... you should be investigating the Alvarez family in Seville. The señor what works in the Alcazar for the King.'

I asked how she knew about a family that lived three days ride away in another city. She told me that the gossip about all the *converso* families reached Córdoba. The Alvarez family were talked of because of their royal connections. She asked whether this information would earn her mercy. I told her I would see what I could do.

I told Brother Tomás. A hard glint appeared in his eyes, and he smiled so broadly that I could see his teeth.

CHAPTER
FIVE

*S*eville

ISAAC IS IMMERSED in anxiety about the future of his family as he finds his way through the twists and turns of the narrow *calles* on his way to the Real Alcazar. A sense of foreboding had enveloped him overnight as he thought about Isabel and their troubling conversation. Something was not right about their after-dinner talk; what was the child thinking? He tries to recall what it was like to be her age. But too much has happened, he has lost too much for him to regain that sense of righteous innocence.

Turning into Calle Juderia he sees people gathering in twos and threes on corners. He is surprised that they are shouting, shaking their heads and fists. The noise swells as he nears the Real Alcazar. Passing into the square, just near La Giralda, – the tower abutting the cathedral – he sees a crowd. Drawing closer, he notices they are crowded round a man atop a wooden crate normally used for transporting oranges. He has never seen anything like this before in Seville. Men stand on corners selling their wares all the time, but they do not attract sizeable crowds, nor do they foment the sense of aggression that is in the air. For a moment he cannot make sense of it. He is fixed inside his head, his mind focused on his family whilst his eyes take in the unfamiliar scene. A man wearing an embroidered orange silk tunic pushes past him, running towards the crowd shouting something, and Isaac regains the world. What is he shouting?

'We've got him. We've got him.' Is that it? Whatever it is, the crowd turns almost as one, consumes the man and like a great shoal of fish moves off at speed.

Isaac tries to comprehend what any of this might mean. Does it have anything to do with Juan. He feels a light tap on his shoulder. Spinning round, he reaches for his rapier. It is Alejandro, his deputy at the Real Alcazar. He is in his middle-twenties and a recent graduate of the University of Salamanca, Isaac's alma mater. He has a straight Roman nose, thin lips and pale blue eyes that give him a delicate appearance. His fine skin is drawn taut across high cheekbones. Always elegantly attired, he carries himself with an aristocratic bearing. He must have many female admirers.

'Good morning Señor Alvarez. I hope I didn't alarm you?' Alejandro glances down at Isaac's right hand which still grips the handle of his sword.

'No, not at all,' Isaac says as he pats Alejandro's arm, 'Good morning to you.'

'Have you heard the news?' Alejandro asks.

'No, I haven't ... what ... what is it?'

'They found one of those boys from the choir at the cathedral, Fernan, behind the synagogue the night before last with his head cut off. They're accusing the crypto-Jews, they say they did it to drink his blood.'

'And they think they've already found the culprit?'

'They believe they have, they don't care about proof, they just want to lynch someone. It's rumoured to be one of the *conversos,* Juan de Mota, I think his name is. He's already in custody. He lives in San Bartolomeo, so the mob is going over there to burn his house down.'

Isaac considers the right course of action. 'You proceed to the Real Alcazar, I will be in a little later. I have some matters to attend to.'

Alejandro bows and strides away.

'Heaven help us all,' Isaac mutters, as he turns for home.

It is closed, as he is not expected. Isaac raps on the heavy oak door of Casa de la Felicidad. Maria opens it. Her hair is down; he has never seen it like this during the daytime. She purses her lips, as though containing her frustration. The news of the murder has travelled quickly. Catalina is probably the source, but no time to ponder that now.

'Where are the children?' he says.

'I've put them in the study with Catalina, asked them to quiz her about the "old days" in Seville. That should keep them occupied.' She manages a slight smile that he does not reciprocate.

'Let's go to the terrace,' he suggests, holding her hand, which she squeezes back.

There is a flask of sherry and two glasses already on the table of the terrace. 'It's that bad is it?' Isaac says.

Maria says nothing. She pours two large measures,

hands him one and paces the long terrace that runs along the front of the house.

Isaac is unsure whether to walk alongside her but thinks that one of them should remain still. Sitting down he gazes into the distance, searching for calm. He takes in the glorious view over the Guadalquivir river towards Triana, that den of thieves. Over the past ten years it has become populated by sailors, taverns and prostitutes. Isaac takes some solace from the sails of the tall ships travelling to and from the Puerto de Indias; evidence of his daily toil in the dead language of contracts.

'How can you be so calm?' she asks him.

'You know it's my way, to think things through.'

'Sometimes more action is required and less thinking.'

Isaac does not know how to respond. 'I've just heard that Juan is suspected of Fernan's murder. I cannot believe it; the mob are just using this as an excuse to cause trouble.' He knows that danger will follow the accusation against the crypto-Jews. The Inquisition will not be far behind. And as a family of *conversos* they will be especially vulnerable.

Maria does not reply.

'What are you thinking?' he ventures, raising his glass to his lips.

'What do I think Isaac? I don't think, I know. I know that whatever piece of scum carried out that heinous crime has just unleashed all hell on us.'

The glass of sherry remains in mid-air. In their fifteen years together, he has never heard such vitriolic language. 'So, my love, what do we do?' Isaac exercises as much caution as he can muster; she needs time, and he requires patience.

'I don't know. I know we need to act, we cannot wait, but exactly what we need to do I am unsure.'

He could have predicted many responses but not this. Maria always knows the correct course of action.

'All I can say is what I know, Isaac: I love you, I love our children, I love our life, but it is all finished. We were protected in Seville by the King. But the symbolism of that boy's decapitated body and the baseless accusations have destroyed our lives. All we can do is save our family. There is nothing else left, nothing at all.'

Isaac holds her gaze and knows she is right.

'You know that I knew the boy, Fernan?' she says.

He looks at her, uncomprehending.

'He sang in the choir at the cathedral and had a beautiful voice. They live in

Triana. His mother, Beatriz, takes in our laundry. She was so proud of him. I have to see them. Catalina knows where they live. You will accompany me tomorrow morning?'

In more ordinary times, Maria would never have invited him to visit the home of the woman who took in their laundry. But these are far from ordinary times. He is always filled with a sense of foreboding on the rare occasions he visits Triana and would rather not go now. He will need all his energy for the days and nights ahead. But it is a waste of time once Maria has set her mind.

Another matter troubles him he chooses not to share with Maria: the murder occurred two nights ago, so why are they only hearing about it now? A lot of *maravedies* must have been spent to buy the silence of those aware of the murder and delay it becoming known. This indicates conspiracy. If this is true, what is the motivation for the murder? Cutting a boy's head off suggests sacrifice. Isaac has never seen or heard any evidence that the Jewish community uses the blood of children in their rituals. It is a ridiculous idea. And yet the gullible, the ignorant, and the malicious believe it; there are enough of them to cause serious discord. Fernan's murder is an act of pure malevolence. Who stands to gain from it? Before Isaac can follow this line of thought, Maria returns.

'Do you think you should visit Juan?' she asks.

Isaac takes a sip of sherry and considers. 'As his friend, yes, I should, but I very much doubt Juan would welcome me. On balance I think it would be better to do nothing at the moment. The only cards we have to play are patience and watchfulness. Besides, I have another appointment this evening.'

Maria reaches out to take his hand. 'Is it not dangerous for you to attend that "appointment"?'

He does not reply and looks out across the river as lightning jags across the sky. Thunder rumbles and he hopes the rain might cool tempers a little. He has little expectation it will.

TWELVE CHAIRS ARE ARRANGED in a circle; two are empty. The *minyan* is complete, they are fortunate to be quorate in the current climate. Eyes closed, each wears a *kippah*, the black skullcap that is the symbol of their faith. The room is almost completely dark, except for two candles in tall brass holders on an oval table in the middle of the circle, and a solitary oil lamp. The windows are closed and the two doors on either side of the circle bolted shut. Isaac breathes heavily in the almost airless room. They do not use names. This precaution, taken at the first meeting five years ago, seems even more prescient now.

They hold hands and intone the Sabbath evening prayers: 'Blessed are you, Lord, our God, sovereign of the

34

universe, who has sanctified us with his commandments and commanded us to light the lights of Shabbat. Amen,' the final word almost whispered. Each of the men opens their eyes and contemplates the two flickering candles for a long moment. Isaac thinks of the commandments the two tapers signify: Zakhor, to always remember freedom from slavery in Egypt, and Shamor, the duty to observe the Sabbath by honouring it as a day of rest. Isaac can achieve Zakhor, though he wonders if what he is going through is just a form of self-imposed slavery. The second is impossible; to refrain from work would make it obvious that he was still at heart a Jew. He comforts himself that violating the restriction is acceptable if it means saving a life. He assuages his guilt further by remembering that breaking the commandment of Shamor means he is saving the lives of his family.

Isaac rises, and picks up the two candles. He places them in the centre of the long dining table that runs along the back wall, where a simple meal of red wine and rye bread awaits the men. Every week he feels the same sting of regret that the bread is not the traditional *challah* and that the meal is not prepared by their wives and enjoyed openly by the entire family. Each of the men washes their hands in a bowl of water and together they occupy ten of the twelve dining chairs. Isaac recites the Kiddush prayer, and the men begin to eat and drink. The silence is broken by a thin, sallow-faced man. 'Will we need even ten chairs next week?' The others stop chewing the doughy bread and sipping the inexpensive wine and appear to consider an answer. Juan de Mota's capture and the lack of information about his fate have hit them hard. There had once been twenty of them.

'We are brothers, and we need to keep our faith, even

more so now. We are the remaining few and we must remember what our ancestors suffered so we could survive,' Isaac says. Chair legs scrape against bare wooden floors.

'Those are fine words Isaac,' a portly man already finishing his second glass of wine says, 'and I agree, but this will be my last meeting, gentleman.'

He stands, finishes his wine, and stretches out a hand to Isaac, who grips it firmly and returns his farewell of, 'Shabbat Shalom.' This process is repeated with each of the men until Isaac is left facing the sallow-faced man across the table. Isaac wonders how he got the thin, red scar that follows the hairline down the left side of his face, from eyebrow to jaw. They sit back down.

'I want you to know, Isaac, that I will keep our faith and I will celebrate the Sabbath every week, but we will not meet under these circumstances again. It is only a matter of time before we are found out. The Edict of Grace changes everything. We cannot evade the Inquisition; it is a wonder that Juan does not appear to have given our names.' He looks deeply into his glass. 'Perhaps in time it will be different.'

Isaac nods and watches as the two candles sputter and struggle to stay alight.

CHAPTER
SIX

THE TESTIMONY OF FRIAR ALONSO

lcázar de los Reyes Cristianos, Cordoba

SEÑORA GRACIELLA'S questioning has given us much to think about. Her accusation of the Alvarez family is of great interest to Brother Tomás . He is clearly familiar with Señor Alvarez, and his connection to the King is important. But he did not take me fully into his confidence.

The silk shawl that the señora liked to wear just to feel its softness reminds me of the convent and the sisters. During my time with them I often speculated who my father might have been – a soldier or a rich merchant. Perhaps even royalty. When I was ten and coming to the end of my time at the convent, I tried to share these notions with Sister Manuela who listened but made no comment. She continued to recite the Ave Maria or the Pater Noster, waiting for me to join in. My Latin had to be good enough for the Friars at the Monasterio de San Juan de los Reyes.

This was important as without fluent Latin I could not confidently set out on the path to priesthood. Sister Manuela did not want me end up as one of the cooperator brothers doing the mundane jobs around the monastery. I am grateful to Sister Manuela for instilling ambition into me at such an early age.

My last day with Sister Manuela came just before I turned eleven. With a lot of hard work, and the Lord's guidance and assistance, my facility in Latin had developed sufficiently for me to gain the Friars' acceptance. It was an unusually cold February and I had slept badly the night before I was to leave. I was grateful for the warmth of Sister Manuela's arms. Pulling me to her she whispered, 'Remember Alonso you have family who think of you and believe in you. The sisters will never forget you and I'm sure your new brothers will grow to love you as much as we do. But when you feel lonely, as you will, remember The Almighty sees you, blesses you and watches over you.' I have never forgotten those words. The sense that The Almighty sees all that I do, knows all that I think, and feel has never left me.

I spent the next decade studying and working happily at the Monasterio.

Before my ordination at twenty I worked in the garden and then in the kitchen with the cooperator brothers. You may be unfamiliar with the inner workings of a monastery; these brothers had chosen to become monks but did not speak Latin. They could not, therefore, achieve a clerical position. The principal work of the clerical brothers was to celebrate the divine office and Mass, which was sung daily by the choir. The primary work of the cooperator brothers was the upkeep of the monastery. They formed a separate community and were subject to their own superior, the

Master Father Bartolome. He was responsible to our prior, Father Santiago – a kind man, much venerated by all of us.

Although Master Bartolome was not much taller than us, his substantial figure and his hard stare made him an imposing character. He did not need to say very much. A curt gesture with his long fingers, a steely glance, or a dismissive nod, told you what you needed to know. And when that didn't work, he would put an arm firmly around you, draw you to one side and whisper in your ear. He left you in no doubt.

I was fifteen when Master Bartolome moved me from the garden and the lands that surrounded the monastery to the kitchen. He did not provide an explanation and I did not think to request one. I did as I was told; we were all at God's mercy. I preferred to be outside, tending the plants or helping to harvest the almond crop, but at least the kitchen was warm in the winter months. I spent my time washing pots and scrubbing floors. I could bear this as I knew that my future as a cleric, thanks to Sister Manuela's wisdom, was all but assured. The cooperator brothers could have no such confidence.

One of the cooperator brothers assigned with me to the kitchen was Andreas. He was the same age as me, but about a head taller. His tunic swaddled his wiry frame, the sleeves flapping and the hem in constant danger of tripping him. The first day I walked into the kitchen he gave me an enormous grin, took me by the hands and said in a mockingly portentous baritone, 'Brother, are you here to save me?'

'I may not be able to salvage your soul but perhaps I can save your soft hands,' I said, matching his serious tone. Andreas bellowed with laughter and I loved him from that moment, and we became great friends. I knew that fraternising with a cooperator brother was frowned upon, especially by Master Bartolome. We were very fond of imitating his menacing tone and authoritarian manner. We were young and meant no disrespect. If only I could have foreseen what our foolishness would cost.

That is enough painful recollection for now. It is the present that should be of more concern. I need to discover the significance of the Alvarez family. Brother Tomás' reluctance to share all the information with me is both frustrating and disquieting. I shall discreetly enquire of the *notario de secreto*. They seem to know almost everything.

CHAPTER
SEVEN

S *eville*

Isaac leaves the prayer meeting profoundly disturbed. One moment he is certain what to do and the next confusion clouds his mind. They could all flee to Lisbon; passage could easily be arranged. But that would be cowardice. A betrayal of both Isaac's faith and his city. Maria would tell him that betrayal is a better choice than death. Isaac is not so sure. The shame of betraying Juan still stings. He needs to atone by staying and protecting his faith.

Screams greet his arrival home. Isabel is chasing Gabriel around the courtyard with a raised hairbrush.

'Wait till I get hold of you. I'll thrash you, you little devil,' she shouts at her brother.

Gabriel easily evades her, weaving around the fountain and the marble bench. 'You'll have to catch me first,' he cries back.

They are so engrossed in their argument they do not notice their father's arrival. He waits for his son to come near and grabs his arm.

'Papa, that hurts!' Gabriel screams.

'Sit down, both of you.' Isaac points at the bench.

Maria appears, but Isaac shakes his head, and she disappears. Isaac sits in the middle of the bench, one child either side of him. He takes the hairbrush away from Isabel.

'What on earth is this nonsense about?' Isaac asks.

The children begin their defences at the same time; a gabble of mutual accusation.

'Enough!' Isaac pauses to consider the best way to deal with this. 'I am going to tell you a story from my childhood. Listen carefully. In the summer of 1469, when I was your age, Isabel, my father, your grandfather – God rest his soul – took me and my best friend Juan, Señor De Mota, to our family house in Pozzoblanco.'

'It's not really a house, it's only a single-storey stone building,' Isabel interrupts.

'True,' Isaac replies patiently. 'But it's important to us. My grandfather bought the estate with the money he earnt from buying spices from the Moorish traders in Cadiz. Anyway, Catalina was with us; she had just started her employment with the family. Your grandmother stayed in the city as she did not want to miss the gossip and preparations for Queen Isabella and King Ferdinand's wedding. We spent our time walking, playing cards and swimming. Juan was twelve, a year younger than me. I was stronger, quicker, taller, and Juan still had his puppy fat.'

Gabriel laughs.

Isaac stares at him until he stops. 'Juan had been an orphan since the age of seven and he looked up to me, like a brother. One afternoon we were supposed to be enjoying a siesta, but we were bored so we went swimming in the river. We crept out after lunch whilst my father and Catalina were asleep.'

Gabriel looks at his father with interest.

'I remember we marched along chanting, "Hotter than hell, hotter than hell."

Gabriel laughs again, this time more quietly.

Isabel asks, 'Isn't that blasphemous?'

'Probably Isabel, but we were young and it's not the point of the story. By the time we reached the end of the dusty track we just wanted to jump into the cool water. There'd been a thunderstorm the night before and the water was black as it crashed and twisted around the rocks. I remember whooping with glee, but Juan was not as good a swimmer. We stripped off our clothes and threw them on the bank.'

Gabriel covers his mouth to stifle his giggles.

'I jumped in and shouted to Juan, "You're a loser." I told him it was warm. He tested the water with his toes and called me a liar. I was annoyed so I dragged him into the icy water. I let him go and he drifted off and began to swim. I waited until he was a good distance away and swam back to the bank. I put my clothes on and hid behind a rock. I heard Juan cry out, "Where are you? Where are you?" But I stayed hidden until he swam to the bank, got out and started to look for his clothes. I let him look for some time. Then I stepped out from behind the rock, holding his clothes above my head and ran as fast as I could back towards the house.'

'That's mean, Papa,' Gabriel says quietly.

Isabel shakes her head.

'I let Juan walk halfway home with just a branch to cover himself with before I gave him his clothes back. I put my arm round him and told him that it was "Just a joke brother, just a joke". I remember he stared down at the ground. When I chanted, "Hotter than hell", he didn't join in.

We arrived at the house and my father was sitting on the porch, trying to keep cool. Juan ran to him and sat in his lap. My father indulged Juan's immaturity.' Isaac looks down at Gabriel. 'My father looked at me and I knew that he knew something was wrong. He asked Juan to get some water and told me to sit next to him. We sat in silence for a while, watching the waves of heat coming over the hill. My father asked me what had happened. I said it was nothing important. But he knew. Then he told me a story from his childhood that I've never forgotten. At the time I didn't want to hear it, but it has stayed with me.

Gabriel kicks his legs against the bench. Isaac waits for him to stop.

'I'm going to try to tell it in his words, as best as I can remember them:

"It was an insufferably hot summer, and I was here with your grandfather. I must have been about seven. One morning he woke me whilst it was still dark, told me to get dressed, gave me a hunk of rye bread, a flask of water and told me to follow him. I could see the stars as we began our walk in the cool of the early morning. We must have trekked for more than three miles; the sun was starting to rise. I was hungry despite finishing the bread, when my father put a finger to his lips and motioned me to stand still. I heard a terrifying high-pitched scream. He pointed to something long and brown wriggling in the grass. We moved closer, it was a hare with a leg trapped in a snare that my father had set. It was weak and near death. My father bent to untwist the wire from its leg and it suddenly leapt out of his grip. It seemed to have used up almost all of its energy in that one burst as it limped towards a tussock of grass.

We followed the hare, there was no danger of it escaping, and I was curious what it wanted. It struggled on, still making that high-pitched mewing sound. Then it stopped and nuzzled at the ground. Then it screamed.

We moved closer, my father still ahead. I saw him pick the hare up by its hind legs with one hand and twist its neck with the other in one swift motion. I will never forget the crack. My father held the hare up by its ears and smiled broadly. I moved past him and discovered three small leverets. They were almost blind and cuddled up to each other for warmth and comfort. Their ears trembled in the cool of the morning air. I reached down and picked one up by its hind legs. I brought my other hand up to break its neck, just the way my father had shown me."

There is a sharp intake of breath from Isabel.

"He put his hand on my shoulder and said, 'No'. He smiled and glanced at the leveret as it struggled to break free. I waited for an explanation, receiving none, I put the leveret back in the nest with his siblings and we returned home. The hare stew we had that night was the best I ever tasted."

Isabel looked down at her hands in her lap.

Gabriel grins and says, 'So, you were a naughty boy as well sometimes?'

'Yes. I did things that I wish I had not. Those are called regrets.'

'Regrets,' Gabriel repeats softly.

Isabel stands and kisses the top of her father's head. She reaches out a hand to her brother and says, 'Come, it must be well past your bedtime.'

Gabriel takes his sister's hand, and they walk into the house.

Isaac wishes his father were alive to seek advice from. But what story could he possibly weave that would bring any comfort in, or meaning to, the current circumstances? He still has to decide on the best course of action. The Inquisition is surely on its way to Seville. Should they seek passage to Lisbon? Or should he fully renounce his Jewish faith? But is it already too late for that? Far too many questions and not even a safe source to seek answers from.

EIGHT

THE TESTIMONY OF FRIAR ALONSO

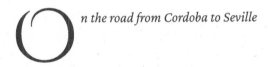

O n the road from Cordoba to Seville

BROTHER TOMÁS RODE A FINE, white, thoroughbred Arab steed while I struggled to keep up on a lumbering cob. In the distance, I saw the red tunics of the two royal bodyguards. It should have been an easy three-day ride from Cordoba to Seville, but Brother Tomás was eager to get to grips with the situation. He drove the horses so hard that by late afternoon of the second day we were within striking distance of the city.

One of the *notario de secretos* had given me the information I required about the Alvarez family. Señor Isaac Alvarez was responsible for the contracts with the Indies. It is rumoured he is a close ally of the King. That is why Brother Tomás is so interested. If the family are in fact crypto-Jews this could give him great leverage with the King. If a crypto-Jew could gain such close proximity to the crown, it would

47

be further proof that Seville required the services of the Holy Office.

Nothing gave Brother Tomás greater pleasure than conquering fresh territory. He believed the King had protected Seville for far too long. The murder of the boy was the perfect reason to purge a city that thought so highly of itself that it did not need the cleansing balm of the Inquisition. I had done everything to ensure we could begin the work of The Almighty swiftly. I had established Castillo de San Jorge in Triana as our new headquarters. I hoped that Brother Tomás would recognise my hard work when we arrived in Seville.

As we cantered for mile after mile, I slipped into a meditative state, my thoughts returning to Andreas. There are many stories I could recount about our friendship. There was one particular event that changed everything for us. I did not realise its import, but I suppose that is true of many events in life. If I were able to change what happened, would I? But not even The Almighty can alter past events. The thought tortures me that my life and Andreas' might have been completely different. It is a bittersweet memory, much like the taste of a blood orange. Even so, I do not want to lose it and the warmth in my heart its recollection brings.

It was after lunch and Andreas and I were following our normal routine: pot washing in the scullery. We were alone, as the other brothers had retired for the usual period of afternoon prayers and meditation. We would join them once we'd finished our chores. It must have been midwinter as I can still recall the icy, numb feeling in my fingers. As usual, I was fussing and moaning about my chafed hands whilst Andreas teased me in a way that nobody else has ever done.

'Why, Brother Alonso,' he began, imitating the deep baritone of Father Bartolome, 'are you so frail that you cannot tolerate chilly water?'

I did my best to ignore him and focus on completing our work.

'Do you not remember the sufferings of our Lord on the cross? Answer me boy,' he continued.

I stifled a giggle and kept my eyes on the dirty pots.

'This attitude does not become you, Brother. You will require great fortitude and courage to carry out your duties as a Friar,' he continued in a booming voice.

I splashed some water towards him, he responded by raising his eyebrows in mock surprise.

'If you cannot suffer a little cold water, how will you meet the monumental challenges that lie ahead?'

He paused and I looked up at him and shook my head, but I knew he would not stop.

'We need to have a quiet discussion, Brother Alonso,' he hissed, expertly capturing Father Bartolome's tone. He walked over to me, put his arm around my shoulder and turned me around to walk out of the kitchen. Father Bartolome stood in the doorway, arms folded under his cassock. He narrowed his eyes at me and then gave Andreas a hard stare. He turned and left. Andreas looked down at me and hung his head. I patted his shoulder.

MY HORSE TOOK A SHARP BEND, jolting me back to the present. We were just outside the small town of Valdezzoras, to the east of Seville. I saw the two bodyguards keeping lookout just ahead and Brother Tomás waiting for me at the top of a hill. He sat ramrod straight in the saddle, his image outlined by the weakening red sunlight. He dismounted and took in the view. By the time my ungainly mount made the top of the hill, Brother Tomás was admiring the fields surrounding this part of the city; a fecund array of almonds, olives and rice. I could just make out the twin strands of the Guadalquivir that encircled Triana. If I soared like an eagle they would appear to form a teardrop cradling the infamous neighbourhood. Seville's power and strategic importance came from this river because it stretched all the way to the Atlantic. Now the Queen and her foolish husband were slavering over the riches that this conduit to the Indies delivered.

'It is a wonderful panorama, Brother Tomás,' I said, a little out of breath.

He grunted.

'A shame Seville does not look quite so wonderful close up. *Picaros*, thieves and prostitutes were flourishing when I was last there.'

'Let us see what we can do about that with The Almighty's divine guidance.' Kneeling he continued, 'Brother Alonso, let us pray for righteous retribution and the power to deliver The Almighty's divine purpose. And then onward! If we ride hard, we will arrive before sunset, and I shall have time to visit the cathedral and meet with Father Gutiérrez. I shall be interested to hear what information about his parishioners he is prepared to share with me. In particular what he knows about the Alvarez family.'

CHAPTER
NINE

S *eville*

TRIANA IS SHAPED like a teardrop surrounded by the Guadalquivir river and nestled against Seville's south-western corner. It is connected to the mainland at its far northern tip by a thin strip of land. It has always been strategically important, connecting the city to the coast and the fertile plains of the Aljarafe. Triana is Seville's last line of defence from the West. Thieves, prostitutes and scoundrels call it home. Fernan had once called it home as well.

It is a brisk twenty-minute walk from Casa de la Felici-dad. The weather is fine, and the exercise gives Isaac time to mentally and emotionally prepare to meet Fernan's parents.

Catalina bustles ahead of them. They cross the river using the Puente de Barcas. As they pick their way across the linked chain of boats the atmosphere changes and the air becomes more oppressive. Isaac scents the damp tang lingering from the last flood and his sense of unease grows. The cause is either the thought of venturing into Triana or the certain knowledge of what they are about to endure. He feels a pang of guilt for attending to his own feelings when they are about to console Fernan's parents for the loss of their son.

They disembark from the last boat in the chain and walk along the wide *calle* of San Jacinto. Catalina takes Maria's arm and leads her quickly through the streets. Isaac follows closely behind, one hand hovering over his rapier. He sees the grim faces watching them closely from windows and doorways. Perhaps it would have been better to come by carriage. He would like to put a handkerchief over his nose to block out the rotting smell. Was it rancid meat? Even human flesh? But this might be too provocative and attract even more unwanted attention. Catalina asks in a hushed tone if the Señora is aware the mob had tried to burn down the house of one of the suspected murderers of Fernan? Luckily it rained and spoiled the would-be arsonists' fun. They wind their way through a narrow *callejon*, daylight decreasing at every turn. At last, Catalina stops and gestures towards a dark doorway.

They are admitted to a small, gloomy room by a tall man with hunched shoulders and sore, red eyes. The room reeks of cinders and salty ham. A woman sits rocking back and forth, hands cupped to her mouth, a low mewling sound struggling to emerge. The man crosses the room and stands behind her, one hand patting her shoulder. The woman pays him no regard.

Isaac hesitantly crosses to Fernan's father and shakes

his hand. The man's grip is weak and clammy. Isaac is afraid if he lets go the man will collapse.

Maria goes to Fernan's mother and pulls her hands away from her face. The woman tries to kick Maria and wails, 'Fernan, Fernan!' Maria pulls Beatriz to her, embracing her until she submits. They fall to the floor, united by motherhood and grief.

Isaac keeps hold of Fernan's father's hand and leads him outside. 'I'm so sorry for what's happened. I did not know Fernan but I have two children of my own and ...' Isaac's voice trails away. 'My wife speaks highly of his singing voice ... I'm so sorry, I do not even know your name.'

'My name is Rodrigo Duarte and my wife is Beatriz, señor.'

'I am Señor Isaac Camarino Alvarez and I wish we had met at a happier time.'

Rodrigo nods, lips pursed, eyes downcast.

'They have released a man that the mob caught yesterday. His alibi was confirmed by his priest. He is a church warden and was at St Ignatius most of the night. He's fortunate they didn't tear him limb from limb,' Isaac said.

Rodrigo says nothing.

'Señor Rodrigo, can you tell me what happened?'

Rodrigo sighs deeply. 'We know only what you know. They found my precious boy in a *callejon* without, without ....'

'Yes, I know that part of the story. Do you know why he was in the *callejon*?'

Rodrigo looks into the distance, through a narrow gap in the buildings, across the bridge towards Seville. 'He was doing something with the cathedral, a choir practice I think, I don't know, I can't keep up with everything Fernan does ... did. I'm a sailor and I'm not here a lot and my wife takes in washing for the neighbours so we can make ends meet. Of course, you know that; it's how you know us.' He seems embarrassed by this realisation. 'Fernan takes care of himself, he's a big boy now.' He glances down the *callejon* and then up at the sky. Isaac notes the use of the present tense.

'What else can you tell me?' Isaac asks.

Rodrigo digs his hands into his armpits and holds himself tightly. 'There's nothing else. I don't know what to say. I can't help you anymore,' his voice is becoming louder.

There are other questions but Isaac knows he is unlikely to get an answer at this time. 'Señor Rodrigo, if you need anything leave word at my office through Señor Alejandro de Cervantes, my deputy, and I will do my absolute best to help you.'

Rodrigo looks up at the sky, swaying back and forth on his heels.

'Do you understand?' Isaac's tone is gentle but insistent.

Rodrigo brushes his palms over his eyes.

'I mean it Rodrigo. Anything at all.'

ISAAC AND MARIA retrace their footsteps in desultory fashion. Catalina has stayed behind with Beatriz. They stop halfway across the Puente de Barcas and stare into the still waters. On the Triana bank a large family picnics on a thin strip of dusty grass, shouting and calling happily as the children chase each other, sword fighting with sticks.

'Did Beatriz tell you anything?' Isaac asks.

'Sometimes you are so obtuse. Do you think we actually talked?'

Isaac ignores this. 'Something is not right,' he says.

'There's nothing right about this.'

'What I don't understand is why was Fernan coming home alone by himself from the city so late at night?' His thoughts turn again to the motivation for murdering a child. It was an act of complete madness by an individual, or a deliberate provocation. If it was the latter, who would gain, and what was their motivation? Finding the answer to that is not his responsibility, he is just a royal administrator. So why is he beginning to feel a sense of obligation? And who to – Fernan, his family, his faith? It cannot be to all three, he must choose. Maria takes Isaac's hand and they pick their way across the bridge of boats to the city.

'PAPA, WHAT'S AN EDICK GRACE?' Gabriel asks. Isaac is in his study still wondering what they should do next. His son stands in the doorway, with a quizzical expression. 'I heard Catalina and Isabel whispering about it, but they wouldn't tell me, they told me to go away.' He crosses his arms defiantly, as he shares news of this great injustice with his father.

'Come in and close the door.' This is the first time he has invited his son into his study for a private consultation, and Gabriel closes the door with a serious expression. Isaac indicates for him to sit in the chair opposite. He regards his son, steeples his fingers and ponders his response.

'Gabriel, when you do something wrong, what do you expect to happen to you?'

The boy turns his lustrous blue eyes to the ceiling and kicks his legs back and forth against the chair. 'Have *I* done something wrong Papa?'

'No, of course not, my boy. Let me try again. Let us say, hypothetically ... just for pretence ...'

'I know what hypotheckikally means, Papa. Mama is a very good teacher you know.'

Isaac smiles. 'So, *hypothetically*, you disobey Catalina and don't, for example, wash your hands before dinner. What would you expect to happen?'

Gabriel looks thoughtful. 'I expect Catalina to tell me off and make me wash my hands.'

'Yes, of course. And what if you repeat your mistake? What then?'

'She'll box my ears and tell Mama.'

'Do you think that's fair?'

Gabriel rolls his eyes and finally comes to a conclusion, 'Yes, I believe so. It's not nice, but it's fair.'

'So, you don't think it would be fair if Catalina were to publish a notice regarding your failure to follow her instructions and ask the neighbours to tell us if there were any other bad things that you had done? And to tell them that if they didn't let us know of your misdemeanors, they themselves might be punished?'

'No. Papa, that's unfair. That is too much, and my friends might start making things up just for fun or to get revenge on me. Pedro has still not forgiven me for stealing his apple and ....,'

Isaac ignores the admission and continues, 'If Catalina were to take such a course of action, this would be "disproportionate"?'

'Yes if "disportionate" means too much, yes it's very disportionate.'

'And that, my dear Gabriel, is what an Edict of Grace is: a disproportionate response to a crime, inviting neighbours and friends to tell tales against each other, with a threat to punish them if they do not. It turns friend against friend, neighbour against neighbour and tears families apart. It is one of the worst things.'

'What will you do, Papa? About the Edict Grace.'

'You are not really old enough to hear this, Gabriel, but I don't think I have a choice.' He takes a deep breath and looks away from his puzzled son. 'Sometimes even your father cannot solve everything; sometimes even he does not know the answer.'

'But I already knew *that*, Papa.'

Isaac stares at him for a moment, then roars with laughter as Gabriel runs into his open arms.

CHAPTER
TEN

'Dear Mother of Jesus,
Look down upon me
As I say my prayers slowly
at my mother's knee.
I love thee, O Lady
and please willest thou bring
All little children
To Jesus our King.'

Isabel and Gabriel monotonously recited the ritual prayer that preceded their daily lessons then looked to their mother. It was after breakfast and Isaac had gone to the Real Alcazar. They were sitting on the large terrace from which they could see the calm blueness of the Guadalquivir and glimpse Triana just beyond. Maria stared into the distance, straining her eyes as if trying to see what was happening in Triana.

'Mama?' said Isabel. Receiving no response, she directed Gabriel towards the door with a sideways glance.

They began to rise from their seats when Maria turned and cast them a baleful look. They sat back down.

'Right children, today we will examine in more detail the land around Seville. We live in the centre of a very fertile plain with many valuable crops. Gabriel can you remind us of those crops?'

'Almonds, oranges, lemons, olives ...'

Isabel cut across Gabriel's laborious repetition. 'Mama, don't you think there are more important things to discuss?'

Maria clenched her jaw and deadened her eyes. Isabel chose not to heed this warning. 'Mama there are things happening that we need to talk about. I cannot sit here discussing almonds pretending there is nothing else going on.'

Gabriel squirmed in his seat.

'Gabriel. Isabel and I will have a private lesson, you are free to do as you wish for the morning. Do not disturb Catalina and do not leave the house.'

Gabriel moved, then hesitated as though ready to complain, but took one glance at the expression on his mother's face and left.

'So, Isabel, now we're alone what are these matters, and why are they so important that they take precedence over your education?'

'Mama, Catalina says a boy was beheaded and that the boy's mother takes in our washing. Is that true?'

'Yes, it is.'

'Why did you not tell me?'

Maria paused, trying to conserve the little reserves of patience she had left. She would need to have a talk with Catalina. 'These matters need not concern us, we do not need to get involved. That is all you need to know.'

'But the talk is that the *conversos* killed the boy, so they could use the blood to make unleavened bread.'

'What do you mean "the talk"? Who has been talking? What have they been saying? "The talk" Isabel, since when do we in this house heed, "the talk"?' Maria's voice reached a crescendo.

Isabel hung her head and stared at her hands. But then, almost imperceptibly, her back straightened and her posture became more confident. Raising her eyes she held her mother's gaze and said, 'So, it is not true, Mama?'

'No, it is not true! Jewish people do not indulge in such practices; they are just as God-fearing and humane as …'

'As we are, Mama?'

'Yes, yes just as we are. Is there anything else, Isabel?'

'Yes, Mama. The Edict of Grace has been issued and the Holy Office for the Propagation of the Faith will open in Seville. Father Tomás de Torquemada himself is coming.' She paused as if expecting a response. Maria made none. 'Does that worry you Mama?'

'Why would it?' Maria looked out at the river and then turned back to her daughter, seeming to have decided. 'Yes. It is worrying. It will cause great suspicion and suffering.'

'But only to those who deserve it?'

'No, Isabel, the Inquisition is indiscriminate, it hides behind a facade of rules and misplaced faith to dispense misery to the undeserving, particularly the poor. You know what they say, "Here in Seville they only punish those who haven't got a deep purse." '

'What, "they say", Mama?' Isabel's remark hung in the air for a few moments. 'Thank you, Mama, you have given me much to think about.' With that, she rose gracefully and sauntered away, her head held unnaturally high.

Maria stayed on the terrace for a long time. What was

this child becoming? She had little idea and even less understanding of what to do about it. Had Maria been like this when she had been a young woman? Isabel's self-possession was disconcerting. Maria was sure she didn't have that kind of poise at fifteen, she wasn't even sure she had it now. She thought of life before she met Isaac in 1478, when he had graduated from the University of Salamanca. She was the only child of Isaac ben Ezra, an eminent physician. He could not save her mother from typhus, and she died when Maria was ten. He passed away from a broken heart a year later.

For one short golden year, after being introduced to Isaac by family friends, she was happy. He was such a gentleman and so handsome. He still was, just a little frayed around the edges. Isaac was a fine dancer, and she remembered joyful picnics by the banks of the river, and raucous family dinners. Her parents had named her Maryam for the sister of Moses. She changed it to Maria when she and Isaac converted to Catholicism shortly after their marriage. Isaac kept his first name, against her wishes. A year later, the Inquisition started burning heretics at the stake.

Lately, she sometimes caught him staring off into the distance and wondered what made him so thoughtful. Did he regret the decisions they had made to protect their family? A part of him did, she decided, or else why would he insist on attending the prayer meetings? Why did he hide the Torah in a chest in his room? Did he really think she didn't know? She had to do something before events overtook them. Isaac was being too thoughtful, too measured for the current times. But what did she have the power to do?

. . .

After a fitful siesta, Maria awoke with certainty. She summoned Catalina and told her to prepare for an outing to the cathedral before dinner. She did not feel safe walking through the streets by herself, now the Edict was in force. Neither did she want to leave the children alone. It would be safer to keep them close, even though logic dictated they would be better staying in the house. Isaac would no doubt have sided with logic. She wondered whether the circumstances were affecting her judgment.

Isabel and Gabriel said they would rather stay at home, but Maria's tone told them this was not an option. Isabel politely enquired what the purpose of the outing was. Maria told her it was just some boring business to do with the choir.

Maria knew that some fresh air would do them all good and expend some of Gabriel's excess energy; it was only fifteen minutes to the cathedral. She walked quickly, Catalina and the children trudging behind. Maria's parasol did little to protect her from the late afternoon sun; Catalina and Isabel flapped fans in a vain attempt to cool themselves. Gabriel seemed unbothered by the heat, kicking and skittering pebbles off the cobbles. As they approached the cathedral square, Maria picked her way around the beggars, doing her best to ignore the foul aroma of urine and sweat. She supposed that not all of them were indolent. As the wealth had grown in Seville from the trade with the Indies, so had the number of people coming to seek work from the surrounding villages. 'Another thing I can blame Isaac for,' she thought with a rueful smile.

'You can wait there with Catalina,' Maria said to the children. She indicated a shaded area just outside the main cathedral doors. Catalina seemed surprised, but Maria did not want her, or the children, to overhear the conversation she felt compelled to have. If she didn't speak to someone other than Isaac, she might go mad. The children took some coins to buy fresh orange juice from the red-capped seller nearby. They disguised the bitter taste with as little sugar as they could get away with, but the children still enjoyed it.

The cool air of the cathedral was a relief. Specks of dust flickered in the shafts of light from the high stained-glass windows. She felt the dry, dusty air catch at the back of her throat. Pulling a silver silk shawl over her hair she stood for a moment, allowing the stillness to seep into her and took a deep breath of incense. Making the sign of the cross she lit two candles, one for each of her dead parents. The service was ending, and Father Gutiérrez de Morales was intoning the concluding rite: 'May Almighty God bless you, the Father and the Son and the Holy Spirit.' Maria joined in with the 'Amen' as it rang around the cathedral. Father Gutiérrez had been the priest at San Pedro when she and Isaac had converted to Catholicism. Since that defining moment, she had always felt comfortable with the elderly cleric. She knelt at a pew and offered her prayers, as the cathedral emptied around her.

'My child, this is a pleasant surprise. Have you come for confession? No, then what is it I can do for you?'

Father Gutiérrez' warm, honey-toned voice made Maria want to close her eyes and just listen. Perhaps that would keep her sense of impending disaster at bay. *Maybe that's why I'm here, to be comforted.* She opened her eyes and Father Gutiérrez's long white beard and disheveled appearance gave her further solace. A fleeting image of her father flashed across her mind. If only she could stay like this without having to speak.

'I need to talk to somebody that I can trust Father, especially now.'

Father Gutiérrez sat patiently beside her.

'I want advice from you but I'm not sure you can say anything meaningful. I want you to solve my problems, but even you cannot do that. And more than anything I want you to save my family.'

'Should I say something meaningful, solve all your problems, and save your family before or after evening mass?' He smiled, his eyes twinkling with delight.

'You know that nobody else talks to me like this?' she said archly.

'But that's why you come, my child.'

'I must sound confused Father, but I just need guidance. And you are the only person in Seville, apart from Isaac, who can give it to me.'

Eight priests approached the pulpit. Their long white tunics were cinched about the waist with leather cords. They gathered in a circle beneath a rope attached to the enormous, bejewelled incense burner hanging from the roof above the pulpit. Taking firm hold of the rope, they pulled in unison, swinging the *incensario* back and forth, dispensing the sweet fragrance of orange blossom.

'They decided to practice before Semana Santa. Last year Father Danilo was almost knocked unconscious,' Father Gutiérrez said.

Maria smothered a laugh with her hand.

Father Gutiérrez pretended to ignore this and said, 'Permit me to talk straightforwardly.'

Maria nodded.

'You feel confused and frightened, you don't know what to do for the best and you think I can offer you some reassurance. Perhaps even suggest a course of action?'

64

Maria pursed her lips.

'You and I both know that what has happened is irrevocable, the Inquisition is coming to Seville, and families like yours are in particular danger. Neither of us can change any of that. Injustice will follow, sacrifices will be made, more innocents like Fernan will lose their lives.'

'And you and your God are happy with this?' she snapped.

'*My* God?'

Maria looked down at her hands.

Father Gutiérrez continued, 'I'm deeply unhappy about all of it, I cannot speak for The Almighty, I am not privy to *His* greater plans.'

'I'm sorry, Father.'

'I understand, my child. I suspect you have already said to Isaac what I am about to say to you: all you can do is your best to protect your family. The only alternative I can suggest is for you all to seek safe passage to the Indies. If that's too far, Portugal or Italy, as many in your position have done. Isaac could surely arrange that?'

'You advise us to run away? We are not cowards. We will stay and face what is to come. We have nothing to be ashamed of and nothing to hide.'

'*You* may have nothing to hide.'

She looked at him, eyes blazing. He held her gaze and she dropped her head and put her hands over her face.

'People talk Maria; there are very few secrets in Seville. Isaac's closeness to the King has protected him up to this point, but there is no earthly force that can shield him from the gaze of the Grand Inquisitor of All Spain.' He did not disguise the insincerity with which he intoned Torquemada's title. 'I will always be here for you to talk to, but you must realise I have little power in the matter,' he said softly.

'The only advice I can give is talk to Isaac and keep your children close.' He paused, but she still had her head in her hands. 'How are Gabriel and Isabel?'

She looked up. 'They are both fine, thank you Father. They are healthy and clever and good company. Sometimes I worry about Isabel ...'

'She must be fifteen or more now. Girls can be difficult at this age, so I am led to believe. Bring them all to Sunday Mass. You have not been as a family since I moved from San Pedro. It would be a wise signal to send to the community. Or you could accompany me on my visits to Triana, to bring some solace to those poor wretches?'

But Maria had drifted away, watching the mesmerising swing of the *incensario*. The fragrant *azahar*, the hypnotic sway from one side to the next, breathe in, breathe out, breathe in, breathe out ...

CHAPTER

ELEVEN

THE TESTIMONY OF FRIAR ALONSO

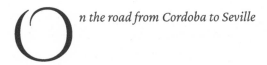

O*n the road from Cordoba to Seville*

WHIPPING the cob to keep up with Brother Tomás had quite exhausted me, but we did indeed reach the outskirts of Seville before the sun disappeared. Brother Tomás slowed his steed to a gentle trot, and I was able to catch up, the two royal bodyguards riding on ahead. He wrinkled his nose against the stench from piles of excrement, both human and animal. Cresting a hill, we saw plumes of thick black smoke below us. As we descended a bitter stench drifted towards us. I lifted the hem of my cassock to cover my nose, but it did no good. Brother Tomás asked, 'What do you know of this?' He indicated several smouldering pyres that stood in our path.

'I am not sure Brother, but I can make a supposition. When last I was here the mobs had rounded up anyone they thought were *marranos* and cut their throats. These are the bodies.'

Brother Tomás coaxed his stallion forward. We rode on, passing through the black smoke of the vast fires. There were hundreds of bodies. I tried to avert my eyes, but it was impossible to ignore the charred flesh, the blackened clothing, the agony of such a death. The acrid smell stayed in my nostrils, coating the back of my throat. Brother Tomás seemed unperturbed.

As we drew nearer to the centre of the city, these foul aromas were replaced by the fragrance of flowers and citrus trees. But our senses were assaulted in a different way: young ladies dressed in fine silks, satins and velvets were sitting on the patios of large houses of newly wealthy merchants. They were waiting to see and be seen. Their number seemed to have increased in the brief time I had been away. One thing remained constant as we travelled deeper into the city: whenever anyone looked up and saw Tomás de Torquemada's commanding visage they crossed themselves and fled. I studied him when this happened and thought I saw him wince. After a short while he pulled his cowl over his head.

Approaching the cathedral, we came upon a large number of people out for their evening *paseo*. It was easy to tell who amongst the promenaders had money: those dressed in scarlet, gold and silver. Everybody else wore undyed cloth in various shades of monochrome.

Brother Tomás brought his horse to a sudden halt and I saw his gaze fall upon a striking, tall woman in a purple satin dress. A fine veil covered the top half of her face. Her eyes darted around, looking for someone. There was something about her bearing, her anxiety and, let me be truthful, her beauty that attracted me. It drew Brother Tomás as well. Two children, a boy of about eleven and a girl who looked a little older, rushed out of the crowd into her arms and she clutched them to her. Then she pushed them away and seemed to have sharp words with them. She brought them in again, one on each side of her. All three turned to face us as they scanned the crowd. The daughter was even more arresting than her mother.

I saw Brother Tomás draw back his cowl, look directly at the woman and make the sign of the cross. She returned the benediction without hesitation. She bent down and whispered something to the girl. They turned away, I assumed to continue searching. Then they were gone, lost in the throng.

We made our way through the crowd to the hitching stone outside the cathedral, dismounted and tied up our horses. Brother Tomás put a hand up to me indicating that I should remain outside whilst he met with Father Gutiérrez. The two bodyguards ascended the steps and remained on watch outside the cathedral doors. I was at a loss as I had expected to be privy to Brother Tomás' conversation.

I stood at the bottom of the steps and surveyed the multitudes. I saw a vaguely familiar face poking and pushing its way through the crowd. She was searching for someone, and then she was there in front of me. She put her hand to her mouth and said, 'Alonso! I mean, Father Alonso.'

I looked closely at her, searching my memory, and then I had it.

'Catalina, it has been a very long time.'

She'd been one of the local women in the monastery at San Reyes who'd taken in laundry and helped with the annual harvesting of the almonds. She was five years or so younger than me and we had grown quite close. I'd thought of her as a little sister. After Andreas vanished I withdrew into prayer and meditation and Catalina became less and less important. I'd not brought her to mind for many years.

'I'm so sorry, Alonso, Father, I mean,' she said, blushing. I don't have time to speak with you. I have lost my mistress and her two children, Isabel and Gabriel. I don't suppose you've seen a fine lady in a purple dress with a boy and a girl?'

'Yes, I may well have done. They were here just a few moments ago. I'm sure they will return. You are employed in Seville?'

'Yes, Father, I work in the house of Señor Isaac Camarino Alvarez. He's an important man at the Real Alcazar. The King favours him.' This was a piece of unbelievable good fortune. Or perhaps The Almighty had favoured me. I was sure that my connection to Catalina would be of great interest to Brother Tomás. Now I would be able to capitalise on my knowledge of Señor Alvarez.

'The family treats you well, my child?'

'Yes, they do.'

'And are they a good, devout Catholic family, Catalina?'

She hesitated before stating, 'Yes, of course Father Alonso.'

'That is very pleasing to hear.'

'And I hear you've done very well, Father? Aren't you now The Grand Inquisitor's right-hand man?' She looked around, seeming to remember her actual purpose.

I smiled. 'I'm sure you've read the Edict of Grace?'

Catalina muttered that she had and looked at the ground.

'Be sure to consider it carefully and let me know if you can provide any useful information. You have a duty to protect your own soul, my child.' I saw the family returning

70

so I said farewell, turned and ascended the cathedral steps. I looked down at the four of them pushing their way through the crowd away from the cathedral. But then the eldest, the girl called Isabel I recall Catalina said, turned to look at me and I thought I saw her smile. She was a most attractive young woman.

MEETING CATALINA again could prove to be very fortuitous. It will give me access to information that should improve Brother Tomás' opinion of me. The intemperate way he's treated me of late is upsetting. Why did he exclude me from the meeting with Father Gutiérrez? Does he not trust me? His actions bring to mind the behaviour of the Master at the monastery of San Reyes. Especially on the day I can never forget.

ANDREAS and I had become firm friends and spent as much time as possible together. We were the same age, much younger than all the other monks and we laughed at the same things. The monk in charge of the kitchen, the *refectarius*, liked and trusted us, allowing us to work together as much as possible. I sometimes caught him smiling, and even laughing, at our silly games. I realise now that I had a hunger to feel close to someone. I had never known my parents and had no siblings or family that I knew of. Andreas was the first person to respond to me with such unbridled affection. For the first time it felt as though somebody really wanted my company. I'd sometimes felt that Sister Manuela's warmth was borne of a sense of duty.

Was it a weakness to seek comfort and companionship?

Was I supposed to have all my needs met by praying to The Almighty?

Andreas' mother told him that his father was a soldier who died fighting in the War of Granada before he was born. Andreas confided in me that he did not believe his mother's story. She was a whore, and he was a bastard. When I asked him why he thought that, he just shrugged and said, 'The way the townsfolk treated us. They showed us no respect.' From the age of ten Andreas stole and fought. His mother did not know what to do with him. Finally, when he was fifteen, she begged Master Bartolome to admit him to the monastery as a cooperator brother. She died shortly afterwards. Andreas once told me he was glad to be an orphan, that it freed him to give all his love to The Almighty.

Late one afternoon, about a month after Father Bartolome had caught us fooling around in the kitchen, I was on my knees scrubbing the kitchen floor when I felt a gentle tap on my shoulder. I turned and saw the Refectarius standing over me, blinking nervously.

He whispered, 'Father Santiago wishes to see you.'

Why would the Prior want to see me?

'And,' he turned, glancing around to see who might be listening, 'the Master will also be there.' He bustled away.

I emptied my bucket, washed my hands and walked slowly to the Prior's chambers, needing time to compose myself. I whispered the Pater Noster over and over. Passing through the garden that formed the central courtyard, I caught sight of Andreas. He was kneeling by a bed of agapanthus, weeding. This was odd. Brothers were assigned to work in only one area of the monastery, he should have been in the kitchen. I coughed, Andreas turned, saw me, hesitated, and returned to his work. I saw him make the sign of the cross and bring his crucifix to his lips.

My knock was answered with a curt, 'Yes,' and I entered Father Santiago's outer chamber which served as his office. He stood, staring out of the window that looked over the central courtyard. Turning, he raised an eyebrow in greeting and held out a palm to a chair in the middle of the room. I sat down and placed my hands in my lap. About ten feet away Father Bartolome sat squarely behind a long, wooden desk. I winced as Father Santiago's chair scraped on the flagstones when he drew it in to sit next to the Master.

'Alonso, you've been at the monastery for more than five years now,' Father Santiago began.

I dipped my head.

'You're doing very well, yes very well,' he continued.

Master Bartolome coughed and looked down at his interlaced fingers, clenched so hard I could see the finger-tips reddening as they dug into the backs of his hands.

'And you are perfectly happy here?'

'Yes, of course, Father,' I blurted out truthfully. I still didn't understand the purpose of this meeting.

'By God's grace in a few more years you will be ordained. The time will pass quickly I'm sure.' He rose, made the sign of the cross and said, 'God be with you my son,' and left.

I was relieved that the meeting was over but perplexed by its brevity. I rose from my chair and made to follow the Prior. Master Bartolome slapped a palm down on the table. I sat back down.

'Andreas has become an excellent friend,' he hissed.

It was a statement, not a question, so I waited. But not as long as Master Bartolome was prepared to. 'Yes ... he has

... we are ...' I managed to get out. 'We help each other with our work.'

'It's always good to have the correct type of friends. The kind that will engage in righteous activity,' he let his words hang in the air between us, continuing to stare directly at me all the while.

I had no idea what he could be talking about. Had somebody told him about our fun? And then I recalled the incident in the kitchen where he had witnessed Andreas' imitation of him. And then I had a far more worrying notion. Was he implying that there was something other than fraternal love between myself and Andreas? I remember taking a very deep breath before replying, 'Yes, Master Bartolome.'

'But if our friends distract us from our duty and our prayers, can they really be our friends?'

I hesitated. I didn't know if this was rhetorical. I decided it was best to remain silent.

'Well?' he asked.

I took another deep breath and blurted out, 'I think it is possible to have friends, enjoy oneself and to still faithfully worship the Almighty.'

'*Enjoy*?'

He spat the word out so viciously that I was too shocked to reply. I looked down at my hands as they writhed against one another in my lap.

He continued to stare at me until we heard the bells for Vespers, at which point he jutted his clenched jaw at me. I left as quickly as decorum would allow. I didn't see Andreas in the garden. I never saw him again.

. . .

I HAVE DONE my absolute best to forget him. But he was my friend, the first human being I ever remember feeling genuine love for. We never had a chance to say farewell. I consider that to be, God forgive me, an act of cruelty by the Master. I am sure he had his reasons and believed he was obeying Gods' Will. I have prayed hard to find it in my heart to forgive the Master, and I will continue to do so.

This indulgence in nostalgia distracts me from my duties. Brother Tomás expects me to find Fernan's killers. If we can find proof that it was the crypto-Jews the King will have no choice but to accept whatever the Holy Office does in Seville. This is a mission that will take time and strength. The King cannot be allowed to stop us when we have only just begun.

CHAPTER

TWELVE

S *eville*

Isaac's desk in the Real Alcazar is situated at the far end of a cavernous corridor of a room that is never warm enough in winter but is blessedly cool in the stifling summer. He endured a poor night's sleep, again. He tries to raise his spirits by remembering how wonderful it is to be in the room where two of the three most important characters of the age met. Queen Isabella received Cristofer Colombo here, on his return from the Americas. Isaac will miss it when they finish the permanent building, a five-minute walk away. Still, another year is the latest estimate and perhaps he will not even be in Seville by then; perhaps not even alive.

He tries to banish the unsettling thought of the third member of that august group, but Maria's account of Tomás de Torquemada's entrance to Seville forces its way to the front of his mind. The previous evening she told him of her conversation with Father Gutiérrez and how irritated she had been to lose sight of the children. She was furious with Catalina and panicked. Isaac knows she would not have done so in more normal times. He had decided not to chastise her or question the logic, or indeed advisability, of taking the children out now the Edict of Grace was published. Isaac remains disturbed by Maria's description of Torquemada's arrival and the way he looked at her. Gabriel was, of course, impressed by the size of the body-guards' swords. Isabel remained silent and thoughtful during her mother's recounting of the episode.

Catalina did not emerge with any credit. Not only had she become separated from the children, but Maria saw her speaking to a Dominican friar in an overly familiar way. When asked why, she told Maria, 'I don't know his name, señora. He started talking to me, something about saving my soul. I wasn't really listening.' Isaac chose not to share with Maria his suspicion that it was probably Friar Alonso, Torquemada's right-hand man. He reasoned that there was enough paranoia and suspicion without adding fuel to the fire.

Isaac pretends to study one of the vast number of contracts that litter his desk. He needs more help. Alejandro is efficient, but they cannot cope with the sheer volume of trade flooding into Seville. Alejandro knocks and enters. Isaac wishes he would wait for permission. He is in his early twenties, newly graduated from the University of Sala-manca, intelligent, energetic, committed. He reminds Isaac of himself at that age.

'I've received word that His Majesty would like to speak with you, Señor Alvarez.'

Isaac feigns indifference and rises slowly. 'Very well

Alejandro. I have finished with this sugar contract. You will need to go through it; there are several shortcomings I'm sure you'll be able to find.' He has not finished with it, has barely started, but he likes to keep the young pretender in his place.

ISAAC SEES King Ferdinand standing by the fountain in the Hall of Justice, surrounded by courtiers and supplicants. He is not an attractive man; his doughy face framed by bushy eyebrows and fashionably long sideburns. Isaac had long ago disregarded physiognomy as a good basis for judging character. He knows the King to be clever, mainly honest, but a ruthless pragmatist. A courtier formally announces Isaac, the King nods and everyone else melts away.

'Isaac. All this trade with the Indies must keep you busy. Not the liveliest of occupations though, I wager?'

Isaac smiles and bows his head in assent.

'There are some far more pressing matters I want to seek your view on.' Isaac became a confidant of the King once Ferdinand learnt of the origins of his family. Isaac's father was a direct descendant of Hasdai Ibn Shaprut, the renowned court physician. Isaac was brought up in the same way that Hasdai had brought up his children: to study Hebrew and revere the Torah but to also learn Arabic and Latin languages. The King views Isaac as a cultured man of integrity and good pedigree. He values his impartial, informal advice. Ferdinand is rumoured to have *converso* blood in his ancestry, though they never speak of this.

'It is always my great pleasure, Your Majesty.'

The King gives him an amused smile, 'Isaac we are alone, you can drop the reverential tone. I need your intellect and your honesty.'

Isaac returns the smile.

'This murder of the boy and the blood libel nonsense will make all hell break loose. Her Majesty is not happy, so she's sent for the "Grand Inquisitor of All Spain", as he just loves to refer to himself. No doubt you've heard?'

'The city talks of little else since the Edict of Grace was published.'

'I'll give him Edict of damned Grace. Here in *my* Seville? What's the man doing?'

'Only what you give him leave to.'

The King regards him sternly. 'Yes, I suppose you're right, but the Queen is relentless and there is little I can do I'm afraid. Is there something you can think of?'

Isaac ponders for a long moment, and then sighs. 'Sometimes we put things in train that cannot be stopped. A series of events have to run their natural course, and unless you can persuade Her Majesty otherwise ...'

The King's silence is sufficient answer.

'Then I'm afraid that there is nothing to be done. You will have to let this play out.'

'Damnable man, damnable Inquisition. I wouldn't mind if I thought the methods they used got to the truth. The "water cure"? What's that going to cure, except your ability to breathe?'

Isaac knows it is futile to interrupt the King when he is in this mood.

'You have my complete trust, but I don't agree with you that there is nothing to be done.' He looks expectantly at Isaac. 'You're far too clever to believe that. We need to know the actual reason the boy was murdered, and why so savagely. Torquemada is using it as a pretext to bring the Inquisition to Seville. If you can find the real murderers and disprove the blood libel, I might persuade the Queen the Inquisition is not required in the city after all.'

'I could ...'

'I want you to think about how we can get proof. She will not settle for anything less than incontrovertible evidence.' With that, he turns and strides from the room, leaving Isaac alone and staring up at the octagonal, coffered, ceiling searching for guidance.

'WHEN I PUT Gabriel to bed, he asked me who the man on the horse was,' Maria says, sipping her sherry. It is a perfect night to be on the terrace. Warm with a slight breeze, a clear star-adorned sky, and the comforting sound of the cicada. Across the river, torches are being lit on the Puente de Barcas, and the silhouette of the Castillo de San Jorge comes slowly into view.

'And what did you say my dear?' Isaac asks, thinking that he cannot escape the Grand Inquisitor today. He wonders if he should tell Maria about the King's request.

'Tell me Isaac, what would *you* have said?'

'The truth,' he replies without hesitation.

'What? That the evilest man in the world just rode into our city on a big black horse, like the devil incarnate?'

Isaac hesitates, 'I've already explained the Edict of Grace to him, so he knows about the Inquisition.' He pauses whilst Maria studies him. 'I would have said it was the man who'd issued the Edict, and that he might hear people talking about him. If he does, he should come and speak to me and I will explain things. But that he needn't worry until I tell him to.'

'Yes, all *very* reasonable. I'm sure Gabriel would be

grateful to you, but he's just a boy. He cannot comprehend the abominations this man will perpetrate.'

'No, my dear, that's why I didn't use those words,' Isaac says, aware the conversation is straying into dangerous territory. He does not want to disagree with her.

Cats yowl and someone shouts from the street below, "Get out of here!"

Isaac rises to look over the edge of the wrought iron railing that runs the length of the terrace. When he turns back he sees his wife, head in hands, shoulders jerking, trying hard to contain her sobs.

'Oh, my dear,' Isaac says. He pulls her hands gently away from her face. She looks up at him, tears staining her cheeks, holds his head in her hands and kisses him delicately on the lips. He nestles his forehead against hers and looks into her eyes.

'Don't you fear that each time we hug, each time we kiss, each night we put our children safely to bed, that it might be the last time?'

He takes her hand and leads her to the edge of the terrace. He puts his arm around her waist and says, 'Look up. Those stars will still be there tomorrow night. When we awake in the morning the sun will rise, life will go on. We have to believe there is a way through this. I could say I have a plan, but that would be untrue. Deep in our heads, in our hearts we have both known this would happen. We have to face it, do whatever needs must to ensure Isabel and Gabriel survive.' He pulls her close and gently strokes her hair. He knows that he has to formulate a plan to save his family. There are few options, none of them appealing. He must decide before events overtake them.

THIRTEEN

'Why *were* you speaking to that seedy little friar outside the cathedral yesterday?' asked Isabel. She was sitting in front of a mirror perched atop an oak chest. Catalina was brushing Isabel's hair with the tortoise-shell comb that was a gift from her father. The house was quiet, Gabriel asleep. Her parents were on the terrace, no doubt sipping sherry, as was increasingly their custom after dinner.

'I already told your mother, señorita. Friar Alonso was asking after my soul and whether I'd done enough to save it from the eternal fire.'

Isabel contemplated Catalina's reflection. Catalina looked away, intent on continuing to count the brush-strokes under her breath. 'Sixty-seven, sixty-eight ...'

'It didn't seem that way. It looked as if you already knew him,' Isabel said.

Catalina met Isabel's eyes in the mirror but said nothing.

'Do you? You know his name after all.'

'No, señorita, I do not, and I know his name because he

82

introduced himself.' Catalina continued counting sotto voce, pulling the brush very firmly.

Isabel yelped and turned around.

Catalina put on a pained expression. 'I'm so sorry, señorita, there was a very tough knot of hair. Sometimes a little pain is unavoidable.'

'Don't do it again, please, Catalina.' Isabel tried for a placatory tone and thought she saw a small smile form on Catalina's lips.

'I'll do my best, señorita.' Catalina continued brushing until she announced loudly, 'one hundred' and put the brush down firmly on the oak chest.

Isabel studied her own reflection, turning her head from side to side, judging the efficacy of Catalina's work. She nodded, rose from the chair and turned to face the servant. Isabel could look directly into her eyes as they were now the same height. She noticed there were more lines around Catalina's eyes and wrinkles on her brow than there had seemed to be just that morning. 'That will be all, Catalina.'

She made to leave the room.

'Catalina.' The servant stopped with her hand on the door handle, 'I thought I heard you say something about the Edict of Grace to that friar.' Catalina did not move, did not appear to be even breathing. 'But maybe I'm mistaken, it was very noisy in the square.'

Catalina turned and strode back. She caught hold of Isabel's wrist and hissed, '*Señ-or-it-a* your mother would be very upset to hear about you accusing me of such things. You should remember you are still a girl, and I look after you, dress you and prepare your *food* every day.' She pushed Isabel's wrist away, said goodnight and left.

Isabel massaged her wrist, eyes wide and jaw tight. *How*

dare she treat me that way. She went in search of Gabriel. She found him in his bedchamber playing with the two white knights and a black bishop he had taken from his father's wooden chess set.

'Gabriel,' Isabel barked. Her brother continued to play. He formed the pieces into a 'v' shaped configuration – the bishop leading, flanked on either side by a knight. He moved them slowly over the floor as Isabel sat alongside him. She looked at him expectantly. Receiving no response, she swept the three chess pieces away with the back of her hand. Gabriel opened his mouth to scream and Isabel put one hand over it and with the other pinched his ear lobe, hissing through clenched teeth, 'If you scream I'll come to your bedchamber one night, put a pillow over your face and hold it there until you choke to death. And then I'll tell Mama that a robber came in and did it. Do you understand?'

Gabriel nodded and a thin line of tears ran down his cheeks.

'You can play your stupid game after I've finished.'

Gabriel rested his chin on his chest.

Isabel took her hand away from his mouth and said, 'Swear you won't scream or tell Mama.'

'I swear I won't scream or tell Mama.'

'Right let's start again. Gabriel.'

'Yes, Isabel,' the boy moaned.

'What did you hear Catalina say to that priest when we were waiting for Mama outside the cathedral?'

'Nothing, I was too interested in the knights.'

'Are you sure you didn't hear her telling him about us? About Mama and Papa?'

Gabriel looked blankly at her, trying to rub the snot away from his nose.

Isabel slapped his hand away. 'Well, *I* heard her say something about cutting ham and about secret prayer meetings. Are *you* sure you didn't?'

Gabriel shook his head and started to say something when Isabel grabbed hold of his ear lobe again, twisting it viciously. 'Are you really, really sure you didn't?' she hissed.

'No, I'm not sure,' Gabriel sobbed as he tried to squirm away.

'Good, you just remember that. Ham and secret prayer meetings. Say it.'

'Ham and secret prayer meetings,' he whispered.

'Again,' she insisted.

Gabriel complied.

'Good boy,' she released his ear and patted his head tenderly. 'Now, get back to your idiotic games.'

CATALINA HURRIED TO TRIANA, but she was not intending to go home. Not yet. She had left the house quickly after the nasty episode with the señorita. She bid a hasty goodnight to the señora, who was in a particularly foul mood. Her silence always made this apparent; when she was happy her voice was heard throughout the house, teasing Gabriel, laughing, chiding Catalina. But today Catalina had not heard her voice at all, just suffered her nasty looks when their paths crossed. Something was amiss.

The weather was mild. Though there was a whisper of warmth in the air that announced the end of winter. The heat of summer would soon follow, and Catalina would despair of having to cook another meal in that stuffy kitchen. The señor, in particular, would become irritable and Catalina would suffer his ill temper. She still had a soft spot for him; she had served him and his father's family for a long time. They never hit her, but the señor and señora had a way about them, of making you know through their looks, their silences and the occasional unkind word, that you had displeased them. And it carried on for days sometimes. She had almost rather the señora shouted at her or slapped her; at least it would be clear and all over with. Justice would have been done and a line drawn.

The señorita had become quite the little madam lately. *Just because she's fifteen now and becoming a woman doesn't give her the right to treat me like a clod of earth.* Her moods and her silences were becoming like the señora's. The way she flounced around, and that grand tone she used when her mother was out of earshot. At least Gabriel was still respectful, mostly. He seemed to still love her. Surely she deserved that much after ten years' faithful service? They paid her well enough, she supposed, but she was still just a servant. And servants had to keep their family's secrets. There would be serious trouble if people knew what was really going on.

She crossed the Guadalquivir using the Puente de Barcas. It was dark but a full moon lit her way, the sky was full of shimmering stars. She would have liked to just stand and bathe in the beauty of the night sky. She picked her way across the boats, thankful the water was still. Beggars and vagrants, of whom there seemed to be more and more of late, used the boats to rest their heads at night. She was not afraid as the bridge was well lit by flaming torches. She arrived at the Triana bank and made her way to the Castillo de San Jorge: the place she knew Friar Alonso had prepared to become the city's headquarters for the Inquisition.

FOURTEEN

THE TESTIMONY OF FRIAR ALONSO

T*riana, Castillo de San Jorge*

I FOUND Brother Tomás standing in his anteroom admiring the Guadalquivir from the latticed window. Evening was closing in and the night watchman were lighting the line of torches on the boats that bridged the river. He must enjoy keeping a close watch on the citizens of his new territory.

It had pleased me to receive the summons from Brother Tomás. He's taken over the former commander's chambers at the *castillo* – a bedchamber and an anteroom. I am satisfied with our newest headquarters. It is well fortified and spacious. Brother Tomás has not commented on the arrangements, as is his prerogative.

'I've been mulling my disappointing conversation with Father Gutiérrez at the cathedral,' he began, without turning around. 'It garnered little useful intelligence. I would have expected a man in his position to know more about the local mores. The only information I extracted were the names of the woman and her two children we saw standing outside the cathedral.' He paused. 'But then you already knew that.'

I permitted myself a smile of satisfaction, but instantly regretted the cardinal sin of pride.

'We'll return to the family of Señor Alvarez later, but first, what progress have you to report?'

'I've been spending almost all of my time ensuring that the arrangements here would be to your satisfaction,' I replied, expecting acknowledgement of some sort.

'I meant what information do you have for me regarding the boy Fernan's murder?' he said, turning to face me.

I blinked rapidly and struggled to find an answer that would appease him.

'You understand we need results? You do recall that the Holy Office receives no funding from Their Majesty's exchequer? We rely entirely on the proceeds from the disposal of the assets we rightfully seize from the sinners we bring to justice?'

I hung my head.

'You need to make it a priority, Alonso, we need to assign responsibility for this heinous crime. I will expect news within the next two days. Surely the Edict must have elicited some response?'

'We have received many hundreds of reports, the *notario de secreto* are finishing their records of all the conversations. We already have over one hundred prisoners in the Torre either being questioned or awaiting interrogation. Nobody who we have information about has been allowed to escape. I assure you I am doing my very best Brother Tomás.'

'What about Señor Alvarez's family? Isaac ... Maria ... Gabriel ... and Isabel.' He seemed to savour their names. He whispered the last, and I thought I saw his tongue trace the outline of his bottom lip.

'Something of great import happened last night,' I paused, hoping to draw Brother Tomás in. His clenched jaw told me I had better talk quickly. 'Catalina, their maidservant, the one I knew in San Reyes?'

He nodded curtly.

'She came to visit me. She is a kind soul, but naïve and gullible.'

'A nostalgic chat?' Brother Tomás enquired impatiently, leaning forward and placing his palms on the desk.

'No, Brother Tomás, although that was the pretext. Once we had finished reminiscing something rather more interesting emerged. As I told you, Catalina worked for Señor Alvarez's father when she was a girl. It was her first position after she left the monastery. She moved into his direct employ when Señor Camarino – his father – died. She appears very loyal to him.'

Brother Tomás drummed his fingers on the desk.

'She suggested that the family was in danger because of certain practices, which she was not specific about. I don't know what they were or who was responsible. She alluded to something that Isabel had done,' Brother Tomás narrowed his eyes at me, 'but would not be drawn on details. I think she believes that by bringing me into her confidence she could somehow protect them, or some of them, perhaps just the children. She's become anxious for their safety since the Edict was published.'

Brother Tomás grunted. 'They are a family of *conversos* and are naturally under suspicion. This requires delicate handling. Normally this testimony would be sufficient evidence to act, or at least bring this Catalina in for further questioning. Even with Señora Graciella's testimony, we require caution, given Alvarez' royal connections. His Majesty favours, even, it is rumoured, to confide in him. If we act precipitately, things may not go well for us, for the Office. How does the maidservant believe that things have been left?'

'I listened with interest and told her I would do whatever I could to protect the innocent whilst bringing the guilty to justice. That seemed to satisfy her.'

'You must secure greater, direct evidence Brother Alonso. I need not remind you of why that is of the utmost importance.'

'But how should I – '

'I have absolute confidence you will find a way.' He stood and turned to face the window again. I didn't leave as he clearly intended me to. His shoulders relaxed a little. 'Perhaps a further, more in-depth conversation with this Catalina. You might like to encourage her assistance by letting her know that if she can't be helpful, I might need to have a more *formal* discussion with her.'

'Yes, Brother Tomás, we must root out these alleged heretics.'

Brother Tomás wheeled round, and I felt myself blinking rapidly again as he shouted, 'There are no *alleged* heretics; only those who choose to repent and those who do not.'

As I closed the door to Brother Tomás' chambers I silently cursed him. What did he expect of me? I'm his right-hand man, not a miracle worker. I made the sign of the cross and chastised myself for such intemperate thoughts. Surely, he understood the gathering of information was a painstaking process? It involved many hours of sifting and sorting the grains, separating the wheat from the chaff as Matthew would have it. I was proud to remember the words from Chapter three of his gospel so readily. Since turning forty last year, I had found I could not always rely on my memory.

I know Brother Tomás favours the bluntness of the rack, but I am unsure if this is always the best route to the truth. He was right though, I needed to act, to discover the truth of Catalina's assertions. I needed to protect the Church as best I could without compromising Brother Tomás' position with the King.

I returned to my room. It was small, cold and high ceilinged with just enough space for a narrow bed, a desk and a chamber pot. I have no window with a view over the river, just an arrow slit through which a dull shaft of light shows the waning of the day. If I stand on my bed and peer to the east, I can make out the tip of the Torre del Oro on the opposite bank of the Guadalquivir. I visited the tower only yesterday to make sure it was proving suitable as a prison to hold those awaiting questioning. Yet another consideration that Brother Tomás did not appreciate.

The sun was setting and I heard the bells for Vespers. I like to say the evening prayers alone. It helps to settle me as I always feel uneasy with the onset of night. It's usually at twilight that Andreas appears. I try to think what he would have said about my circumstances. But I could not harness the imagination to do so, though I was sure it would have been something humorous. That would have helped, if only for a few moments.

I knelt by the bed, clasped my hands and softly recited,

'O God, come to my assistance. O Lord, make haste to help me. Glory to the Father, and to the Son, and to the Holy Spirit. As it was in the beginning, is now, and will be forever. Amen. Alleluia.' I opened my eyes to complete darkness and was certain what I needed to do.

CHAPTER
FIFTEEN

S *eville*

TWO DAYS after his difficult conversation with Maria on the terrace, Isaac is on his way home from the Real Alcazar and looking forward to a family lunch; in particular, the rice pudding Maria has promised. The remainder of last years dried figs have arrived from the orchard they maintain outside the city near Valdezzoras. The figs will pair very well with the pudding.

Pushing open the door to Casa de la Felicidad he is surprised to hear the deep tones of a man's voice. He stands in the open doorway, startled to see Maria sitting beside the fountain next to a Dominican friar. Isaac notes her fixed smile and rapt expression. The friar rises from the marble bench and advances towards him. He has a long, sallow face; gimlet eyes separated by a large, hooked nose bring to Isaac's mind an eagle.

'My apologies, Señor Alvarez. I should have contacted you before visiting you at home. I was in the *barrio* and Señora Ximenes invited me in, and has been so hospitable,' he turns to smile at Maria. 'My apologies, señor, I am Friar Alonso de Hojeda,' the prelate announces.

Isaac manages a smile but cannot think what it might be appropriate to say. Why was this man in his *home*? Were soldiers about to storm Casa de la Felicidad? If they found his Torah they were all lost.

'Brother Tomás has, of course, heard of your valuable work with the Indies.'

Isaac notices that Alonso is blinking rapidly.

Alonso glances at Maria. 'Brother Tomás asked me to visit you at the earliest opportunity as someone who might be helpful to the Holy Office for the Propagation of the Faith.'

Isaac resists the temptation to reply sardonically to the friar's pomposity. Maria widens her eyes at him and nods encouragingly. He grips Friar Alonso's outstretched hand and takes a moment to study his small, dark eyes. It is a predatory face. He continues to clasp the friar's hand, snatching a moment to decide how to manage the encounter. He assumes that it is only because of his connection to King Ferdinand that this conversation takes place at his home and not the Torre.

'Why of course, Friar Alonso, you are most welcome. We know that you are in Seville on important work.' Isaac wonders if his smile appears to Alonso as the rictus he feels it to be.

Gabriel rushes in to hug him.

Isabel follows, hands clasped demurely in front of her. She murmurs, 'Good afternoon, Papa.' Alonso's eyes appear to linger over Isabel's form.

Isaac returns Gabriel's hug and smiles at Isabel. 'Well, where are my manners, Friar Alonso! Would you like to stay for lunch? You are most welcome, though I'm sure you have many pressing matters to attend to regarding the work of the Holy Office.'

'Of course, our work on the glorious mission never stops, but one must always find time to sustain oneself with good food and enjoyable company. Besides, it would be rude of me to turn down such a gracious invitation.'

Isaac beams, and with a flourish shows the way into the main part of the house. He avoids any eye contact with Maria.

It is the family's routine to enjoy their afternoon meal on the terrace, but this would be too informal a place to dine with Tomás de Torquemada's deputy. Maria hastily confers with Catalina and the formal dining room is prepared, whilst Isaac shows Friar Alonso the view from the terrace. They engage in small talk, with Isaac resorting to pointing out landmarks such as the Torre del Oro and the Castillo de San Jorge. Friar Alonso seems remarkably animated and interested but Isaac is relieved when Gabriel appears to ask them to come to lunch. Isaac wonders why Alonso had not taken the obvious opportunity to discuss more serious matters, or to reveal the real purpose of his visit.

The dining room is just large enough to accommodate all of them. A cloth that Maria, with Isabel's help, had embroidered with an elaborate design of purple agapantha, covers the trestle table. Isaac and Alonso take the high-backed chairs at either end. Maria sits with Gabriel on a wooden bench on one side with Isabel opposite. In the centre of the table is a large bowl of mutton stew, accompanied by a dish of asparagus, a basket of rye bread, two carafes of red wine and two jugs of water.

'I'm so sorry for the poor fare, Friar Alonso,' Maria says.

Isabel looks to the heavens. Isaac hopes he is the only one who notices.

'What nonsense, Señora Ximenes, it is a feast. It smells delicious,' Alonso sniffs the air ostentatiously. 'Although, I think you have cooked it using olive oil?'

Isaac continues pouring wine into the adults' goblets and tries to ignore this dangerous question.

'Yes,' Maria replies, 'my mother told me that olive oil was healthier than lard, so I've always followed her advice. We need to respect our elders and it doesn't worry us that some people call it the smell of the Jews, does it, Isaac?' she says lightly.

'No, my dear, of course not. As you say respect for ones' parents and the health of ones' children are far more important than some old wives' tales. Wouldn't you agree, Friar Alonso?'

Alonso ponders Isaac's explanation for a moment before replying, 'On balance perhaps you are right, but the opinion of our neighbours is so important, especially now.'

Neither Isaac nor Maria take the bait. Gabriel rocks back and forth, Isabel staring at him.

'Well, let me serve you Friar Alonso,' says Maria as she places food on everyone's plate and then waits expectantly.

Isaac feels the pause stretching awkwardly out. 'Friar Alonso would you like to say Grace?' Has Alonso just set another trap, is he waiting for us to start eating without saying a blessing?

Alonso bows his head, closes his eyes, and intones, 'Bless us O Lord, and these your gifts, which we are about to receive from your bounty. Through Christ our Lord. Amen.'

Isabel's "Amen" is particularly loud, Gabriel's only a mumble. They eat in silence with the occasional "Delicious" from Alonso punctuated by slurping noises from Gabriel at which Isabel kicks him under the table. Catalina comes in to clear. Isaac notices her staring at Alonso and grimacing as she leaves, arms piled high with plates. The friar gives no indication that he notices her attention. They wait for her to return with the pudding.

'I'm sure you will find the figs delicious Friar Alonso. They are from my father's estate at Pozzoblanco, just out near Valdezzoras. It's about an hour away.'

'I'm sure I shall, Señor Alvarez. Do you plan to spend from St John's Day to Michaelmas there? That's the usual pattern for those who enjoy the luxury of owning a country estate?'

'I'm sure we will, or rather the family will. I expect I will still be dealing with sugar contracts. And I'm not sure it's a luxury worth enjoying Friar; labour and maintenance costs are so high.' Isaac notes with alarm that Alonso seems extremely interested in the estate as he tries to elicit some detail about its value. Isaac deflects these questions with generalisations. He is grateful when Catalina returns with the rice pudding and the promised plate of dried figs, aware that he says a little too loudly, 'Ah, here are the figs!'

Apart from administering violent retribution to Gabriel under the table, Isabel has taken almost no part in the meal. She refuses Maria's offer of rice pudding and takes just one fig. She coughs and asks, 'Friar Alonso, can you tell us what progress has been made by the Holy Office since you arrived in Seville?'

Isaac and Maria simultaneously turn to stare at her, and then just as quickly turn away.

'That is an interesting question. I have been spending

my time attending to, what shall I say, logistical preparations in order that everything should be as Brother Tomás
decrees.'

Isabel is rapt.

'We have also gathered much information since the
Edict was published and are examining it. As you can
appreciate it is very time consuming. We have also been
busy at the Torre with our ... *other* methods of discovering
the truth.'

'You mean interrogation and torture, Friar Alonso?'
Isabel asks.

'More wine, Friar Alonso?' Maria asks hurriedly, but
Alonso covers his goblet with the palm of his hand.

'Let me just say, in answer to your question, señorita, in
the present company,' he glances at Gabriel, 'when heretics
refuse to confess their sins, they need encouragement to do
the right thing. And the righteous purpose of the Holy
Office is to save souls from damnation.'

Isabel is about to continue when Maria intervenes,
'Have you received any information regarding the murder
of the choirboy, Fernan?'

At that moment Catalina returns and starts to clear
away the dessert bowls.

'We have, señora,' Alonso turns to look at Maria and
holds her gaze while he continues, 'but I'm sure you understand I cannot make any comment at the moment.'

Maria nods.

'Although, I have received information that you knew
the family, Señora Ximenes?'

Isabel coughs and reaches for a glass of water. She
narrows her eyes at Gabriel.

'Ham and prayers,' Gabriel mutters almost in a whisper.

'I'm sorry, my boy, what did you say?' Alonso asks.

'Ham and prayers,' Gabriel repeats more loudly.

Isaac and Maria turn to glare at him. A sly smile creeps over Isabel's face. A loud crash of broken crockery and Catalina's cry of "Christ's fingernails" distracts attention from Gabriel. Isaac considers nudging a goblet to the floor, just to add to the mayhem, but this might be a little too dramatic.

'I'm sorry, my boy, what was that you said?' Alonso repeats.

Gabriel looks at Isabel who nods almost imperceptibly as he whispers, 'Ham and prayers.'

'Yes, I thought that was what you said. What do you mean by that?' he asks with a smile.

Gabriel, now sitting on his hands rocking back and forth, starts to cry.

Catalina lets out a loud shriek, everyone turns to look at her outstretched bloodied palm, a large shard of white porcelain protruding from it. She staggers to one side, clutching at the back of Isaac's chair for support.

'Oh my God!' Maria screams, and rushes to her side. 'Gabriel, go to the apothecary and ask Abu Ali Sina for wormwood and honey.'

Alonso grabs Gabriel's wrist, pulling the boy towards him, 'What *did* you say?'

Gabriel's wailing grows even louder, and Alonso lets go of him. He runs to his mother, who ruffles his hair and brushes her palms over his eyes. 'Now go along Gabriel, run as fast you can to the apothecary,' Maria says, glaring at Isabel.

Isabel looks from her mother to Alonso and then down into her lap.

Alonso surveys the scene and makes the sign of the cross. He smiles at Isabel. Shortly afterwards he makes his excuses and leaves.

SIXTEEN
THE TESTIMONY OF FRIAR ALONSO

T *riana, Castillo de San Jorge*

I COULD NOT HAVE PREDICTED the way my visit to Señor Alvarez' house would turn out. Brother Tomás smiled broadly when I told him of the evidence: cooking with olive oil and the boy Gabriel's chant of "ham and prayers". Add to this, Señor Alvarez continuing to be known as "Isaac" after converting; not to mention that unkempt beard of his which the Jews seem to favour, and we had more than sufficient proof. Even without the rumours that Señora Graciella had alluded to.

Brother Tomás was in the midst of issuing an instruction for the arrest of the entire family when a messenger arrived with a missive for me. I am still unsure, even as I write this, whether the timing was fortunate or unfortunate. If the message had not arrived we would have sent the guards immediately to arrest Isaac and Maria and lock them away. Brother Tomás generously planned to become guardian to those two, poor children. If only Andreas and I had enjoyed such benevolence and guidance. I cannot help but regret the Master's intolerance.

We cannot blame the children. Gabriel is much too young, and Isabel is surely without blame; she merely requires guidance. She is an intelligent, and indeed beautiful, young lady. I'm sure she will flourish under Brother Tomás' expert tutelage.

I'm digressing and have not explained the import of the, perhaps, untimely message we received. We were in Brother Tomás' chambers at the *castillo*. It was from Señor Alvarez requesting to meet with me. I have rarely seen him surprised, but that was Brother Tomás ' reaction to the message. It stated that Señor Alvarez wished to discuss the matter of Juan de Mota. I was pleased to be able to readily recall the details of his case, informing Brother Tomás accordingly.

We presumed that Señor Alvarez intended to plead for de Mota, perhaps he really thought we would release him. Surely, he is not so foolish? Brother Tomás favoured me by laying out our options: ignore the note and continue with the arrest of the family or allow the meeting to take place. My view was that there was nothing to be lost by allowing Señor Alvarez to come, and perhaps much to gain. There might well be further incriminating evidence. I was happy that Brother Tomás agreed with me.

I was therefore disappointed, especially after I had concluded such a full briefing on the matter, when Brother Tomás informed me that *he* alone would meet with Señor Alvarez. I thought better of arguing the point and left to compose a reply making the appropriate arrangements for the meeting.

CHAPTER
SEVENTEEN

*S*eville

'It's so thoughtful of you, my dear.' Maria could not recall the last time she had said those words to her daughter. Isabel bowed her head in acknowledgment of the compliment, picked up the basket of dried figs, fresh oranges and a loaf of Catalina's rye bread. Maria sat on the marble bench in the courtyard at Casa de la Felicidad. It was two days after the meal with Friar Alonso. The basket contained the last of the season's fresh oranges and all that remained of the dried figs. Maria wondered why Isabel had been so attentive since the disastrous lunch, almost as if she felt guilty. She chided herself for doubting her daughter's motives and reminded herself to be grateful for what she had.

Maria had spoken to Isaac about Gabriel's strange behavior at the lunch. They concluded that discussing it with Gabriel would only make things worse. He must have overheard one of their conversations and picked up on one or two words. The children were already worried enough by the Edict and the Inquisition. Gabriel had woken from nightmares almost every night, calling out for his mother. They agreed to settle for telling Gabriel that he must be cautious about repeating words that he overheard. They knew how "fortuitous" Catalina's injury had been and Maria had made a point of being kind to her.

Maria knew that something had to come of the incident. Surely Alonso would not let it pass? She half expected to be awoken in the middle of the night by officers of the Inquisition. Feeling helpless was new; as was the resentment she felt towards Isaac. Why did he have to attend those prayer meetings and put the family in such jeopardy? Part of her knew she was being unfair, that his principles and values were a part of why she had fallen in love with him. But he was a man, her husband, the father of her children, and a confidant of the King. Surely he had the power to do something? Her frustration grew, and with it, her silence.

Maria wondered what would have become of them all by the time the orange blossom appeared again. Even that seemed a long way off; so much had already happened this year. She told herself she should just concentrate on getting through to the festival of Semana Santa, which was only a few weeks away. Focusing on the renewal and rebirth of the Holy Week would awaken the optimism it usually engendered. 'Give my very best wishes to Fernan's parents and let them know I will visit next week.'

'I will, Mama,' Isabel replied, as she passed the basket to Catalina.

Maria watched as they walked through the door leading

to the street. Catalina turned and looked at her for just a moment. Maria thought she saw fear in her eyes. But fear was commonplace now. If even half of the rumours she heard were true, there was no hope for any of them. The Edict had pitted neighbours and family members against each other.

Last evening, Catalina had told them of one such story she had heard from a neighbour's servant. The eldest son, just nineteen, from a family of rich merchants, was accused of attending illicit Jewish prayer meetings. The family assumed the allegation came from a scorned girlfriend, though they had no proof. He was kept in the Torre for a week in a crowded cell with barely room to stand, and fed bread and water once a day.

One morning, just as the sun was rising, he was taken to the interrogation chamber. Six executioners entered, stripped him naked and forced his arms back so that the palms of his hands were turned outward behind him. They fastened his wrists together with a rope connected to a hand crank. They turned the crank, drawing the wrists together by degrees so that eventually the backs of each hand touched. Both shoulders were dislocated and, so the servant told Catalina, he vomited blood. This torture was repeated twice more, after which he returned to the dungeon, and a surgeon attempted to set the dislocated bones. He confessed, though the family maintained it was false. He would be burnt at the stake at the next *auto-da-fé*.

Was this Seville now? Was this their future?

THE WORDS on the contract swim before Isaac's eyes. They seem to have a life of their own, he cannot even control *them* now. He sits at his desk in the Real Alcazar trying to concentrate. After the lunch with Friar Alonso, he had an audience with the King and told him of the prelate's strange behaviour in arriving unannounced at his home. The ensuing conversation was elliptical and highly unsatisfactory. The King told him to provide information regarding Fernan's murder. Isaac could not do so and he realised that Ferdinand felt he was wasting his time. He knows if, somehow, he can bring Fernan's murderer to justice it will give him more influence with the King. If he can disprove the blood libel, the basis for the Inquisition's activities in Seville will be weakened. And it might bring some solace to poor Rodrigo and Beatriz. But he does not accept that is his place to investigate such matters.

Isaac walked away from the audience with a verse that Samuel ibn Naghrillah wrote about a monarch occupying his thoughts:

> 'You are caught in his tongs:
> With one hand he brings you into the flames
> While protecting you from the fire,
> Which with both hands he sets against you.

Words from five hundred years ago that precisely sum up his situation. But, Isaac speculates, perhaps they also capture the circumstances that Ferdinand finds himself in? Caught between his wife and the Inquisition, trying to protect his beloved Seville whilst maintaining amicable marital relations. And all the while, both he and the King are all too aware of the looming spectre of Torquemada.

Isaac has never felt more alone. He cannot even talk to Maria, he does not have the answers she expects. He realises his sense of isolation is probably why he went to see the King. It had been a mistake; he needs proof, not anecdote and speculation. Isaac becomes aware of Alejandro's presence. How long has his deputy been standing there tapping a sheaf of papers against the side of his desk?

'What is it, Alejandro?' Isaac asks, trying to keep impatience from his voice.

'You have a visitor, señor,' Alejandro replies, 'Señora Ana de Palacios, I told her you were busy and could not see her.'

Isaac wonders what Juan's wife wants with him, and why she is visiting him at his place of work. He considers sending her away, but on reflection it might be better to hear what she has to say. Alejandro has had the common sense to ask her to wait in the small anteroom that adjoins Isaac's office. Perhaps he has underestimated his deputy, and he might be trusted after all?

Señora de Palacios is dressed in black and sits in the only chair. She waves a small fan listlessly in front of her face. 'Don't you think it gets hotter earlier every year now, Isaac?' she says in a weak voice.

Isaac is puzzled. He responds as though she has not said anything, 'My dear Ana, I'm so sorry you felt you had to come here. I have been meaning to visit you, but I thought that might expose you to even more danger. In fact, should you be here at all?'

She covers her mouth and nose with the fan and widens her eyes coquettishly at him. 'Oh, you know why I'm here Isaac,' she says in a low tone. Ana is tall and graceful. Isaac has always found her attractive. Her large, blue eyes fix on him, and for a moment he almost forgets where he is. Then she narrows her eyes and a shadow passes across her face.

He coughs, crosses his arms and looks at her. 'I'm afraid I really don't know, Ana. Would you like some water?'

'What I *want*, Isaac, is my husband. He wouldn't be where he is if it wasn't for *you*,' she hisses.

'My dear Ana, I'm so sorry about Juan, but I have no power, especially now the Edict of Grace has been published.'

'You are the leader, Isaac; you always were even when you and Juan were children. He would have never attended those prayer meetings unless you had persuaded him. I hear you are remarkably close to the King.'

Isaac forces himself to be patient and consider his response, 'I have said Ana that I have no power in the matter. My hands are tied.'

At this image her eyes widen, she leaps from the chair and advances towards him until he can feel her breath on his face. 'I wish your hands *were* tied behind your back and that you *were* suffering what my poor Juan is suffering in the Torre del Oro,' she whispers hoarsely.

Isaac places his hands on her shoulders and she collapses into his arms. He helps her back into the chair and kneels down beside her. 'Ana, I am so sorry, but I am not responsible for this. If there was anything I could do I would do it. We are scared for our own lives.'

'You should be,' she says. 'They won't tell me anything about Juan, I have had no news since they took him. I don't even know if he is even still alive,' she pauses, and her tone becomes gentle. 'Find out for me Isaac, please. It's the least you can do.'

'But what if I can't, Ana? I'm not a miracle worker.'

'For the sake of your family, perhaps it's time you became one.'

. . .

CATALINA AND ISABEL were returning home from the visit to Triana, finding their way over the Puente de Barcas as quickly as they could. They were both in a sombre mood; the visit had been difficult. Beatriz and Rodrigo welcomed them and thanked them for the food. But the conversation was forced and Beatriz had been taciturn. Catalina noticed that Isabel struggled to deal with the atmosphere and became increasingly upset. They were both grateful when it was time to leave. When they reached the Seville side of the crossing Isabel took Catalina's arm as they headed towards home. Catalina looked down at Isabel's hand and then straight ahead.

'Was the story you told us last night about that poor boy true?' Isabel asked.

Catalina thought for a moment and said, 'I have no reason to believe otherwise, señorita.'

'I can't believe that men like Father Alonso would really do things like that.'

'That, and far, far worse, señorita.'

'What could be worse?'

'Better you don't know.'

'Fernan was about the same age as Gabriel. I hadn't appreciated that.'

Catalina did not respond, waiting for Isabel to continue.

'Who would do such a thing? For what reason?'

'When love for The Almighty becomes mangled and tangled then men find a reason for doing all sorts of evil,' Catalina replied.

'I'm scared Catalina, I'm confused, I don't know what to think sometimes.'

Catalina stopped, turned to Isabel and took both her hands in hers. 'You listen, señorita.'

She paused as if weighing the risks of continuing.

'It's easy to lose your way in evil times such as these. Men and women do foolish things, they believe they are doing the right thing for The Almighty but they forget about their loved ones.'

She paused for breath.

'Perhaps even people such as you and me might do things we are not so proud of.' Catalina raised a questioning eyebrow.

Isabel looked down and nodded. 'I thought I was doing the right thing.'

'I knew it was you egged the young master on to talk about, "ham and prayers," Catalina said.

'The Edict of Grace said we can save our souls by telling the Holy Office of anything we think is wrong.'

Isabel paused.

'But now I'm not so sure. I don't understand why people - children - need to be tortured. It doesn't seem right, it doesn't feel like something The Almighty would want to happen.'

'I've been with your family a long time. Your mother and father are good, God-fearing people. We should *both* remember that in the days to come.'

Isabel squeezed Catalina's hands, linked an arm through hers and they walked on together.

CHAPTER
EIGHTEEN

S *eville*

ISAAC THINKS a brisk walk to the Castillo de San Jorge will do him good. He hopes the outcome of his visit will be equally beneficial. He sent a boy yesterday to request a meeting with Alonso and received an invitation to come after None prayers. Twenty *maravedies* just to deliver the message and another twenty when the boy returned. Seville was becoming more extortionate by the day. Although, he reminds himself with a bitter smile, that was hardly the most significant challenge nowadays.

Work delays him, and it is drawing onto Vesper prayers before he leaves the Alcazar. It is warm and he feels the sweat prickling his scalp underneath his hat as he hurries along Calle San Gregorio. He passes the Torre del Oro and wonders why the Almohads gave themselves such a challenge in making it twelve sided. It has been a watchtower for over three hundred years now, a noble use compared to the heinous purpose to which it is now put.

He feels his heart racing as he approaches the entrance gate to the *castillo* and shows the invitation to the guards. One of them leads him up a narrow, winding stone staircase, and leaves him in a tiny, bare room with only a small arrow slit affording any light. The guard shuts the heavy metal door with a loud slam. He imagines this is what it feels like to be in a cell and is startled to realise this must be what they want him to feel. There is nowhere to sit, so he stands and waits.

The door clangs open and Brother Alonso rushes in, full of apologies for keeping him so long. He takes Isaac's arm and leads him along a dimly lit corridor towards a large oak door. The prelate knocks timidly, dips his head, and slips away into the gloom. Isaac barely has time to register the strangeness of this before a voice booms, 'Come in!'

He pushes the door open to see Tomás de Torquemada sitting at his desk reading some papers. Torquemada looks up from his work and smiles, though it does not reach his eyes. He comes from around the desk and greets Isaac as though he is a long-lost friend. They are the same height, but Torquemada is much broader. He clasps Isaac's hand with a powerful grip and says, 'Welcome. I'm so sorry if I have kept you. As you can imagine, the affairs of state keep me terribly busy, but I don't have to tell you that do I?'

The voice warm and gentle, Isaac wonders if this is really the "Grand Inquisitor of All Spain."

Torquemada shows him to one of the two chairs near the fireplace, pours glasses of sherry, gives one to Isaac and asks, 'How is it that I might help you?'

The only explanation for the enthusiasm of this greeting is that Torquemada knows he is a confidant of the

King. Isaac senses he might have greater influence than he appreciates. He takes time to savour the sherry, an exceptionally fine vintage.

Torquemada watches him closely and says, 'Yes, it's from Jerez. My private collection.'

The warmth of the sherry settles Isaac's nerves. He attempts to take a measure of control by asking, 'How are you settling down in Seville Father Tomás?'

Torquemada responds with some dull logistical details and opines on the difficulty of getting competent hired help.

Isaac feigns interest. What he really attends to is the voice in his head which asks him what the hell he is doing here and how he intends to get out of this room without inflicting further damage on his family. Why had he let the guilt he feels about Juan expose him to this danger?

'I'm sure you have excellent assistance from Friar Alonso in these matters.'

Torquemada looks puzzled but nods thoughtfully.

Isaac wonders whether his reply had been a non-sequitur. He looks over Torquemada's shoulder out of the window at the setting sun; it was almost Vespers. Torquemada's face is disappearing in the gloom.

Isaac clears his throat, 'Father Tomás, I was visited yesterday by Señora Ana de Palacios.'

'Oh yes, de Mota's wife. What did she want?' Torquemada leans forward.

Isaac hopes the astonishment he feels that Torquemada knows who Ana is does not register on his face or in the tone of his voice. 'Juan and I were acquainted when we were children in Cordoba. Ana, Señora de Palacios, has not heard from him for two weeks since he was arrested in the street. She asked for my help. As Friar Alonso so graciously favoured us with his presence in our home I thought I might trouble him by asking for his assistance.'

'Well, de Mota was arrested for the murder of the boy Fernan before the Holy Office began its duties in Seville, so he is not officially part of our investigations ... at the present time. That might change should other information come to light.'

'He is still alive then?'

'Yes, I believe so, barely I expect. The murder of a child is a serious business. And the rumour is that the boy was murdered for his blood. Why the Jews feel the need to use a boy's blood in their heathen rituals I do not understand. He's being held in the dungeons in the Torre. Would you like me to have him brought over?'

Isaac struggles to keep the sherry glass still as he fights the tremor in his hand. He sees Torquemada watching the glass and a distant image of trapped leverets springs to Isaac's mind. The memory of a hot summer afternoon with Juan is suffused with warmth and regret. 'No, thank you, that won't be necessary. Juan is no longer a close friend of mine. I just felt sorry for his wife. Perhaps it might be arranged for her to visit him?'

Torquemada is silent. He turns to look at the dying light over the Guadalquivir and picks up a small silver bell from his desk. A servant appears at once and lights two small oil lamps on the desk and then the three torches in the sconces lining the far wall. 'The sunlight dies quickly in Seville.' The light from the torches brings Torquemada's face back from the shadows. He steeples his fingers in front of his face and continues as though he has not heard Isaac's request.

'You know that de Mota's crimes are very serious? We suspect him of being part of a group of *marranos* conducting illicit prayer meetings.'

Torquemada allows this to hang in the air as the servant leaves the room.

'He denies all knowledge. Though I have yet to meet him and we have not yet employed the special powers granted to the Holy Office by Their Majesties and confirmed by His Grace Pope Sixtus.' The mention of the monarchs is, Isaac supposes, an invitation of sorts.

'My wife has been concerned about Juan de Mota. She is quite close friends with Señora de Palacios.'

'Ah yes, Señora Ximenes. We have yet to be introduced, but I believe I may have seen her outside the cathedral on my arrival in Seville. I formed the impression that she was a very pious woman. And I believe you have a daughter, Isabel.' Torquemada's tongue passes slowly over his bottom lip. 'I saw her at the cathedral as well.'

'Yes, and a son, Gabriel,' Isaac adds quickly.

'Yes of course, a fine son as well, a pigeon pair.' Torquemada pauses. 'It is a shame for such a devout woman to be so worried. I believe she serves a wonderful mutton stew.'

'Friar Alonso has been reporting back in detail, I see,' Isaac attempts what he hopes is a jocular tone.

'It's an important part of his job,' Torquemada seems puzzled that Isaac does not appear to appreciate this.

Isaac pulls thoughtfully at his beard and realising he has no choice replies, 'You must dine with us one of these nights, but we will provide finer fare than just mutton stew.'

'Brother Alonso will make the arrangements soon. I will see what I can do to arrange for de Mota's wife to visit him at the Torre. And I will find out what I can do to make him more comfortable in the meantime.'

Isaac does not respond.

'I believe Señora Ximenes knew the family of the decap-itated boy, Fernan?'

'Yes, the mother took in our laundry.'

'A terrible business. Have you heard anything more about it?'

Isaac shakes his head. As the bells ring for Vespers, all he can think is how to explain to Maria that the Grand Inquisitor of All Spain is coming for dinner. The image of a pair of tongs and a large red fire flashes through his mind.

'Shall we pray together, my son?' Torquemada tilts his head down and stares at Isaac from beneath raised eyebrows. He rises and moves towards the two kneelers situated on the floor in front of the prayer desk. He eases himself down, clasps his hands together and sonorously recites the Ave Maria, 'Hail Mary, full of grace, the Lord is with thee.'

Isaac kneels beside him as he continues, 'Blessed art thou amongst women, and blessed is the fruit of thy womb, Jesus. Holy Mary, Mother of God, pray for us sinners, now and at the hour of our death. Amen.' The Grand Inquisitor's breath reeks of garlic and sherry.

Isaac recites the prayer in a low, hesitant tone. They finish and cross themselves. Isaac is surprised to see how easily Torquemada gets to his feet; he is sprightly for his age.

'A little ... rusty, my son?' Torquemada smiles.

'No ... Father ... just a little tired, that's all.'

'Perhaps you would like me to hear your confession?'

Isaac now knows for certain he is being toyed with. He draws himself up and says, 'Another time ... Father. It is late and I must get back to my family.'

Striding home beside the Guadalquivir he considers what a blessing it would be to throw himself into the river to rid himself of the stench of his own hypocrisy and Torquemada's foul breath.

ON THE OTHER side of the river, Fernan's mother also hears the bells for Vespers as she stands in her doorway gazing up at the full moon, suffused orange by the dying sun. Beatriz remembers Fernan's beautiful singing voice. The choirmaster told her he had perfect pitch, whatever that was. She makes the sign of the cross and then pushes the heels of her hands into her eyes to stem the steady flow of tears. How kind it was of the señora to send that basket of food. She recalls how Fernan loved eating figs with rice pudding. The señora is a good woman. Then the tears start again. She goes inside, closes the door and hopes that nobody can hear her stifled sobs.

CHAPTER
NINETEEN
THE TESTIMONY OF FRIAR ALONSO

T*riana, Castillo de San Jorge*

BROTHER TOMÁS SUMMONED me and recounted the most important elements of his meeting with Señor Alvarez. He now believes even more strongly that Isaac is key to unmasking a ring of *conversos*. Had it not been for his relationship with the King he would have incarcerated Alvarez immediately. There was something in his tone that told me he was enjoying this game. Perhaps it made a change from our more brutal methods. I thought it best to agree to wait a little while longer before arresting the family. We should see what comes of the meeting between Señora de Palacios and her husband.

Even so, I am still surprised by his hesitation, I had thought his relationship with the Queen was strong enough for him to act decisively. Is Brother Tomás too concerned about the King's ambivalence regarding the methods of the Holy Office? Perhaps he is trying a different approach so that he can conclusively report to His Majesty that less direct methods do not work? Brother Tomás reasoned that it might be interesting to see who else we could snare in our trap before snapping it shut.

I left him to his thoughts and went about arranging for Juan de Mota's wife to see her husband. I was to be in attendance so I could report all that was said, and perhaps as importantly, what was not.

WELL, what an interesting couple Juan and Ana are. I did my best to be discreet. The scratching of my quill on the parchment may have broken the illusion of invisibility that I tried to create by standing statue-like in the corner of the cell Juan shared with at least ten other loathsome creatures. I had arranged for them to be temporarily billeted else-where to encourage Juan and Ana to be as open with each other as possible.

On reflection, perhaps it would have been better to leave one of the more intelligent prisoners in place and promise him his freedom for faithfully reporting the couple's conversation. If Brother Tomás wasn't so concerned about His Majesty's opinion, we could have just used our usual methods. It might have saved a great deal of time and trouble. I'm going to reconstruct the conversation from my notes and my memory in as much detail as possible:

'Ana, my darling,' Juan said as she entered the cell. She brought her hand to her mouth, clearly startled by his appearance.

Doubtless he had lost some weight in the past ten days,

though I cannot swear to that having never set eyes on him whilst he was still a free man.

He held out his hands to her and pulled her towards him saying, 'How are the children?'

All I could hear in response were some muffled sobs as Ana buried her head in his shoulder. She finally emerged saying, 'They miss you terribly,' and then the wailing started in earnest.

When she gained control of her emotions she asked when he would come home. I wondered how she could be quite so naïve. Juan responded that perhaps he might be some time yet, at which she burst out crying *again*. I almost called a halt to things then – it was becoming insufferable. But then it became interesting. I shall set it down as near verbatim as I can from my notes:

> *Ana: How are you?*
>
> *Juan: Very well, my dear, given the circumstances of course.*
>
> *Ana: Yes, you look ... quite well.*
>
> *Juan: My dear, please don't start crying again. Do you have any good news?*
>
> *Ana: Yesterday I went to see Maricela, the dressmaker. You remember her? I ordered a new blue silk ballgown before Christmas? Do you remember?*
>
> *Juan: Yes, my dear, I do. Is it ready? How does it look?*
>
> *Ana: Well, there's been a problem in sourcing the right quality of cloth. The dressmaker says he's trying to secure another shipment from Portugal by next week. He's waiting for confirmation though. If he doesn't hear soon, he'll send someone to talk to the merchant.*
>
> *Juan: But he sounded confident? It sounds promising?*
>
> *Ana: Yes, I think so, my love.*

Juan: Well that's good. And are you meeting our other friends? Do
people ask after me?
Ana: Everybody is so busy at the moment. I suppose Semana Santa is
only a few weeks away ...
Juan: Well, that's something to look forward to.

There is no need to make record of the further sobbing from Señora de Palacios at this point, I will leave that pathetic sound to your imagination. Exactly how stupid do these people think we are? Shipments from Portugal? Such an obvious escape route. I wondered whether there was some more subtle game being played.

But when I reported the conversation to Brother Tomás, he confirmed my initial response. It offended him that these people took the value of their souls so lightly and believed they could dupe us so readily. We agreed that the time for patience and politicking were over.

CHAPTER
TWENTY

S*eville*

MARIA WAS bored and felt suffocated. Once the children were in bed, she told Catalina she would go to evening prayers at St Ignatious which was only a short walk away. Catalina muttered something about the wisdom of being out alone at the present time, but Maria ignored her. Isaac was not back, he had said something that morning about perhaps being late, about meeting Alejandro. She had paid little attention.

The air outside Casa de Felicade was blessedly cool. Walking along the deserted *calle* towards the church Maria fondly remembered the Sundays the family had attended mass conducted by Father Gutiérrez. She realised that everything had been much simpler and accepted, perhaps for the first time, that they could never return to those days. They had to move forward, but into what version of their futures, and how much control did they have over their fates? A sense of foreboding overtook her, and she had the feeling of being followed. Turning, all she saw was a decrepit beggar trudging along behind. The old woman overtook her and without a word turned into the *calle* leading to St Ignatious. She moved quickly for a woman of her age. Maria watched until the beggar woman was out of sight.

Maria eventually followed her into the same *calle* and entered the church. She was adjusting to the gloom when she heard her name whispered from the shadows of the porch. She stood completely still, too frightened to proceed.

'Maria, it's me,' a disembodied female voice hissed.

Maria walked cautiously towards the voice – she thought she recognised it. The porch was dimly lit by an array of votive candles that members of the choir had lit on their way in. Her fear gave way to a momentary sense of guilt, as she had forgotten to light the customary two candles in remembrance of her parents. The figure before her was dressed in a drab, shapeless woollen tunic that almost touched the floor, her head covered in a linen veil secured by a ribbon. It was the beggar woman. Maria stared at the woman's face and wondered why this peasant was trying to talk to her.

'It's me – Ana,' she whispered and reached out a hand to pull Maria into the dark interior of the porch.

'Why are you dressed like that, Ana? What are you doing here?'

'The Inquisition's *familiares* are everywhere, one cannot be too careful. I didn't think it wise for us to be seen together,' Ana replied, her polished accent at odds with her appearance. 'My disguise fooled you, didn't it?!'

Although Maria had known Ana since her marriage to

Isaac, she was unsure whether she could trust her. She wondered what the purpose of this visitation was. She regarded Ana with a cool gaze, waiting for an explanation.

'I've been to see Juan at the *castillo*. Isaac arranged it for me. He's in a terrible state, they cleaned him up and dressed him in some fresh clothes to make him look presentable. But they couldn't hide what they'd done to him.'

Maria waited as Ana fought back tears.

'He couldn't tell me much as there was a Friar there all the time taking notes, face like an eagle. Alonso, I think he was called.'

'I'm glad that Isaac could be of help to you, Ana, but you didn't give him very much choice, did you?' Ana looked down at her bare feet and Maria almost felt sympathetic. 'What more do you expect us to do for you now Ana?'

'Juan has kept quiet so far, he hasn't said anything about the prayer meetings.'

Maria waited.

'If he had, Isaac wouldn't still be enjoying his liberty.' Ana let her words sink in for a few moments. 'But I don't know how much longer he can hold out, and we don't have any money coming in. The children and I are almost starving. I'm surprised they haven't already seized our property and put us out on the street, but it can't be much longer. You need to help us get out of Seville. Isaac has good connections with the shipping agencies.'

There we are. Now we get to the heart of it. She advanced towards Ana, who nervously took a step back, and raised her hand. Ana flinched, but Maria rested the hand on her shoulder and said, 'Ana, have you thought through the implications of what you're saying?'

Ana narrowed her eyes and moved Maria's hand from her shoulder.

Maria bent down until her mouth was close to Ana's ear and whispered, 'You know that if Juan says anything about those meetings you will be implicated too? You realise what the consequences will be for you and the children, don't you?' She stood straight again and saw Ana's jaw tighten as she crossed her arms. Maria decided she had pushed far enough for the moment and said, 'I will talk to Isaac. Meet me here tomorrow after None and we will make some arrangements. I must go, Ana. Tomorrow?'

Ana nodded.

As Maria made her way up the aisle towards the chancel, Ana licked her thumb and first finger and pinched the wick of each of the votive candles, extinguishing their flames one by one.

'THANK YOU FOR INVITING ME, SEÑOR,' Alejandro says as he and Isaac take a table in the Bar Averno. It is the same corner table beneath the single window that Cristobal Arias and his friends occupied the day Juan was arrested. There are only half a dozen other customers. The barkeeper's daughter serves them a plate of Serrano ham, a basket of rye bread and a carafe of red wine. Isaac notices how her eyes linger over Alejandro. Isaac sees her blush and she rushes away.

'Think nothing of it, Alejandro, I should have done it before now,' Isaac replies. A look of surprise crosses his deputy's face. Isaac considers taking a risk, in their present predicament it seems more dangerous not to. He chooses to regard Alejandro's consistent work ethic and apparent loyalty as a sign of good character – that he might be trusted.

They talk about the latest contracts before Alejandro

asks, 'Have you looked at the inventory information regarding the Holy Office's property seizures? I put them on your desk yesterday.'

'No,' Isaac replies. He pauses with a hunk of bread close to his lips. He is conscious he has not been as efficient for the past few weeks. 'How is that any of our business?'

'Strictly speaking, it isn't, but His Majesty asked that we take a careful look. As if we didn't have enough to do already,' Alejandro says, taking a long draught of wine.

Isaac decides not to take the invitation implicit in Alejandro's words. 'We must do as we are told Alejandro.' No sooner has Isaac spoken he feels guilty for the rebuke, as gentle as it is.

'Of course, señor, I didn't mean to make a complaint,' Alejandro replies, picking at a small piece of ham.

'No, of course not, Alejandro, I know that.' Isaac considers his choices. 'You are quite right though, we have more than enough to cope with and I'm not entirely sure why the King should add to our burden.'

'You could say that it's the price we pay for our effi-ciency and excellent reputation,' Alejandro counters. His mug empty, he looks towards the barmaid who hurriedly delivers another carafe.

'I suppose we could look at it in that way. I'm not sure why Their Majesties don't provide the Inquisitors with funds. Asking them to rely on property seizures provides a perverse incentive,' Isaac says, closely watching Alejandro's reaction, who nods, slowly. 'Have you looked at the papers?'

'Yes, I glanced through them ... they are about to seize the property of Juan de Mota,' Alejandro takes a large mouthful of wine.

'Really?' Isaac feigns indifference.

Alejandro places his mug deliberately on the table and breathes a long sigh. 'Señor, I know de Mota is your friend and this is a hard time for you. I want you to know that I understand, that I ... sympathise,' Alejandro whispers the last word. He glances around the bar, leans towards Isaac and says, 'I am from a family of *conversos* too.'

ON HIS WAY home Isaac thinks about his conversation with Alejandro; it had been both promising and worrying. A germ of an idea has been planted, a plan of action that could keep Maria and the children safe. Upon entering Casa de la Felicidad he sees Maria sitting on the bench by the fountain enjoying the cool of the night. She looks beautiful by the light of the gibbous moon and he feels a surge of love. Maria pulls him down next to her and embraces him, resting her head on his chest. She holds his hands and looks into his face. They talk intently in whispers, exchanging their news. He tells her his plan. She cocks her head to one side listening to every word her husband says. Then she holds Isaac's head in her hands and kisses him tenderly on the lips. They link arms and look up at the moon.

BOOK II

March, 1495

CHAPTER
TWENTY-ONE

S *eville*

ISAAC FLOATS, eyes closed, arms and legs outstretched, imagining himself a star shining brightly in the night sky. He feels a surge of power. Sensing the cool water lapping against the side of his face he lets himself drift. Feeling the water caress every part of his naked body. Sun warms his skin, almost too warm, making his eyelids tingle. Tasting saltwater on his lips. *Salt?* That was strange. He thought he was floating in the river and that Juan was somewhere nearby.

Then he hears waves crashing against the shore and is comforted. The sound of the waves gradually comes nearer, changing into something more jarring. Turning into a muffled knocking that grows insistent until it becomes a clear banging sound accompanied by a woman's voice calling, 'Señor, señor, *señor.*'

Opening his eyes with a start, Isaac finds himself alone, spread-eagled face down across his bed. He slowly raises his head, the effects of the wine dulling his senses and sending a searing bolt of pain across his forehead. Hazily, he recalls last night's events. After the carriage left, with Alejandro escorting Maria and the children away from Seville, he felt bereft and did something he could never remember doing before. He went to the terrace and finished a carafe of wine sitting alone contemplating the *castillo*.

He sits up and realises he is naked, sees his bedding strewn across the floor. The woman's voice keeps calling, calling to him. He finds a nightshirt and a robe and tries to make himself decent. He opens the door to the sight of Catalina sobbing uncontrollably.

An hour later, after washing his face and dressing for work, Isaac sits with Catalina on the marble bench in the courtyard of Casa de la Felicidad. It is warm and all he can hear is the bubbling of the fountain and the murmur of pigeons. He thanks God for this relative peace but knows the stillness is about to be sundered by more sobbing. Catalina positions herself as far away from him as possible. Isaac knows it is improper for him to be sitting with Catalina like this, but he wants to break the news to her in as kind a way as possible.

'So, Catalina, it is now obvious to you that the señora and the children are not here,' Isaac begins tentatively.

He watches Catalina's downcast face closely.

'There is nothing to be concerned about. They have simply left Seville for a while so as not to endure the preparations for Semana Santa. You know how trying the señora finds this time of year.'

'But, señor, why so sudden?'

Isaac pretends to hesitate, trying to convey a sense of great sorrow in both his facial expression and tone of voice. 'You have known my family for a long time, haven't you?'

'Some might say too long, señor,' she smiles weakly.

'And we can't keep things hidden from such trusted retainers, can we? You will have noticed certain matters over the past few weeks.'

'You mean after Friar Alonso's visit, señor?'

Isaac is unsurprised by this turn in the conversation. He and Maria have rehearsed the various possibilities.

'No, Catalina that was not what I meant at all,' he says, and the servant looks down at her hands in her lap. 'I'm sorry, I'm not making a particularly good job of this, so let me just say plainly that you will be aware the señora and I have been arguing over Isabel's behavior. We decided it would be best for all of us if we took some time apart from each other to get a little, a little ... perspective. Do you understand Catalina?'

It was important she believed the story as they knew that Catalina could be indiscreet. The tale she would tell needed to be convincing to the Inquisitions' *familiares*, whom it would inevitably reach. They are counting on Catalina being almost as exasperated with Isabel as they are.

'Señor, I knew there were some problems, but I did not realize it was that bad. I am so sorry.' Then she asks the questions that Isaac and Maria have carefully rehearsed the answers to.

'But why did they not take me with them? And why so suddenly in the middle of the night?'

'We decided Isabel needed time alone to talk things through with her mother.' He pauses, hoping this will allow her time to see the sense in this. 'And besides, Catalina, you know how much I need you here to look after me when I'm so busy at the Real Alcazar.'

'I know that, señor.'

'And they left at night because, as you know, it's much cooler to travel then.' The story has the benefit of all good lies in that it holds a significant degree of the truth.

Catalina rises from the bench. 'Thank you for telling me the truth, señor. As you say, I've been with your family a long time and I'll do my best through the good times and the bad.' She pauses and Isaac fears she is about to cry again, but she sits back down. She wrings her hands as she says, 'I think I may have done something awful.' She looks towards the fountain.

Isaac waits and thinks about how right they were not to trust anyone. 'Don't be afraid. You can tell me anything.'

In between sobs and moans, it all tumbles out, how she visited Friar Alonso, who she now admits she has known from when she was a girl. She claims she was trying to protect the family, that she told Alonso how pious they were. How she told him what a good family they were and how concerned she was. 'I thought it for the best. I thought Friar Alonso would help to keep us all safe.'

Isaac listens and wonders if it was more likely she had gone to get insurance for herself when the family inevitably fell under the Inquisition's close examination. It does not make any difference one way or the other. If she has said anything incriminating about the family to Alonso it is too late now. But one thing troubles him, 'I can understand why you might do such a thing out of fear.'

She nods eagerly.

'But ... what I don't understand is why neither you nor

Friar Alonso mentioned that you knew each other when he visited. Can you explain that to me?'

'I trusted Friar Alonso. He is a devout man. When I talked to him at the *castillo* he said we must keep our meeting to ourselves. It wouldn't be good to alarm you and it was better that he did his work in secret. He said it would work out better for you that way. I believed him, but when he came to the house I was surprised. I've been confused ever since. I didn't know whether to tell you or not. And the more days that passed, the more difficult it was.'

Isaac strokes his beard.

'I'm scared that what *I* did led to the señora and the children leaving so suddenly.'

'No, no, you need not concern yourself about that; you are not to blame.' Isaac is troubled by these revelations. He recalls how Catalina deliberately injured herself to divert attention from Gabriel's unfortunate choice of words. She had not needed to do that. 'Is there anything else you need to tell me, Catalina?'

She hesitates before saying emphatically, 'No, señor, that is all, and I'm sorry if I've caused trouble. May I be excused? I have a lot of work to get on with.'

Isaac watches as Catalina goes to the kitchen and thinks the conversation has gone as well as it could have. Has she has really told him the whole story?

TWENTY-TWO

'How did you sleep, my dear?' Maria asked Gabriel as he sat up in bed, tousle-haired and sleepy-eyed. She knew the answer as she had endured his restless legs for the entire night. Gabriel crawled into her bed at some ungodly hour saying that he wanted to go home and see Papa. He cried and she didn't have the heart to ask him to leave.

Maria had given up on sleep and was sitting in a chair by the bedchamber window watching the sun's rays begin to outline the distant hills.

'I don't know, Mama. I'm too tired to talk,' Gabriel replied, collapsing into her lap.

They had arrived at the estate close to midnight. Alejandro stayed a short while to ensure they were settled then returned to Seville. He needed to be at the Real Alcazar at his usual time in the morning to ensure that suspicions were not raised.

Isabel had cast several surreptitious looks in his direction during the journey. To Alejandro's great credit he remained focused on his conversation with Maria or looked out of the carriage window. He could not have seen very much but she was grateful for what she took to be his discretion. Perhaps Isaac was right, and they could trust him. They would soon find out.

'Mama, I'm hungry,' Gabriel whined.

Maria kissed him on the forehead and went out to the main room where she had left the basket of fruit and bread.

'Thank goodness Isabel is still asleep,' she thought. She was not ready to face interrogation by her daughter.

At the same moment Maria kissed her son's forehead, ten riders galloped along a deserted track, raising a large cloud of dust in their wake. They rode in single file, nine of the men wore the red tunic of the royal bodyguard. The tenth rider wore the black habit of a Dominican friar, face obscured by his cowl. He was some way behind the main group and was struggling to keep up. He joined them as the royal bodyguards crested a hill and brought their horses to a halt, the rising sun beginning to outline their forms.

The lead rider pointed down the valley to a single-story stone house and trotted down the hill towards it, signalling the others to follow with his drawn sword.

'Mama, when are we going home?' Isabel asked. She woke up as soon as Maria started to look through the basket of food to arrange breakfast.

'We've only just arrived, Isabel,' Maria said brightly.

'But there is so little to do here, Mama, and I really don't understand why we are here so early in the year. Everyone else is still in town. Enjoying themselves. And if we stay here too long, we will miss Semana Santa.'

'We are here now, and we just have to make the best of it. I'm sure your father will come and join us just as soon as he can arrange his work with Señor Alejandro.'

'Will Señor Alejandro be coming to visit us?' Isabel asked, the hope and excitement clear in her tone.

Before she could think of an appropriate answer, she heard Gabriel calling from the bedchamber, 'Mama, Mama, riders are coming.'

Now that the horses were trotting over open ground, Alonso coaxed his horse to the front of the group. He managed, with some difficulty, to persuade his horse to fall into step alongside the lead rider and said, 'Captain, what is your plan?'

The captain turned to Alonso and then stared straight ahead. After a few moments he said, 'I don't have a plan, I am just here to follow your orders, Father.'

Alonso considered this and regretted he had not sought more detailed instructions from Brother Tomás. He could think of only one course of action: gallop down the hill at full speed, dismount and ask the men to smash down the door.

The captain turned to him again. 'We could just tether the horses and knock, Father.' He waited. 'It is only two children and their mother that we are expecting to find, after all. And you have a warrant for the mother's arrest issued by the Inquisition.'

Alonso thought he detected disapproval in the captain's tone. He ignored it and tried to affect an air of quiet contemplation by freeing one hand from the reins and tapping a forefinger against his lips. 'Yes Captain, you read my mind, that is exactly what I was about to suggest, and I think....'

But the captain had already picked up the pace and was cantering away to carry out his duty.

MARIA RUSHED BACK to the bedchamber in response to Gabriel's cries. She looked out of the window and her heart sank. She had hoped it would take them longer to get here. How had they found out so soon? She had wanted the morning to settle the children and get them used to the new surroundings. She had at least hoped to give them something to eat. Why on earth couldn't they have had the common sense to wait until after breakfast? She watched them tether the horses. She picked up her shawl from the chair, took Gabriel's hand and went out to meet them.

'How lovely to see you again, Señor Garcia, there was absolutely no need for you to come out so early,' Maria said to the caretaker of the Verdazzo estate.

'We thought you'd be hungry,' Señor Garcia said pointing to the basket held by his daughter, Juana.

'And it is good to see you as well Juana. My how you have grown,' Maria said, 'I hope your mother is well.'

CHAPTER
TWENTY-THREE
THE TESTIMONY OF FRIAR ALONSO

T *riana, Castillo de San Jorge*

MY EMBARRASSMENT and shame were absolute. How was I to know the family had access to two estates? One had belonged to Isaac's father, Pozzoblanco, and the other to Maria's family at Verdazzo. We'd rode confidently into the estate at Pozzoblanco, the royal bodyguards smashing the door open to find absolutely nothing. I will make sure that one of the *notario de secreto* pays for this; it was most certainly their fault, not mine. But when I told Brother Tomás he didn't agree. I will not sully the pages of this testimony with his foul, intemperate language – may God forgive him.

Our plan – Brother Tomás' plan – had been to capture the entire family at their home. But information from one of the *familiares* told us that they had seen a carriage leaving Casa de la Felicidad at the dead of night, heading out of Seville towards the family estate. We didn't know who was in the carriage. But if we could catch the family fleeing the city, it would provide greater evidence to convince His Majesty that the Alvarez family were heretics.

And so, I will have to suffer yet another lengthy ride in the company of the captain and his men. They didn't try that hard to contain their amusement and I had to use all my patience to tame my anger. It would do no good to show my genuine feelings. I will remain silent for the whole ride out to Verdazzo, that will teach them a lesson. I will keep my own counsel from now on. Someone will pay dearly for my mortification.

CHAPTER
TWENTY-FOUR

S *eville*

AFTER A DAY in which he accomplished extraordinarily little at the Royal Alcazar – his mind drifting away to the family at the estate – Isaac is once again sitting with Alejandro at the Bar Averno. It is busy and noisy this evening, but he does not see anyone he knows. The corner in the window that Cristobal Arias and his companions normally occupy is taken by a lady dressed in black, her face shrouded by a thick veil. She appears to be alone.

A crowded tavern does not make an ideal setting for the confidential conversation that Isaac intends, but asking his deputy to Casa de la Felicidad risks inviting even more suspicion.

'You delivered them safely? How did they seem? Were they happy? Were they settled?'

Alejandro leans in.

'Yes, señor, though I did not stay long, so I cannot be certain of their mood,' he replies cautiously. 'Gabriel seemed excited and happy, I'm not exactly sure why. Perhaps the novelty, the fresh air?'

Isaac smiles at this small piece of good news and reaches over to grasp Alejandro's shoulder. 'That is something, I suppose. And Isabel, how did she seem to you?'

Alejandro hesitates, 'She was ... noticeably quiet during the whole journey.'

Isaac grimaces.

'Perhaps she will take time to get used to the new circumstances?'

'I have made the arrangements for Señor Garcia to take to them to Cadiz this evening, to embark a ship tomorrow that will take them to Lisbon. I only pray to God that all goes well,' Isaac says.

'I'm sure it will.'

'Do you really expect it to?'

Alejandro pauses. 'In all honesty I do not know, but all we can do is pray and hope, señor, hope and pray.'

Isaac looks into his mug of wine and tries to hold back the tears. He is struck by a sudden conviction that he knows what he should be doing. The murder of Fernan is at the heart of everything, but it has become lost in the storm of events. Or perhaps he has been avoiding it? Investigating this murder would be a treacherous endeavour and he is not even sure where to begin without drawing further attention to himself. If he could provide information to the King to disprove the blood libel, perhaps that would slow Torquemada down, perhaps even end the Inquisition in Seville. This might be idle speculation, but it nags away at him. Or should he just forget the whole business and get on the next ship to Lisbon?

Isaac is afraid to sound foolish; he does not understand how to conduct such an investigation. He needs to find a calm place to just sit and think.

'I'm sorry Alejandro. I must go.'

He rises and takes Alejandro's hand.

'Thank you.'

Isaac knows that it is now too dangerous to return home. He will have to stay with members of the prayer group, moving every night.

MARIA SAT on the porch at the Verdazzo estate watching the sunlight slowly fade behind the hills. It was chilly in the evenings here and she pulled her shawl closer around her shoulders. It was of fine Indian silk and had been given to her by Isaac's mother on the occasion of their wedding. She resisted the temptation to dwell on the past and wondered how Isaac was coping. *Will we ever be together as a family again?* There was some consolation: at least she did not have to suffer Torquemada at her dinner table. Rather a dramatic solution. That this could, in any way, be considered comforting, brought a wry smile to her face.

She turned to listen to the children's voices coming from inside the house. They were playing chess and she thought they were arguing. She listened more closely and realised it was just good-natured teasing from Isabel. They had begun to relax during the day. Perhaps it was the fresh air. 'How am I going to break the news to them of what is about to happen?' That when Señor Garcia returned in a few hours with a carriage it would be to carry them off to Cadiz to board a ship bound for Lisbon.

Maria knew that the story she and Isaac had concocted of an outbreak of the plague in Seville would not fool Isabel, and that her questions would unnerve Gabriel. Should she take Isabel into her confidence? No, the girl had been so unpredictable of late, better to get them safely aboard the ship first. Better to adhere to the plan she had agreed with Isaac.

She wondered what she now truly felt about her husband. She couldn't rid herself of the thought that he was to blame for all of this. Why did he have to continue with the prayer meetings? She understood he was a man of principle, she still loved him for that at least, she hoped. Why didn't he just read the Torah and pray at home? She could understand the need to practice one's religion communally, but not in the current situation, not when it put your children's lives in danger.

She found it difficult to find it in her heart to forgive him. Children, family, should be the most important things in life, shouldn't they?

ISAAC STANDS outside the door to the church of St Pedro. He left Alejandro to the attentions of the barkeeper's daughter at Bar Averno having been overcome by an irresistible need to pray in a house of worship. The synagogues have long been demolished or closed, and he certainly cannot risk a meeting with his Jewish friends. The church is the only place he can go. *We all pray to the same God, don't we?*

There is nobody around except an old beggarwoman on the other side of the *calle*, with her hand outstretched. He thinks he noticed her when he left the bar. He is not in a generous mood. Hesitant now, starting to doubt his conviction that this was what he needs. He pushes open the door and slips inside to what appears to be an empty church. None of the votive candles in the porch are alight. He lights three, automatically making the sign of the cross, bringing his fingers to his lips and whispering, 'Maria, Isabel and Gabriel.'

He makes his way up the central aisle towards the chancel. He hears a slow grating sound. Is it the door he can hear opening? He turns, but it is closed. Isaac pauses, eyes straining to look past the shadows, but sees nothing, no one.

He looks at the statues and images that form the apse behind the altar. There are nine bronze and golden images arranged in rows of three. The central column comprises Christ on the cross, Saint Pedro and the Madonna. He looks closely and all he feels is a sudden rage. He paces up and down the aisle, clenching and unclenching his fists. This feeling of being consumed by waves of anger is a new sensation. He enjoys submitting to the fury, instead of always being measured, always being in control.

He should pull the statues down and smash them. Why should this family have more importance, more love, more reverence than his own? What are principles set against the love he feels in his heart for his own family whom he might never see again? Is this all his fault? He has only tried to do his best, to follow his faith and protect his family.

He sees the large golden chalice, used to drink the so-called blood of Christ, on the altar. Scenes from the passion of Christ are engraved on its base and the cup is encircled with large, red garnets. Even in his rage he appreciates the exquisite craftsmanship. The beautiful depiction of Christ's suffering offends him. He feels the anger swell further and overwhelm him. What did Jesus really know of sacrifice? Was the pain of spending one day on the cross comparable to a father's pain at having to endure the thought of never seeing his children smile again? And the so-called Messiah was rewarded with resurrection and spent the rest of his days in heaven at his father's right hand. *What is my reward to be?*

He lunges towards the chalice, picks it up, raises it towards his nose taking in the faint smell of alcohol and metal. He brings the cup back behind his head and flings it with all his might at the Madonna. It rattles off the statue and clangs onto the stone floor, the Madonna seemingly unscathed. Isaac raises his fists at the image of Christ on the cross and half shouts, half sobs, 'You bastard, you bastard.'

The beggarwoman raises herself from the shadow of the last pew and shuffles silently out.

MARIA FANNED herself to keep the humid late afternoon air at bay. She was so lost in thoughts of Isaac that she did not notice Isabel sneak up behind her until her arms were around her neck. Maria tried to contain her surprise and laid her palm on her daughter's hand.

'It's so quiet out here, Mama, and the air smells so fresh. I love it,' Isabel said as she broke the embrace and walked to the front of the porch.

'This is a big change, Isabel, I'm so glad. What has come over you?'

'I really couldn't say, Mama,' Isabel replied as she looked out at the hills.

Gabriel exploded onto the porch, lunged at Isabel and shouted, 'You're it!' and ran out onto the dusty field that surrounded the house.

Maria gave her an encouraging look and shooed her

away with the back of her hand. She watched the children trying to catch each other and wished Isabel would let herself be this way more often. She was trying too hard to be a young woman; she was still a child. Maybe it wasn't too late. Perhaps she should return to Seville and they should face whatever was to come as a family.

As this thought occurred to her she saw a horseman crest the top of the hill, his shadow outlined by the dying sun. Shielding her eyes with the fan, she thought she saw a group of horsemen gathering. Señor Garcia must have returned, bringing some more food. Why were there so many men with him? It must be some of his workmen she supposed. Maria rose to greet them, hoping they wouldn't stay too long. It would be better to get this over with.

ISAAC HEARS them before he sees them, feels his stomach tighten with fear before it forms in his thoughts, becomes aware of the metallic taste in his mouth before he can utter a word. The top notes of the blaring trumpets and the steady beat of the kettledrums as he makes his way through the streets to another safe house. He pushes through the gathering crowds and finds a secluded doorway to watch the procession.

The musicians first, then the ministers of the Holy Office for the Propagation of the Faith, followed by the city nobles bearing the arms of the Inquisition: a cross flanked by an olive branch to the right and a sword on the left. Alonso brings up the rear, shambling along a on a large white cob. Their purpose: to announce Seville's first *auto-da-fé* by parading through the city publishing notices on all the grand buildings. It will take at least two weeks to make the lavish preparations for the ritual burning of the heretics.

Isaac wonders what Isabel and Gabriel are doing right now. He listens intently as the parade passes slowly into the distance, then turns and strides away. *So, we all have a small sliver of time to take action to protect ourselves and our families.*

TWENTY-FIVE

T *riana, Castillo de San Jorge*

MARIA SAT ON A THIN, hard mattress and looked through the one narrow slit in the wall that afforded a view towards Seville. She saw the light dimming over the blackening water of the Guadalquivir. She had been sequestered for the past week in an apartment in a dark corner of the *Castillo*; guarded both day and night, only Catalina permitted entrance. Although the room was small and plainly furnished, she was glad her confinement was not at the Torre.

The relative comfort was surprising as was the fact she had not been tortured. Yet. *What game is Torquemada playing?* She took some solace from knowing she was near to Isabel and Gabriel, although she had not seen them since their capture at Verdazzo. Catalina visited every day and tried her best to keep Maria's spirits up with news of the children.

She heard footsteps, the sound of bolts being pulled across and assumed that Catalina had come to light the lanterns.

'Good evening, Señora Xemines,' Torquemada boomed.

Maria turned and took a sharp intake of breath at the sight of the Grand Inquisitor. She composed herself, smoothed her dress and began to stand.

'There is no need for such formality, señora. My visit is purely a pastoral one.'

Maria remained on the bed and held his gaze.

Torquemada indicated a single chair in the corner and raised his eyebrows. Maria nodded and he sat down.

'I trust your accommodation is to your liking?'

Maria remained silent.

'Much more preferable to the chambers I could have placed you in at the Torre.'

Maria did not respond. *If he expects gratitude, he will be sorely disappointed.* She gave him an infinitesimal smile that quickly disappeared.

'I'm sure Catalina provides you daily news of your fine children. They are both well and reasonably happy, I think. You must be proud of them, particularly Isabel ... such an attractive personality, such a lively mind.'

Maria's eyes flashed a warning. It was his turn to return a thin smile. She knew he was trying to provoke her into saying something rash. Continued silence was her best course of action.

'We would really like to talk to your husband, señora. Would you know where he might be?'

Maria gave him another smile, this time a little broader. *I can be provocative too.*

'If we could discuss matters in a civilised fashion, a satisfactory conclusion *might* be reached. A conclusion that would not require your removal to a dungeon at the Torre.'

Maria continued staring directly at him. She noticed he was tapping his foot against the bottom of the chair leg. *Perhaps I'm unnerving him, just a little?*

'It would be most beneficial if we could talk to your husband. For all of you. Just to clear up certain matters that have come to my ... to the Holy Office's attention,' his tone was harsher now. 'You can only keep silent for so long,' springing from the chair and stepping towards her, 'your circumstances can change very quickly!'

I will not show any weakness, not give you anything to prey upon.

Torquemada took another step towards her, but at the sound of the bells for Vespers he stopped. He looked out through the narrow opening in the wall and took a deep breath.

'I must say my prayers. I shall pray for your soul, and for your children's. In fact, perhaps I shall pay them a visit before bedtime. I always have such interesting conversations with Isabel.'

Maria fought an urge to lunge at him and pummel him with her fists. She dug her nails into her palms, using the pain as a distraction until the door clanged shut behind Torquemada. She beat the bed with her fists and then drew her arms around her. *Where on earth is Isaac, and what is he doing to free us?*

THE NEXT MORNING, Isabel picked up the mitre of the white bishop, circled it over the board and then flicked its base to knock over Gabriel's black knight. The two children were on the floor of a large apartment in Castillo de San Jorge where they had spent the last week since being captured. Catalina sat in the corner embroidering a small piece of cloth. Alonso, following Torquemada's instructions, had ensured it was comfortably furnished. The children had been playing for over an hour and the game was nearly complete.

'Why do you do that *every* time?' Gabriel asked.

'I'm just teasing you, silly boy,' Isabel said, as she tousled his hair.

'It's not the proper rules of the game you know. That's not how Papa taught us to play.'

The mention of the señor brought a small gasp from Catalina, and her embroidery needle hung in the air. She opened her mouth but then, seeming to think better of saying anything, continued her needlepoint.

'And anyway, that's checkmate,' Gabriel said, as he swept his Queen across the board through the channel now left undefended by the white bishop.

Isabel raised her hand as if to sweep the pieces aside, but instead cupped Gabriel's face in her hands and said, 'My dear, sweet brother, you are so clever.'

Gabriel stared up at her, as if assessing her sincerity. He had no opportunity to respond, as a loud creak from the door announced the entrance of Torquemada. Catalina hastily put her embroidery away underneath her chair, stood up, smoothed her dress, curtsied and bowed. The children remained on the floor. Torquemada tapped his foot until a loud cough from Catalina brought them to their feet. They stood to attention in front of the purple chaise longue. Catalina nodded at them. Isabel understood the prompt, tugged at Gabriel's hand and whispered, 'One, two, three'.

'Good morning, Father Tomás, how are you today?' they

chorused, Isabel's voice much the louder. Gabriel stood as close as possible to his sister, trying to edge behind her.

'I'm very well children, very well,' Torquemada bellowed. 'Playing chess, I see, excellent exercise for the brain. Her Majesty is very fond of a game. But I hope you have been looking after your spiritual duties?' He smiled at them.

'Yes, of course Father Tomás,' Isabel said, 'we'd just been saying our prayers and had only just started playing. Isn't that so, Catalina?'

Catalina glared at Isabel and said, 'Yes, señorita.'

'Good to hear, very good,' Torquemada was unusually hesitant, as though at a loss how to proceed. He glanced out of the window at the Guadalquivir, shimmering in the morning sunshine, the reflected light flickering on the ceiling. He broke his reverie by asking Catalina to take Gabriel out for a walk, as he had, 'Some matters to discuss with the señorita.' Catalina hesitated but Torquemada's stare indicated she was not being offered a choice.

As the door closed behind Catalina and Gabriel, Torquemada drew a chair closer to the chaise longue. He patted a velvet cushion close to him. She glanced at the position Torquemada suggested, then carefully sat down further away, towards the middle of the chaise longue. She spread her hands, trying to occupy as much of the seat as possible.

Torquemada began, 'You and your brother seem happy enough?'

'Of course, Father Tomás, why wouldn't we be?' Isabel let her reply hang in the air.

Torquemada's raised eyebrow suggested he was unsure whether this was a rhetorical question.

Isabel noticed him look distractedly at her hair.

'Of course, of course, there's no reason why you

shouldn't be my dear. And your dear mother is comfortable in her apartment ... for the present time.'

'When will we be able to see her? We haven't seen her for almost ten days. And what of our father?' The words tumbled out, shattering her illusion of calm detachment.

Torquemada cocked his head to one side, narrowed his eyes and gave her a thin smile. 'We are searching every nook and cranny of the city for your father, and we will find him, I can assure you. As to your mother, well, we shall have to see what happens.'

He rose slowly from and moved across to sit in the space Isabel hoped he would not try to occupy.

She squirmed a few inches further away and bunched her hands into fists.

Undeterred, Torquemada reached out one of his large hands, engulfing Isabel's left fist and stroked it with his thumb.

'There's no need to be afraid, my dear.'

His breathing became deeper as he looked into her dark brown eyes, seemingly unaware of the alarm registered there. He moved his face towards hers, still stroking her fist with his thumb, the tip of his tongue glistening with saliva as it slid over his bottom lip. The crucifix hanging around his neck rose and fell in time with the quickening rise and fall of his chest.

The door flew open and Gabriel burst in. 'Sorry! I forgot my cap and the sun is getting in my eyes.'

Torquemada stood and saw Catalina standing in the doorway, arms crossed, staring at him.

Isabel thought that he looked lost.

He tilted his head as if remembering something. This seemed to help him regain his composure. 'It's time I was on my way. I have the procession to attend this afternoon as the prelude to tomorrow's *auto-da-fé*. Isabel, Gabriel, you will be able to see it through the spyglass if you go to the top of the castle tower. I'm sure Catalina will be pleased to accompany you?'

'As you wish, Father,' she replied, continuing to stare at Torquemada.

'I think it will be instructive for you all, in particular you Catalina.' He looked at her until she finally dropped her gaze. He grunted with satisfaction and left without a further word.

'TELL … ME … THE … TRUTH … CATALINA,' Maria's enunciation of each word left the maidservant in no doubt what was expected of her. Catalina had come to see Maria immediately after Torquemada left to prepare for the *auto-da-fé*, ostensibly to bring lunch. Catalina could not understand why the señora was not on the rack, why she was even still alive. She did not understand the subtleties of the game that was being played, any more than she comprehended the rules of chess.

Maria listened as her maidservant told her a little of what had happened that morning and of the plans for the afternoon's procession.

'It's been a week since I last saw my children. Torquemada has been to see me once, as though he were calling on me to ask after my health and drink sherry. I have not been tortured and I do not know where Isaac is. What is going on Catalina?'

'Señora, I have my suspicions, but I don't understand. I'm so confused and I know it's all my fault. I've been feeling so guilty. I have prayed for God's forgiveness.' Catalina began to cry.

'Enough of this. We have discussed it over and over, and yes, some of this is your fault, but you didn't bring the Inquisition into being and your caterwauling will not make sufficient amends. I do not need your tears, your contrition, or your self-flagellation.'

Maria registered Catalina's puzzlement and tried a different approach.

'I forgive you, Catalina, just accept it. What I need from you now is your loyalty and accurate information about the children. So, for the love of God stop crying, and talk,' Maria hissed at her, conscious of the guard listening outside.

Catalina continued her jagged sobbing.

Maria crossed the room, took her by the left shoulder with one hand and with the other delivered a sharp slap across her face.

Catalina stopped crying. Her eyes blazed at Maria with indignation and she raised her hand. Just for a moment Maria thought she might slap her back. Instead, Catalina brought the hand to her own face to feel the livid red patch of skin, and said, 'Yes, yes, señora you are right.'

Maria poured her some water from the flask on the bedside table. They both sat on the narrow, hard, bed and turned to face each other.

Catalina sipped the water, placed the mug on the table and took a deep breath. 'Señora, this is what is happening,' and Maria listened as Catalina revealed the truth she had been withholding for the past two weeks.

Maria sat in silence until Catalina had run out of words and breath. 'He thinks he can deflower my daughter whilst I remain a hostage. He believes Isabel will sacrifice herself to save me. And I suppose that in his perverted mind he believes he is seducing, not raping. He probably believes this is a lesser sin and that's the only reason he doesn't take her by force.' She took Catalina's hand and asked, 'There is still no news of the señor?'

Catalina shook her head.

Maria gazed through the arrow slit, into the shaft of weak sunlight at her beloved Seville. She turned to Catalina, took her head between her hands and kissed her on the forehead. 'Catalina there is only one solution, it will require all of our strength and if you help me, I believe God will forgive all of our sins. I need to know that I can trust you. I *can* trust you, Catalina, can't I?'

Maria watched as Catalina made the sign of the cross and brought her crucifix to her lips.

It's not as if I have any other choice.

TWENTY-SIX

T riana, *Castillo de San Jorge*

LATER THAT AFTERNOON CATALINA, Isabel, and Gabriel did as Torquemada suggested and stationed themselves at the highest part of the *castillo* with the spyglass ready. The children took turns to look through the eyepiece and report to each other what they saw. Catalina was alternately absorbed by Isabel's detailed descriptions and frustrated by Gabriel's curt and superficial utterances.

'I can see an awfully long stage with what looks to be two marble columns placed at either end. There are stairways built from the stage that seem to connect to some apartments above it, where people are sitting and watching what's going on.'

'Some boys playing trumpets.'

'There's a separate structure topped by a cupola which I think is where the prisoners will be held. The whole stage is beautiful, with rich velvet crimson curtains and wonderful Persian carpets that look similar to the ones we have at Pozzoblanco.'

'Lots of people. I'm trying to look for Papa.'

When it was Isabel's turn again, she pivoted ninety degrees to her right and said, 'A man on a horse is leading the procession as it sets out from the cathedral. It looks like Father Tomás. He's surrounded by so many guards wearing green and black and gold. They look wonderful.'

She walked along the battlement maintaining the spyglass at a steady height. 'They've reached the plaza where the stage is and I can see about twenty Dominican friars, just like Friar Alonso, coming forward carrying large candles to greet the procession.' She paused. 'But now I can't really see anymore, it's getting too dark.'

Night was falling. The friars' candles were joined by hundreds more, and the plaza appeared as if it were almost in daylight. Torquemada ascended the stage to boisterous clapping and loud cheers that drifted on the wind to the children. He stood at the edge of the stage and looked out across the vast crowd, made the sign of the cross and held his hands aloft, palms outstretched in recognition of their adulation. He led them in prayers. The wind carried the low murmuring to the battlements of the *castillo*. The children joined in mechanically with the "Amens".

SLEEP DID NOT COME EASILY that night to anybody in the city, least of all the thirteen *marranos* condemned to death for secretly practicing Judaism. All but one claimed they were innocent, that they were good Christians. All, except Juan de Mota who confessed to being a Jew. His reward? To be the last to burn the next day. The other twelve *marranos* would receive clemency and be garrotted before being roasted. The thirteen spent the night with the confessors provided by the Inquisition. Juan refused anything to do with them. He lay on his side in the corner of the cell repeating sotto voce the special Jewish prayer for protection at night: 'In the name of Adonai the God of Israel, may the angel Michael be at my right and the angel Gabriel be at my left, and above my head the divine presence.'

THE FOLLOWING morning Isaac is awoken at five o'clock by the ringing of bells throughout the city. This ensures that all bear witness to the *auto-da-fé*. This will remind everyone of what they will face after death at the Last Judgment. He makes his way from his latest hideaway. He is now an expert on the cellars and hidden rooms of Seville. He positions himself outside the derelict synagogue, from where the procession will begin.

Isaac watches as an orange seller's cart catches its wheels in the cobbles. The mans' wares spill out across the plaza. Three youths scramble for the fruit. The leanest one is stronger than he looks; he fights off the others and scoops up an armful of fruit. One of the oranges escapes him and rolls towards Isaac. The vagrant boy scuttles after it; his speed and agility are impressive. Isaac lifts the heel of his boot and traps the golden treasure. As the boy grabs for it Isaac applies a little more pressure, but then thinks better of depriving the boy. Oranges from Seville are a prized delicacy after all, even this late in the season. And the boy is in need of sustenance. He grabs the fruit and looks up at Isaac with a huge grin. He stands beside Isaac, peeling and greedily consuming the orange - juices smearing his blackened face. Isaac gives silent thanks that his own son is alive and well cared for, even though he remains in danger.

Loud cheers from the mob draw their attention. They see the cause of the outburst – a white stallion ridden by Tomás Torquemada has ambled into view. Isaac grimaces at the thought of his family being held captive by this man. The carts carrying the effigies of those who have already been tortured to death follow Torquemada. These sculpted figures will burn by proxy for heresy.

Then stumble the *reconciliados*: those who have recanted and who will only suffer whipping, imprisonment and the confiscation of their property and land.

Next the *relajados*; still proclaiming their innocence in piercing wails. They wear a white conical hat and *sanbenitos*; these blessed sacks decorated with vivid red flames and garish demons. Every *relajado* has a cross to carry and is accompanied by a confessor who walks besides them admonishing them to repent. The crowd press in from every side, urging them to listen to their confessors.

Isaac sees Juan. He claims the honour of burning last; permitted to watch the roasting flesh of the others. He is gagged. The crowd knows this indicates his refusal to repent, even though he has admitted he is a *marrano*. But he will not apologise for keeping his faith. He is spat on, kicked and punched. Ana, dressed in black, walks beside him doing her best to shield him from the worst of the abuse whilst begging him to recant.

Alonso shambles along at the rear on a white cob. Struggling in front of him is a heavily laden mule. It is bedecked with silver plates engraved with gold calligraphy, its neck hung with gold and silver bells, and bearing a purple chest inscribed with ornate copperplate. Inside the chest are the trial records and details of the confessions.

Isaac feels a surge of emotion swell in his chest – he supposes it is pity. But perhaps it is guilt. He has done nothing to help Juan escape the Inquisition. Isaac turns, mounts the steps of the abandoned synagogue, removes his cowl, kisses the tip of a long, thin bladed dagger and points towards Juan. He means it to be a salute, it is all he can think of in the circumstances.

The disturbance in the crowd at this strange sight draws Juan's attention and he lifts his head and tries to raise a hand. Ana turns to see who her husband acknowledges. She wails and shouts, 'Isaac, Isaac, Isaac.' But he has gone.

He hurries through the narrow, dark *calles*. He steps around a gang of children – none more than six years of age – splashing in the stream of piss that meanders through the cobbles of Calle Verde. Removing his cloak, he throws it into a dark corner, but not before taking out the wide-brimmed hat he has concealed in its large interior pocket. He places it on his head. It will have to do. He navigates back to the far side of the plaza just in time to witness the procession arrive to loud cheers from the baying mob.

The crowd swells towards him, shoving him back towards the steps of the cathedral. A tall man sways backwards and Isaac holds out a hand to push him away and feels the rough wool of his tunic. *A peasant come into the city for the day to see the fun.* He brings a handkerchief to his nose to block the fetid smell of unwashed bodies and the acrid aroma of excrement.

The tall peasant's much shorter companion calls out, 'It don't seem that long the Holy Office been open in Seville and look how many heretics they caught.'

The taller man snorts. 'What, you think the Holy Office been too hasty?'

'No, I didn't mean to say that at all, you twist my words.'

'None of 'em are innocent. It's better to endure the agony our Good Lord put up with, than to suffer eternal damnation.'

'Even if they've not done anything?'

'Better a few moments of pain than to burn for all eternity,' the taller man says with finality.

Isaac elbows his way through the crowd towards the top of the cathedral steps and looks across at the *auto-da-fé*. On the far side of the plaza is a wall of boxes, three tiers high. In the centre of the bottom row Queen Isabella and King Ferdinand sit in the royal box that juts out towards the central platform. Isaac cannot see them clearly, cannot tell whether the face of the man he thinks of as almost a friend betrays the horror he probably feels.

On each side of the royal box sits row upon row of clerics – the priests in their black vestments, the Dominican friars in their white habits. The two terraces form an enclosure that provides a clear view of the central platform.

Men carry bundles of wood and clumps of straw up the stairs at either end of the platform, placing them at the base of the stakes. They arrange the wood and the straw in a circle around them, leaving a narrow entrance for the condemned to enter. They take great care to distribute the straw evenly – Isaac knows this will ensure the fire spreads quickly.

The pyre in the middle is different. It is mainly wood, with only a scattering of straw. This fire will catch more slowly, prolonging the agony. This is the stake reserved for the unrepentant. For Juan.

The procession arrives. Torquemada dismounts and ascends the stairs to join their Majesties. Isaac is again surprised at how sprightly he is for his age. Perhaps his conviction lends him energy. The conviction that has led to this, to Juan's death.

The *reconciliados* reach the stage accompanied by loud cheers from the mob and a round of applause from the seated clerics. Their reward for recanting. The presiding bishop reads their names from a scroll and they are dragged one by one to the centre of the stage to be flogged. The crowd hushes as the crack of the whip on bare backs echoes across the plaza. After the first flogging, Isaac averts his eyes from the blood that spatters and pools on the stage.

He looks again when he hears the jeers for the *relajdos* as they are led towards the stakes. One girl looks about the same age as Gabriel. An old man can barely walk and is helped to his appointed place. Still screaming out their innocence, refusing to recant. Isaac looks for Juan, but his recompense for honesty will be delayed until the *relajdos* have begun to burn. His will watch their roasting flesh slip away from their bones as they cry out.

The men smear each of the *relajdos* shirts with sulphur. This will make the flames burn more quickly and shorten their incineration. They are led through the pyre to the stake and bound with thick metal chains. The executioner takes a firebrand and sets each pyre alight. The crackling of burning wood is the only sound as the crowd are silenced. Isaac supposes it is awe and fear mixed with gratitude that it is not them, perhaps tainted by the realisation that it soon could be. One wrong word from a neighbour in the right ear is all it will take.

Thin white tendrils soon become black guttering smoke that accompanies the screams. Isaac feels the charred stink of bitter smoke in his nostrils.

Juan is led up the stairs towards the pyre mainly built of

wood. He stares straight ahead, silent, as the crowd mutters and murmurs, expressing their disgust. The executioner rips his shirt from him, no sulphur for Juan. The keening of a woman rises above the noise of the crowd. Isaac knows it is Ana. He sees her as Juan looks down and smiles at her. The executioner binds him to the stake and Ana's wails become louder until her voice cracks and is drowned by the crowd's rising cheers.

Juan looks directly at Isaac, then closes his eyes and raises his head to heaven. Isaac can make out the movement of his lips – a prayer, he assumes. The executioner tosses the firebrand into the pyre at Juan's feet then turns and opens his arms to receive the approbation of the crowd. The cheers reach a crescendo as the flames slowly form, and Juan begins to howl.

Isaac closes his eyes and whispers the Jewish prayer for the dying, 'O God, full of compassion, who dwells on high, grant true rest in the exalted spheres of the holy and the pure who shine as the resplendence of the firmament, to the soul of Juan de Mota.' He opens his eyes and does not close them again until Juan's body has melted away into the inferno. *I will have vengeance, no matter how long it takes.*

TWENTY-SEVEN

THE TESTIMONY OF FRIAR ALONSO

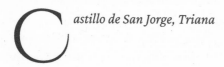 *astillo de San Jorge, Triana*

BROTHER TOMÁS WAS MOST UNUSUALLY effusive in his praise. There was so much preparation and organisation that I've barely slept for a week. But it all went without an obvious hitch. I say "obvious", as something did happen, or nearly happened, that could have spoilt the day for Brother Tomás. Fortunately, he did not *seem* to be aware of it, so busy was he with his duties and so rapt by the executions.

And now it's too late to bring it to his attention. I have to hope I was mistaken. I've been searching my conscience as to why I did not tell him of my suspicions. Perhaps it is to do with what Catalina told me of his recent behaviour towards Isabel? That woman is treacherous, and I have to do something about her. But I need to set it down somewhere to relieve myself of the burden of the memory. I dare not share my deepest thoughts with anyone else.

It was a little after dawn and I kept my cowl on to protect me from the bitter chill. I took my appointed place at the back of the procession, riding my white cob. It appeared the whole of Seville had come to witness the *auto-da-fé*, the inconsiderate crowds pressing in from all sides – we had barely enough space to push our way through. The guards did their best to keep the peasants at bay for which I was grateful, as their body odour was overpowering. On several occasions, I found myself cut off from the main procession.

Brother Tomás gave me the great honour of riding at the back with the mule carrying the evidence chest. He asked me to keep watch on Juan de Mota. His wife, Ana, walked alongside begging him to recant, telling him it wasn't too late to save his reputation. At one point I heard her wail, 'Think of the children Juan, please, please.' I almost pitied her. I knew Brother Tomás had permitted this to happen, in the hope she would persuade Juan to confess and provide the names of his conspirators. He planned to arrest her after her husband's execution.

After about an hour of laboriously trailing our way from the cathedral to the plaza, I looked around me. To my left I saw a tall figure dressed in a long black cloak standing on the steps of an abandoned synagogue, his back to the door. It was not only his height that caught my attention but the ostentatious removal of his hood. Then he raised a thin-bladed dagger to his lips and held it out towards Juan de Mota, as though in salute. There was a disturbance in the crowd as those nearby hastily moved away, fearing he was about to attack. Their startled cries drew de Mota's attention and he raised his head towards the figure and tried to raise a hand in recognition.

Ana turned to see who Juan was acknowledging, as she

did so the figure pulled his hood up and vanished into the crowd. Ana began to wail and sob. I thought I heard her shout, 'Isaac, Isaac, Isaac,' but couldn't be sure over the incessant chatter of the crowds. I felt something stir inside me. I think I was moved.

IT IS NOW deep into the night and I cannot sleep after the report I received earlier this evening. Just after Vespers, a guard brought news that a group of soldiers had found a woman's body on the bank of the Guadalquivir – on the Triana side of the Puente de Barcas. It could have been suicide – the guards told me that there was no blood or any visible wounds on the body – but I don't believe that. One of the soldiers recognised the body as that of the woman who had been walking alongside Juan de Mota at the *auto-da-fé*. When I told Brother Tomás, he did not seem surprised, said he would, "mull it over" and bade me goodnight.

I did not share my suspicion with Brother Tomás that it was Isaac who had murdered her. He had reason. His best friend was dead, and Ana knew what little influence Isaac possessed had not even been sufficient to prevent her husband's execution. Surely, she would want to avenge herself by revealing what she must know about Isaac? Perhaps my hesitation was again caused by what Catalina had implied about Brother Tomás' behaviour towards Isabel. She alluded to it by saying that he had been spending a lot of time with Isabel alone, praying apparently. Catalina had held my gaze for a moment too long.

Why would she imply such a thing if it were not true? I almost tremble to commit it to words, but I have nobody to confide in. I'm beginning to doubt the purity of Brother Tomás' intentions.

If I reveal who I believe to be the perpetrator I also reveal to Brother Tomás that I withheld information from him about Isaac's actions during the procession. I cannot do that. He would then have sufficient cause to order the immediate arrest of Isaac. The King could not prevent it. And that would be Isabel's last hope removed. Why do I care so much? This question troubles me. If only I could sleep peacefully. I hope Ana does; God rest her soul.

CHAPTER
TWENTY-EIGHT

S *eville*

'I DON'T KNOW how much longer I can stay here,' Isaac says.

'I was pondering the same question myself,' Alejandro mutters.

They sit at a small wooden table in the cramped, damp cellar of Alejandro's house, early on the morning after Seville's first *auto-da-fé*. It is still dark. Isaac had slept fitfully, sitting in a chair covered by a horsehair blanket which was abominably itchy. A few candles cast some dim light into the deep shadows. The officers of the Inquisition had, of course, already searched Alejandro's house so he hopes it is now safe. They both know it is just a matter of time before the officers return.

'I'm running out of choices.'

'You only have one, señor,' Alejandro replies in a whisper.

Isaac stares at him, setting his jaw. He scratches at his beard, even more unkempt than usual.

'We both know you cannot stay here for even one more minute, let alone another night. Nobody else from the prayer group will take you in, especially after the murder of Ana de Palacios. I cannot decide whether her death is fortunate or unfortunate for you.'

Isaac's silence dares him to continue.

'It is unfortunate for your reputation, as everyone believes you murdered her because you assumed she would give evidence against you to the Inquisition. It is fortunate for your immediate salvation for just that same reason.'

'You mean the few honourable people left, who are not creatures of the Inquisition, but who are prepared to see me as one of their own?'

Alejandro nods. Isaac's understanding seems to embolden him and he continues, 'But, pardon me, what on earth did you think you were doing appearing at the parade to salute Juan de Mota?'

Isaac remains silent, a thin smile forming on his lips. He ignores Alejandro's question. How could this boy understand a lifetime of friendship extinguished by cowardice? Why should he explain his guilt, his shame, his anger? Yes, he had acted irrationally, instinctively for once. And it felt good, it felt right. Instead, he asks, 'And what do *you* believe is the truth of the matter?'

Alejandro takes a moment. 'The man I knew and respected before the Inquisition arrived would never stoop to murder; it would be impossible for his conscience to bear. But in times like this, when one is terrified not only for oneself but also for one's family, then, anything is possible. But no, Señor, I don't think you murdered Ana de Palacios. *I* might have, given exactly the same circumstances.'

Isaac tries to stand but can only crouch under the low ceiling. His temper is not improved by the ache in his back from bending all the time. He looks down and says, 'You seem very certain that I only have one way to proceed. Out with it man, out with it.' Isaac's voice rises with impatience, 'What is it?'

'Before I come to that, there is one further suggestion I should like to make.' He takes a deep breath. 'You could go to Torquemada and give yourself up in exchange for Maria's life.'

Isaac narrows his eyes, and then smiles. 'You expect me to be angry at you, don't you?'

'Yes, I did think that might be your reaction.'

'You should know me well enough to realise I've already considered turning myself in. We both know that Torquemada will detain me and find an excuse to keep both Maria and I imprisoned. Then execute both of us. And I use the word "execute" precisely. These are not religious acts of salvation. And then where would that leave the children?'

'I agree, señor, but I had to ensure that you had at least considered the matter.'

'What else?'

'It seems to me,' Alejandro continues with conviction, 'that the event we all seem to have lost sight of is the hideous crime that started this.'

'Go on,' says Isaac.

At the same moment Alejandro was pondering the most judicious way to respond to Isaac, his daughter felt herself shaken awake.

'Señorita ... señorita ... señorita,' Catalina whispered, 'I have something important, you must read it now.'

172

Isabel struggled up through layers of consciousness and sat upright. 'What is it Catalina. Better be important,' she said, clawing at her unkempt hair.

Catalina's pursed lips and the beseeching look in her eyes told her that it was. Isabel took the letter and tore it open. She saw her mother's hand and let out a whispered, 'Yes!' She smiled and looked up at Catalina, expecting to see her joy reflected back, but instead saw that she was struggling not to cry. She read:

'MY DEAREST, *dearest darling daughter,*

This is the hardest letter I have ever had to write but I know it will be much harder for you to read. Please read it three times before you say anything to Catalina or do anything. You will need to take the time to think and reflect on its contents; do nothing and say nothing to anyone until you have.

Once you have read it, you must burn it; this will be one of the most important things you will ever do. Once you have digested the contents of this letter I hope you will understand, and forgive, my course of action, for I truly believe it is the only way to protect both of you, my dearest Isabel, and my darling Gabriel.

My child, when I first held you in my arms and smelt you and kissed you and cradled your head, I thought I would burst with the love I felt flooding through my body. You were such a beautiful baby, and I knew I would do anything to protect you; but I didn't realise what our city would become. I didn't foresee the intolerance, ignorance and fear that seems to drive us all now. If I had, I would have urged your father to have removed us from Spain long ago and settled somewhere more agreeable. The Indies perhaps? England or Portugal? It would not have mattered, anywhere else would have saved us from this. But at the time, I thought that it would be a cowardly course to pursue. Now it is too late for me, but not for you and Gabriel. I know it and I know that The Almighty will protect you.

I ramble as I try to find the strength to commit to paper the truth or the various truths I should say ...'

'Hurry, señorita, the castle is stirring and there are things we must do,' Catalina said interrupting Isabel's flow. She looked up at Catalina, only hazily comprehending her words. Isabel returned to the letter, tutting.

'Let me come to the point: the first thing you need to know is that your father is still a practicing Jew. He converted to Catholicism only to do what he could to protect the family, but he could never square this with his conscience. I forgive him. He is my husband and the father of my children but, still, his beliefs and his principles will make us all pay a heavy price. I know that you had your suspicions as you grew older. I know that some of your poor behaviour was due to your awareness of what you perceived to be your father's hypocrisy. I have come to see your father's actions as sincerely carried out with the best of intentions. I beg you to think about this and to do your very best to forgive him.'

The sound of footsteps outside broke Isabel's concentration again. Catalina went to the door to bar the entry of whoever might be there, but the footsteps halted, and then receded.

'... to forgive your father. The second thing that you should know – it is almost too obvious to state it –Torquemada is an extremely dangerous man. There is no delicate way for me to put this, my dearest daughter, but he intends to seduce you. He believes you will succumb to his evil intent in order to save me. We need to take that opportunity away from him.'

Isabel rested the letter on her lap and looked up at Catalina, too afraid to carry on reading. Catalina returned her gaze and nodded encouragingly.

'*This is what you must do now* ...' Isabel read the rest of the letter, trying to comprehend and memorise the details of the plan her mother had laid out. She brushed the silent tears away from her face, told herself to stop; now was not the time. She read the letter twice more, just as her mother had entreated her to and then ripped it up, placed the pieces in the empty bowl by her bed and set light to them with a candle. Isabel watched until the flames had completely died away and then with the tip of her right index finger traced a '?' in the ashes.

As Isaac waits for his deputy's advice, as Isabel fights bewilderment, as Alonso tries not to bask in his success, as Torquemada ponders his next move, as Fernan's mother struggles to prepare breakfast, as Juan and Ana's children awake as orphans, the sun begins its shimmering, fiery ascent above the Guadalquivir and the bells of Seville and Triana ring out, calling the faithful to prayer.

CHAPTER
TWENTY-NINE
THE TESTIMONY OF FRIAR ALONSO

T riana, *Castillo de San Jorge*

DIOS MIO, dios mio, dios mio. I knew from the beginning there would be death, but I believed with all my heart it would be justified and that the righteous would be spared. The good and the pure would be identified by the Holy Office and our shared faith, our community, would be strengthened. I did not foresee what we would do to the mothers and their children. Now four blessed, innocent children are left motherless and another boy lies dead. His mother no doubt beyond any consolation.

But this must all be in God's master plan. Surely my part in all of this is as a servant of his will? I had no choice but do his bidding for his greater glory. I must be held accountable, but all of my actions were directed by God and at Brother Tomás' behest. I am not culpable; I am merely a vessel, a vassal.

Pretty, clever words are worthless! I cannot excuse myself, I cannot, I cannot, I cannot. What does The Almighty require me to do next? Even Brother Tomás seems at a loss. I have never seen him so perplexed as he is now at the events of the last twenty-four hours. I hear rumours that His Majesty is greatly disturbed by the suicide of Ana de Palacios, but most particularly by the death of Señora Ximenes during interrogation by Brother Tomás.

For the first time, I have doubts about our methods. What is gained by depriving innocent children of their mothers? I never knew mine because she could not, or would not, tend to me. She gave me away. What have we come to, that we justify removing children from their loving mothers? Is this The Almighty's will? I do not believe it anymore.

Brother Tomás asked Señora Ximenes, 'Are you prepared to die to protect your husband? Will you sacrifice yourself to save his already damned soul?' Her hands and feet bound to the *escalera*, clothes drenched in sweat, smelling of piss and vomit. And yet she had such grace in her reply, 'I would do anything to protect my family from evil. And you, Father, are evil.' He moved towards her and I thought Brother Tomás would strike the señora. Instead, he signalled for the *escalera* to be tilted back, ready for the next jug of water. The señora rocked her head violently, trying in vain to evade the water. I heard her screams, muffled by the muslin cloth. I watched as the life drained away from her eyes. I watched in silence, doing nothing, saying nothing.

His Majesty demands to know why both these women had to die. I cannot decide on which side of The Almighty's ledger my deeds should be written. If the King becomes actively involved, I do not want to be caught in his tongs, roasted over the fire whilst waiting for judgment. And yet, if

I survive, I will be returned to the protection afforded by Brother Tomás.

And the children, the children, dear God the children. Gabriel and poor pretty Isabel have disappeared.

CHAPTER
THIRTY

S *eville*

SEVILLE IS LAID out before Isaac like a shimmering ocean glistening in the moonlight. The blackness is pierced by the tiny pinpricks of candles in windows and by lanterns carried by the few people abroad at this time of night. He hears the bells toll eleven o'clock. From the summit of La Giralda no other noise reaches him as he basks in the cool breeze.

It had been easy enough to hide; he put his cowl over his head and joined a group of monks wending their way up the ramps. The Sultan who built the original minaret constructed them so he could easily ascend by horseback to admire the view. Isaac gave weary thanks to the Sultan's foresight. As the sun went down, he hid in a dark corner shrouded by his cloak, the guards' cursory look at sunset not enough to discover him.

Alejandro brought Isaac news of Maria's death earlier that day. She had not survived Torquemada's questioning. Isaac said, 'thank you,' packed up his few belongings, shook Alejandro's hand and left. He remembers the puzzled look in Alejandro's eyes. *Had he thought he would scream and shout?* Isaac had been expecting the news and knew the time for emotion lay in the future. He allowed himself to be subjugated to violent feelings in the church and regrets his actions. He has vowed not to act so intemperately again. The children, and his own soul, are his priorities now.

He wonders how Maria's death had happened. The water torture, the *escalara* perhaps? He curses himself for such crass thoughts.

Instinct drove him to the top of La Giralda. To be nearer to God, to be nearer to Maria? He tries to work out why Torquemada allowed her to die in this way – surely burning her at the stake at the next *auto* would have been justified? It could only have been an accident. A mistake, a loss of control. Which means Maria refused to give the Inquisitor what he wanted. She had not recanted, not given evidence against him, or revealed the names of the prayer group. He vows not to waste the opportunity Maria has given her life for. *I will not act rashly; I will not lose control.*

Alejandro had passed on the news from Catalina that the children were being treated well, and she said that Isaac was not to worry. Isaac believes there is no immediate danger and that Torquemada has little to gain by torturing or executing the children. They are more use to him as hostages. He believes they are safe, for now. He places his faith in his fragile connection to King Ferdinand.

A sob wells up from somewhere deep in his chest. He needs to see Maria, to hold her once more. He could go and join her. He places his palms on the cold stone ledge of the parapet and looks over the edge into the darkness.

'HOLD MY HAND PROPERLY YOU IDIOT,' hissed Isabel. Gabriel tugged at her arm and dragged his feet. She put an arm around his shoulder and hugged him to her. He had been sobbing ever since Catalina had left them outside the gates of the *castillo*. As instructed by her mother's letter, Isabel did not share their intended destination with Catalina. The guards were not surprised to see them as the trio regularly took morning walks along the banks of the river.

Catalina had crouched down to hug Gabriel to her with one hand and with the other passed a small dagger to Isabel. It was the blade that Isabel sometimes saw on Mama's dresser in Casa de la Felicidad. Memories of home threatened to unleash a flood of tears, but she chose to focus on the beauty of the dagger. The handle was encrusted with small purple sapphires, the hilt finished with curlicues that lent the dagger a prettiness that made it appear innocuous. The blade was about the length of Isabel's hand. She slipped it into the pocket of her dress before Gabriel could see it. She looked intently at Catalina, trying to convey that she had the determination to use the dagger if the need arose.

Catalina hugged Isabel to her and whispered, 'I will lead them a merry chase for as long as I can, but you must move on quickly, find your father. Maybe you can send word to Señor Alejandro? Good luck my dears. We will meet again in this world, or the next.' She kissed the top of both of their heads, made the sign of the cross and gently pushed them away from her.

The children hurried away crossing the Puente de

Barcas and into the gloom of Triana. Isabel turned to look for Catalina, hoping to see her waving, but she had already vanished into the early morning mist.

Now she stood hugging Gabriel to her at the nexus of a maze of *calles* trying to decide which one to take, trying to remember which one led to Fernan's house. From the dark shadows behind them Isabel heard a rough voice whisper, 'Well, well, well look at this pretty pigeon pair!'

ISAAC CANNOT NOT BEAR the burden of Maria's sacrifice. He knows she questioned his choices, becoming frustrated by his principles, believing that family should be more important. But she gave her life for him, for *his* principles, to protect their family. He bows his head and places his forehead on the cold stone. Her sacrifice cannot be in vain.

Then, as though the stone had cooled his fevered brain enough for rational thought to take over, he has a flash of insight: Alejandro is right, this madness started with Fernan's murder. That was the incident, the supposed pagan Jewish ritual, that gave Torquemada the excuse to bring the Inquisition to Seville after so many years of trying to overturn the King's veto. It was all a little too convenient. And Fernan's murderer had still not been found. The Inquisition seemed happy to place the responsibility on Juan. That he had no connection to, or reason to kill, the boy didn't seem to matter. Facts did not matter, doubt was not entertained, only belief counted.

Alejandro was right to remind him of the way this had all started. It confirmed his own instincts that he should have found the courage to trust long ago. If he can unravel the mystery of Fernan's death he can present the King with evidence that might bring an end to the Inquisition, at least in Seville. Alejandro had told him that his only remaining move was to present His Majesty with some proof that the Jews did not commit Fernan's murder.

But he had nothing to give his Majesty, nothing to trade. Isaac knew that Ferdinand was well disposed towards him, especially given their shared family antecedents. But without evidence there was no possibility the King would move against Torquemada, or risk conflict with the Queen.

He pulls back from the edge, his mind made up. He has to go back to Triana and speak with Fernan's parents again. It all led back to the night of the child's murder. They must be able to tell him something more, to set him on the trail to putting everything right.

CHAPTER
THIRTY-ONE

T *riana*

'LOOK AT THIS PRETTY PIGEON PAIR.'

Isabel turned to face the growling voice, whilst hugging Gabriel to her. She was surprised to see a tall, emaciated figure emerge from the shadows of a taverna – from the voice she had imagined a burly man. He advanced into the dim light that pierced the narrow *calles* and Isabel could see he was barely dressed. His clothes were in tatters and he wore a blue cap. She recalled seeing similar caps worn by the sailors on the ships as they sailed past the family when they picnicked beside the Guadalquivir. This sudden flash of happier times made her want to cry.

The man shambled towards them and Isabel became aware of his stink, the smell of rotting rubbish. She noticed the loose flesh on his face and the patches of pale skin, surrounded by livid, red lumps.

He held out a hand that looked more like a claw and said, 'Give me everything you have, and I promise not to hurt you.'

'Get away from us!' Gabriel screamed from behind Isabel.

The claw reached out to Gabriel and Isabel backed them both away. She was conscious there was only solid wall behind them but could not risk running. She would escape, but the creature would have enough time to grab Gabriel. A flash of anger burnt through her. Why had Mama left her to deal with all of this? Her letter had alluded to the possibility she might not survive the inevitable interrogation once it was known the children had escaped. Isabel accepted she would probably never see her mother again – not in this lifetime. But acceptance did not erase the deep hurt of being abandoned.

As the creature advanced, and the gap to the wall grew ever smaller, she realised that he was a leper who must have escaped from the San Lazaro Hospital. Her hand closed on the dagger in her pocket. The man staggered forward. He was almost upon them and Gabriel began to wail. Isabel took the dagger out and pointed its tip towards the leper. He smiled, revealing a gaping mouth with only a few rotten teeth. Then, without any warning, he lurched violently to his right and crumpled onto the cobbles, his body seeming to lose its form in the remains of his clothes.

Isabel thought she saw a familiar face and then an arm reaching out to her. But fear got the better of her and she thrust the dagger into the hand. She saw a streak of crimson erupt violently; then came a piercing scream.

. . .

Isabel regained consciousness with a start and gasped for breath. She was lying down. She felt a damp cloth on her head, a hand stroking her hair and heard a soft, female voice say, 'Don't you worry my dear, don't you worry, all will be well.'

It's Mama, she's alive, thank heavens I don't have to do all of this by myself anymore. She raised herself from the bed; her brain felt detached from the inside of her head and her stomach churned. She kept her eyes closed, cried, 'Mama,' and reached out for the soothing hand, only to feel its roughness. Her mother's hands were soft and smooth; these were hard and calloused. She opened her eyes and saw Señora Beatriz, Fernan's mother, sitting beside her and Señor Rodrigo, his father, standing behind looking anxiously on.

'You're safe now, my dear,' Beatriz said, 'though heaven knows what would have become of the pair of you if my husband hadn't happened upon you before that monster could do you harm.'

'Where's Gabriel?' Isabel suddenly remembered him, feeling guilty for not having done so sooner.

'I'm here, Isabel.' He was on the floor playing with some roughly carved wooden soldiers. She slumped back onto the bed. She wanted to scream, to wail, to smash things. But she needed to remain calm for Gabriel. It was what Mama would have wanted. And Papa would come soon. She knew he must.

'You took a knock when you fell over,' Rodrigo said, 'just after you gave me that nasty little pinprick.' He raised his bandaged hand so Isabel could see.

'I'm so sorry,' she gulped out between loud sobs.

'There, there dearie,' Beatriz consoled her by stroking her hair again, 'it's all turned out for the best. A bit of bloodletting won't do him any harm. Might put some sense into him,' she said, chuckling. 'It was lucky he came along, mind. He gave that leper a right shove, and a good kicking afterwards. Serve him right for preying on children. He should be grateful that Rodrigo let him go.' She turned to smile at her husband.

Rodrigo returned the smile and then grinned at Isabel.

She tried to smile but managed only a grimace. Isabel collected her thoughts and said, 'Thank you for everything, but we have to find our father, we have to find him quickly.'

'Don't you worry, all is in hand, you just get some rest young lady,' Rodrigo said.

As Isabel returned to oblivion she thought she heard one of them mutter, 'He'll be here soon enough, we must be ready.'

Ready for what? Isabel wondered as she drifted back into the darkness.

THIRTY-TWO

THE TESTIMONY OF FRIAR ALONSO

S *eville, Torre del Orro*

I DON'T KNOW who is becoming more unhinged by all of this, myself or Brother Tomás. At least I am aware of it and can talk to you and confide in you about what I am becoming. Who does Brother Tomás confess to, Father Gutiérrez?

Catalina's questioning at the Torre has lasted almost twenty-four hours. And yet she has told us almost nothing. She will not confirm that Señor Alvarez is a *crypto*. Of the children, all she will say is that she accompanied them on their usual walk, and they ran away from her.

Brother Tomás instructed the *inquisidores* to keep Catalina on the edge of death for almost two days. He told them to end the water torture and move her to the rack. I suppose that is an escalation of sorts. I could barely watch or contain myself whilst listening to her screams. Especially after what happened to Señora Xemines. Catalina kept repeating, 'Gabriel', and 'Isabel', and 'I don't know where they are.' I'd thought Catalina devious, but her first priority has always been to protect the children. She did not seek to use them to bargain for her soul.

Brother Tomás instructed me to try a different approach. He decided that she either knew nothing or possessed extraordinary levels of resilience that torture could not overcome. And, I pray to The Almighty for forgiveness, I agreed without hesitation or any protest at such further dissemblance. I console myself it would not have done any good to argue with Brother Tomás. But at least I, and The Almighty, would know that I had tried.

The *inquisidores* left the dungeon and I entered alone. Brother Tomás listened outside the door. I approached Catalina's inert form. A putrid smell of her unwashed body assailed me, and I gagged. She seemed to have grown smaller, and the end of a loose tress nestled in a sunken cheek. Hands tied above her head, her body in repose, awaiting its next violation. She opened an eye at my approach and tried to scream, but only a cracked wheeze escaped. I took a cloth, dabbed at her brow, and untied her hands. I helped her to sit up and sip some water. She leant against me.

I whispered my suspicions regarding Brother Tomás' behaviour towards Isabel. Gently helping her to raise her head I gave her a hard look, hoping she would understand the message that Brother Tomás believed I was giving her. I needed both Brother Tomás and Catalina to believe they could trust me.

It occurs to me I was no better than Isaac and the other *cryptos*: trying to serve two masters. I don't know how to unpick the morality of this. All I know is that my heart went out to Catalina. Perhaps she brought to mind Sister

Manuela. Perhaps I could not bear the thought of children losing their parents and it reminded me of my own parentless childhood. I was not driven solely by my duty to the Holy Office. Perhaps I should have been, but I do not possess the same purity of conviction as Brother Tomás.

Raising my voice I said, 'It is just you and I, Catalina, we are alone. I want to help Isabel and Gabriel find their father and escape from Seville. You can trust me, after all we share a connection from our previous lives.' She dipped her head weakly, but doing so seemed to cause her great pain and she sobbed. I offered her some more water.

Catalina moaned and said, 'I don't know anything for certain.'

I turned my head at movement from outside the door. She widened her eyes at me and started to moan, but I stroked her hair and made calming noises. She knew something. I waited, put my arm around her shoulder and said, 'My child, my child everything will be for the best, everything will work out according to God's will.'

I shudder in self-disgust at the recollection. She whispered a name and I knew where the children were. Now I had yet another choice: should I reveal the name to Brother Tomás or keep the information to myself? A few weeks, even a few days ago, I would not have hesitated, the decision would not have cost me an ounce of conscience. But I knew too much now, had seen too much. I closed my eyes and prayed for guidance.

CHAPTER
THIRTY-THREE

S *eville*

ISAAC KNOWS that leaving the safety of La Giralda is fraught with danger, let alone journeying through the streets to Triana. Torquemada will pull on all the threads leading to every dark corner of the web of informers that Seville has become. There is nobody he can trust, apart from, perhaps, Alejandro. He has already done so much for the family. Isaac does not feel he can call on him or endanger him again. And then it strikes him – help is closer at hand than he realises. Wrapping his cloak around him and drawing the cowl over his head he hurriedly descends the ramps of La Giralda.

'THIS IS SO DELICIOUS,' Isabel said as she took another spoonful of vegetable broth, 'Gabriel, you should really try some.' She was trying to create some sense of normality. Isabel realised the strangeness of even attempting to do this. She felt like two people: Gabriel's sister forced to act as a parent, and a bewildered child numbed by grief.

Her brother was still playing on the floor with the wooden soldiers; it was all the activity he appeared capable of. He was sullen and lacked enthusiasm. He looked up at Isabel, sitting at the table with Señora Beatriz. Isabel thought she saw fear in Gabriel's eyes, but also hatred. For her? She didn't believe she deserved that; she certainly wasn't going to feel guilty for things she had thought but not acted upon. Were these sins of omission? The Holy Office would think so, would have expected her to inform on her parents, on her father in particular. She was realising what an extremely dangerous game she had played when she encouraged Gabriel to say, 'ham and prayers.'

'Gabriel, please,' she pleaded, 'the broth is just as good as Catalina's.' Gabriel dropped his head and Isabel thought he might be crying. She got down from the table and hugged him. He permitted her to do this, and then turned his face into her shoulder to stifle his sobs.

A sudden, loud rapping noise made them all turn to look at the door. Isabel curled her fingers around the dagger that was still in the pocket of her dress and pulled Gabriel even more tightly into her.

FATHER GUTIÉRREZ HAD JUST FINISHED READING the Terce prayer. He enjoyed this time of day, a period of three hours before the mid-day prayers, which left him undisturbed and able to think, pray, and reflect. As he stood at the cathedral doors and bade farewell to the small congregation, he wondered whether increasing fear of the Holy Office was keeping people at home, even during daylight hours. *Surely it should be the opposite, that more people would want to be seen to acknowledge and publicly display their faith?*

He walked through the nave and was approaching the sacristy, intending to change his vestments, when he heard somebody whisper his name. He looked up at the statue of the Madonna in puzzlement. *Was a miracle about to happen?* There it was again, a hissed, 'Father Gutiérrez,' echoing around the cathedral. He looked into the shadows of the ambulatory and saw a crouching figure. Then the dark mass straightened and started to move towards him. Father Gutiérrez cried out, 'Reveal yourself, if you mean to do me harm ...' - but as he saw a familiar face emerge from the shadows, he exhaled. 'Good God in heaven.'

ISABEL STOOD up as Rodrigo opened the door. Alejandro strode across the room, held Isabel's hand and said, 'My poor, dear child.' She collapsed sobbing against his chest and was joined by Gabriel who wrapped himself around her legs.

'My dear children, I'm here to help you now,' Alejandro said.

'How will you do that? You are not our father,' Gabriel said.

'I helped you once before. Do you remember Gabriel? And I can do it again.'

Gabriel tilted his head to the left as though in reflection and seemed to take some comfort from the memory. Satisfied, he returned to his toys.

Alejandro sat at the table and politely refused the offer of food and drink from Señora Beatriz.

'How did you know we were here, Señor Alejandro?' asked Isabel.

'Your father asked Señor Rodrigo to contact me if he ever needed help. I doubt he thought it would quite be in this way,' said Alejandro, with a rueful smile. 'We have little time; in fact, we have none at all. We must go right away.'

Father Gutiérrez strode away from the cathedral, across Plaza del Cabildo. The monk accompanying him walked, with apparent diffidence, two paces behind, palms clasped across his midriff, head down, cowl shadowing his face. Father Gutiérrez kept the first and middle fingers of his right hand raised, forming a circle with his thumb and two remaining fingers as he made the sign of the cross to almost every person they passed.

As they approached the Puente de Barcas the two soldiers guarding the crossing moved their right hands across their bodies to reach for their sheathed swords. Their red uniforms made them appear almost identical. The one on the left was a head taller, appeared older and sported a fine beard. His confident stance indicated he was in charge. The monk slowed and fell further behind Father Gutiérrez, who kept moving forward expecting the soldiers to give way. They did not.

'Good morning Father,' the taller soldier said. All he got for an answer was a slight nod from the priest. 'We have strict instructions from the Grand Inquisitor of All Spain to inspect the bona fides of anyone attempting to cross.'

'That may be so, but we are about God's business, bringing solace to our poor brothers and sisters in Triana. Let us pass,' Father Gutiérrez' tone made it clear he did not expect further obstruction.

'Forgive me, Father, but this is a serious business. We are on the look-out for the murderer of Señora Ana de Palacios. The accused is Señor Isaac Camarino Alvarez, who works at the Real Alcazar. We've got a rough likeness of him drawn by the hand of the Grand Inquisitor himself. There's no end to his talents it seems,' he glanced down at his companion.

'Yes, I know of Señor Alvarez and if I see him, I will be sure to let you know. Now, with God's blessing I bid you good day.' The priest made to pass but the soldiers stood firm.

'Father, forgive us,' said the shorter guard in a conciliatory tone. 'We know who you are, but we have no idea of the identity of the man accompanying you.'

Father Gutiérrez signalled with the palm of his left hand for the monk to come forward. He did so slowly, head bowed.

'Reveal yourself,' said the bearded soldier.

The monk did not respond.

'Let's have a look at you, Friar, if you would be so kind,' said the shorter one.

The monk removed his cowl and looked directly at the soldiers. The taller solider took out a piece of parchment paper from his trouser pocket, unfolded it, studied it, and showed it to his companion.

Isaac takes the lead now the guards have allowed them to cross into Triana. He still remembers the way from the time he and Maria visited Fernan's parents. That awful day is deeply imprinted in his mind. He starts to allow the memory of Maria to invade his consciousness but knows that to do so risks losing every fragment of sanity he has left. He forces himself to focus on the children.

'I'd been meaning to do something about my beard for a long time Father, so thank you.' Isaac has removed his cowl to get some fresh air, not that there is much of that in Triana.

'It wasn't the neatest of shaves,' the priest replies, 'I'm rather out of practice, but it achieved its purpose.'

'Yes, it fooled the guards,' he says quietly. Isaac needs to hear himself speak, even if it was only to utter the obvious, to prevent his mind returning to Maria. 'Almost there now, Father.'

They turn a corner into a very narrow, dark *calle* that leads to the house where he is almost certain the children are. Isaac pulls his cowl back and allows Father Gutiérrez to move ahead He doesn't know what awaits them, and he needs to be ready to make a quick escape.

They approach the door, and the priest calls out, 'Señor Rodrigo, it is Father Gutiérrez, please open up.'

To Isaac's surprise the door is immediately flung open and over Father Gutiérrez' shoulder, he sees Beatriz. Her eyes widen and she raises her hand to cover her open mouth.

CHAPTER
THIRTY-FOUR
THE TESTIMONY OF FRIAR ALONSO

T *riana, Castillo de San Jorge*

BROTHER TOMÁS AWAITED me as I emerged from the darkness of Catalina's dungeon.

'Well?' he asked.

I needed time to think, to make a judgment on the best way to proceed. I couldn't parse the best outcome. Should I reveal what Catalina told me? What was the right, most moral way to proceed? 'Forgive me, Brother, I feel quite faint,' I whispered, as I leant against him and then fell to the floor, careful to slow my fall by holding on to Brother Tomás' cassock.

I "AWOKE" to the ringing of the None bells as my door was thrown open. It was mid-afternoon so I must have been in my cell for about an hour. Brother Tomás had instructed the guards to take me there, and they did so rather more roughly than I thought necessary. I *had* just fainted, after all. Keeping my eyes closed I used the time to pray for God's direction. I opened them to see Brother Tomás standing there, arms folded.

'Well?' he snapped. This was the second time he had used that word; I knew there would not be a third invitation.

WHEN I ASKED The Almighty for direction, his guidance was that children are precious, and we must do all we can to protect them. Whilst "asleep" I considered misdirecting Brother Tomás by leading him to a false location. I feared I could not carry off such a blatant lie, that he would see through the deception all too easily. It was best to tell the truth but at the same time provide Isabel and Gabriel with time to escape. I listened to The Almighty's guidance and decided that Isabel and Gabriel's safety must be my primary concern. Perhaps I have another selfish reason. But I will tell you that another time. And besides, it is pressing, time I mean. I need to finish this entry before attending Matins. I cannot draw any further suspicion by missing prayers.

Brother Tomás insisted on accompanying me and four soldiers to Triana. I wonder whether this was the moment when he began to have doubts? Regarding my loyalty, I mean. I knew that he always harboured doubts about my administrative capabilities. Was he now questioning my allegiance to him, to the Church?

I suggested we ride to Triana but he had, quite rightly, spat back at me that the horses would be no good in the narrow *calles*. I purposely gave him the opportunity to belittle me, believing his anger would make him lose his reason. The quickest course of action would have been to ride to the Puente de Barcas and then walk. My ruse provided the children with another hour or so to escape. My machinations had so far given them perhaps two hours, a slight advantage, but it was all I could manage. I prayed it would be enough.

The rest of this part of the story can be quickly told. We arrived at the house of Fernan's family and Brother Tomás instructed the soldiers to barge the door open and we followed them inside. The small room smelt of rancid ham and acrid, smoky cinders. I wanted to put my hand to my nose to block out the nasty smells but did not want to offend Fernan's mother. I almost retched.

Brother Tomás made himself comfortable at the table. I remained standing, the guards stood watch outside. He asked Fernan's mother who had visited the house that day. She said they had been on their own for the entire time. She said her husband was out looking for work and she did not know when he would be back. I saw Brother Tomás scan the room, eyes steely, bottom lip jutting out in concentration. I realised I was holding my breath, hoping he would not see what was just next to my right foot. But, of course, he did.

'What's this?' Brother Tomás picked up the wooden toy soldier from the floor and dangled it between thumb and forefinger.

Fernan's mother looked at the toy, then down at the floor.

'Forgive me, señora, for reminding you of a painful truth, but your only son is dead, is he not?' Brother Tomás asked.

Fernan's mother did not look at him.

'So, who has been playing with it?'

'It must have been one of the local lads, sometimes they come and play,' she said without conviction. She did not meet his eye.

Brother Tomás' cry of, 'Guards!' shattered the painful silence. He instructed two of them to search every inch of the dwelling. They interpreted this as a license to smash everything, which would not take long as the family had few possessions. I did not see them complete their task as Brother Tomás mercifully told me to accompany the other two guards in taking Fernan's mother to the *castillo*. Another woman for him to torture.

THIRTY-FIVE

T *riana*

IT WAS NOT an unusual sight in Triana: a tall gentleman dressed in a silver doublet, black cape and hose ambling arm in arm with a pretty señorita. Any onlooker would see the señorita, dressed in a red silk dress, and think she had once come from a fine family. Only closer inspection of the dirty hem of her dress and the frayed lacework around the neckline would betray her current station. And, of course, the brown cap pulled down over her eyes, was further confirmation of her social descent.

She seemed to need to support the gentleman who, any passerby would presume, had been drinking all night. The gentleman stumbled as he lowered his head to say something that made the señorita's face light up with laughter. The jollity would have appeared a little false to a close listener. But deception would not have been unexpected, given the assumed business relationship between the two.

'I hope Rodrigo and Gabriel remain unnoticed,' Alejandro said to Isabel.

She responded with a laugh, and Alejandro pretended to stumble again.

'It was a clever plan of yours to travel to the cathedral separately,' he muttered.

She laughed again and whispered, 'Let's hope it's successful.'

Isaac's head throbs, as though blood were pounding through his body and drowning his mind. He and Father Gutiérrez stride away from Triana as fast as possible whilst trying not to draw attention. Isaac knows he is close to finding the children, but Alejandro has beaten them to it. Again, he wonders just how far he can trust Alejandro. Fernan's parents tried to reassure him about the plan for Rodrigo and Gabriel to take a separate route to the cathedral from Alejandro and Isabel.

If only I had stayed at the cathedral things would have been so much easier. But he could say that about so many of his decisions. If only he had honestly renounced Judaism, if only he had informed on Juan, if only he had got his family to safety sooner. And what if he has misjudged Alejandro? Is he an agent of the Inquisition? Was he at that very moment delivering Isabel to Torquemada? The questions continue to make his head pound with anxiety.

Father Gutiérrez looks across at him. 'Fretting won't help.'

Isaac responds by increasing his pace.

· · ·

Isabel and Alejandro were nearing the *calle* leading to the Triana crossing of the Puente de Barcas when Isabel noticed two men staring at them. Their clothes were so dirty it was impossible to make out their original colour. One was taller than even Alejandro, wore a brown hat and a dagger sheathed at his belt. The other was stocky, with a crop of unruly red hair and held a large club tipped with gleaming metal spikes. Isabel tugged at Alejandro's arm and walked faster. The two men moved agilely to block their access to the bridge and stood before them.

Alejandro drew himself to his full height, looked at the men and placed his right hand on the hilt of his rapier. The two men did not move, did not react. Alejandro shepherded Isabel behind him. Simultaneously, the taller one took the large, curved dagger from his belt and his red-haired friend raised the club to head height with graceful ease. Alejandro unsheathed his rapier halfway.

'There's no need for that,' said the tall one, 'is there, Roja?'

'No, indeed there ain't, Señor Ramos,' Roja mocked.

'Then stand aside,' replied Alejandro.

'We will, once you pay the tax,' said Roja.

'Gentlemen, I'm sure we can come to some arrangement,' Alejandro said.

'Gentlemen is it?' sneered Ramos. They both laughed exaggeratedly and moved a step closer. 'The "arrangement" is this,' Ramos continued, 'listen well as we'll only ask the once.'

They both lowered their weapons, Alejandro supposed this was meant as a conciliatory gesture.

'You leave the little señorita with us, and you are free to go about your business. Seems like a fair deal, don't it, Roja?'

Roja nodded.

Alejandro looked thoughtful, as though he were giving the proposal genuine consideration. 'Gentlemen, I will give you one hundred *maravedies* as your tax, and that's an end of it.'

The two *ladrones* exchanged a glance and Alejandro thought that maybe his offer would satisfy them. But Roja shook his head and the two of them advanced quickly. Alejandro unsheathed the rapier, pointed its narrow tip at them and planted his right foot behind him.

'She must be a real goer, for you not to want to part company with her,' Ramos chuckled.

'Run, Isabel, just run,' Alejandro shouted. She made a break to her left, towards the *calle* leading to the bridge but Roja cut her off. Isabel retreated to stand behind Alejandro. Ramos and Roja circled them, brandishing their weapons, taunting them to make a move. Alejandro noticed a small crowd had gathered. They were chatting, pointing and laughing.

Roja swung the club lazily and Alejandro took a step back, but Ramos moved swiftly to grab Isabel. Alejandro swung his sword towards Ramos and nicked him on the upper arm. Blood seeped through his shirt sleeve, but Ramos did not seem to notice. Blade pointed in one hand, he held Isabel's neck in the crook of his other arm and dragged her backwards to a safe distance, her heels catching on the cobbles. He held her in front of him and tightened his grip on her neck. Roja swung the club again to keep Alejandro at bay. Isabel screamed, some in the crowd laughed.

'Now what?' Ramos taunted as Roja stood his ground, preventing Alejandro from advancing.

Alejandro considered his options. None of them appealed, all of them ended with at least one of them dead.

Then he saw Isabel reach inside her dress and something metallic flashed through the air. Ramos cried out in anguish, staggered backwards, forced to release Isabel. She let out a loud scream, lunged forwards and flashed the dagger across Roja's stomach before he had time to complete the swing of his club. He slumped onto his knees, dropping his weapon and looked up at the advancing Alejandro.

'Isabel?' Alejandro shouted and she replied with a nod. Alejandro saw Roja reaching for the club and slashed the rapier across the top of his arm. Roja fell slowly forward, his face smashing into the cobbles. A pool of deep crimson formed a ring around his head. The crowd started a slow hand clap. Alejandro walked towards Ramos who was scuttling backwards whilst clutching at the gaping wound in his leg.

'That *puta* stabbed me,' he screeched. Alejandro pointed the blade at the *ladrone's* throat. Ramos was breathing hard and he held up a palm and shook his head.

'No Alejandro, please, it's enough,' Isabel called out, 'let's just go.'

The crowd's clapping reached a crescendo as they chanted, 'Finish him, finish him, finish him.'

Alejandro glanced over at them, hesitant. He placed the tip of his rapier on Ramos' chest and turned to look into Isabel's pleading eyes. He pushed the blade a little deeper into Ramos' chest who screamed in pain. The crowd cheered. Alejandro looked into his eyes, sheathed the rapier, drew Isabel to him and they disappeared into the *calle*, accompanied by the booing and hissing of the crowd.

CHAPTER
THIRTY-SIX

S *eville*

ISAAC LOOKS at his two sleeping children, he can just make out their shapes in the gloomy candlelight. They are turned on their sides, away from each other. They are so still; he cannot even tell whether they are breathing. He never wants to close his eyes again. When he believed he had lost them too, it felt like something had been torn from his chest. He cannot let that happen again, he cannot not fail to protect his children, whatever the cost, whatever the challenge. Reaching down, he tousles Gabriel's golden locks, kneels closer, kissing him tenderly on the brow. Gabriel turns in his sleep and mutters, 'Mama.' Isaac whispers, 'shh, shh, my dear.' Isabel sleeps with her knees pulled close to her chest. She has always done this. He recalls gently straightening her legs when she was sleeping, but always finding her in this foetal position in the morning.

They are at the cathedral, in Father Gutiérrez' chambers, adjoining the sacristy. There are two rooms, a bedchamber and a sitting room. A soft murmur of voices comes from the sitting room. He supposes that Rodrigo, Alejandro and the priest are considering what has happened, plotting what to do next. Were they *plotting*? Isaac is surprised he has even considered the word. Surely it was only a plot if you were thinking of committing evil? No, they were not plotting, they were planning. But what exactly? Isaac feels a painful twinge in his back as he moves quietly away from the bed. Yes, he is definitely getting old. Carefully closing the bedchamber door, he goes to join his fellow planners.

The three of them sit leaning forward, heads close together, muttering. Isaac watches. He has moved so quietly that they are unaware of his presence. He feels a sudden surge of warmth in his chest. Is it love? No, it is love's close ally: friendship. This is a startling realisation. Isaac has no time to reflect on it as Alejandro raises his head and beckons him to join them. They make space for him to draw up a chair, and the four of them sit in a circle. This reminds him of another circle of friends, a circle that would never be closed again. Isaac sits straight in the high-backed chair, fingers interlaced on his lap, waiting.

'Your thoughts Isaac?' Father Gutiérrez asks.

'I'd be interested to hear yours, all of yours,' Isaac replies, looking at each of them.

Rodrigo bows his head. Perhaps he feels at a social disadvantage and is wary of contributing as an equal? But he has lost a son; that gives him every right to take a full part in what is to come.

Alejandro putters his lips, exhaling noisily.

Father Gutiérrez raises his eyes heavenward, tapping his first finger on his lips.

Isaac smiles and asks, 'Am I really that difficult to talk to?'

Alejandro laughs and Rodrigo risks a nervous glance at Isaac.

'This is all very fraternal, but we are wasting time,' Father Gutiérrez says. 'It is simple, Isaac,' he continues, 'you cannot stay here after tonight. Then we believe you have four choices. Firstly, claiming sanctuary in the cathedral offers only brief respite. Torquemada will claim the Inquisition is carrying out God's Will, and that he has the authority to enter the cathedral and arrest you, and the children. I may escape punishment, but Alejandro and Rodrigo will certainly not.'

Silence appears to show the group's agreement, so the priest carries on. 'Secondly, you can try to escape Seville and seek passage to Portugal, or even the Indies. This means permanent exile.' He pauses, waiting for his words to sink in. 'Your third choice is to give yourself up to Torquemada, appeal for mercy and for the lives of Gabriel and Isabel.'

Alejandro shifts in his chair and Rodrigo emits a dry cough.

Father Gutiérrez continues, 'If you take this course of action you will be executed, whether or not you recant. Then the children will be placed in Torquemada's care.' He looks at each of them in turn and they return his gaze. He stands up and declares, 'Or you can try appealing to an even higher authority.'

'By which you mean The Almighty, Father?' Isaac asks.

'No, Isaac, I do not. Prayer provides solace and perspective, but I do not believe The Almighty tells us how to act.

We have our judgment and our free will to do as our conscience dictates.'

'You mean I should consult His Majesty?'

'Well, *that* is your fourth choice. His Majesty still has much power, if he chooses to exert it. He is sympathetic towards you, even more so after Maria's passing. I can arrange for you to meet His Majesty.' He looks at Isaac with a stern expression. 'However, he is pragmatic and will expect that you have something to offer him, at the very least a well laid out plan. Only you can decide whether the meeting is the right choice. You have already lost much, you must choose the path most likely to protect those that you love,' Father Gutiérrez concludes.

Isaac looks at Alejandro and Rodrigo who both nod. 'Well then,' Isaac says, 'please make the arrangements, Father.'

CHAPTER
THIRTY-SEVEN
THE TESTIMONY OF FRIAR ALONSO

T riana, *Castillo de San Jorge*

FERNAN'S MOTHER did not survive the water cure. Brother Tomás led it himself, and in his haste and fury, pushed too far, too fast, yet again. I realise that I did not even know her name, God rest her soul. Brother Tomás did not appear unsettled by her death. Although the next steps on the path may be unclear to him, he is still firmly focused on the final destination, when all heretics will recant or be purged. I admire him for this fixity of purpose. He appears completely untroubled by doubt, no matter how many lives are lost in order to save souls. There is a purity to this, I suppose.

He has gone to the Real Alcazar to seek audience with His Majesty. Queen Isabella has gone to Cadiz to take the sea air for a few days. Brother Tomás instructed me to remain at the *castillo* to co-ordinate the search for Fernan's father. I should, at least, find out *his* name.

BROTHER TOMÁS RETURNED from the Alcazar an hour ago and went to his chambers, not even asking me about the search for Fernan's father. I have dared not seek admittance to his chamber. There is shouting and the sound of furniture being thrown from his chamber. Perhaps His Majesty had not even granted him an audience?

When Brother Tomás emerged you might have thought nothing was amiss. He was calm and controlled, though the steel in his eyes seemed to flash even more brightly. He informed me that he was travelling to Cadiz to meet with Her Majesty and would return the following day. This would be an arduous journey as it would require hard riding to travel there in just one day. He would have to travel through the night. This seemed like a reckless move. At first, I didn't understand, and was on the point of saying so when I realised his absence might be advantageous.

It perplexes me why he has not instructed me to put all our efforts into finding Señor Alvarez and the children. Believing it wise to hold my tongue on these matters, I asked him instead if we might keep Catalina in a cell for the next few days to recover before further questioning. I reminded him that she had, after all, been of use and might have more information. He agreed in a dismissive manner, as though she were no longer of any consequence.

After Brother Tomás departed, I sat in my cell and considered what was really happening. If the King had not agreed to see him then Brother Tomás could not be sure whether or not Isaac's family still enjoyed his protection. His Majesty was caught between his allegiances to his Queen, The Almighty, and his love for the city. It made the King unpredictable. Brother Tomás was going to appeal to a higher authority, or so he believed. He will be absent for at least two days. I have to use the time wisely to think and then act decisively.

I owe you an apology. This testimony represents not one, but two dangers: of it being discovered, but also of my currently fevered mind exaggerating and distorting what I choose to record. I need you to believe my testimony is the absolute truth. It will be my only legacy. I have regretfully concluded that I need to take a sojourn from recording my thoughts. With the grace of The Almighty I shall return and report to you with full honesty the resolution to all of these matters.

You have my solemn promise that I will spare no one, not least myself.

THIRTY-EIGHT

S eville

ISAAC WADES through ankle deep water. He hopes it is only water. He tries to ignore the acrid smell and focus on the pain in his lower back. The underground passage had been constructed for much smaller men. It is impossible to avoid the moisture from the ceiling that drips onto his bare head. Father Gutiérrez is shorter and leads the way with ease. The torch he holds in front of him gives sufficient light to see the next step, but the remainder of the passage remains in total obscurity.

Isaac gives thanks it is less than a five-minute trudge through the passage that connects the cathedral to the Real Alcazar. They accessed it through a small door in the catacombs and they will emerge at the rear of the royal chapel in the Alcazar. The passage is principally used by Father Gutiérrez when he visits to hear the King's confession.

Protocol dictates that Ferdinand visit Torquemada for confession but he does so only occasionally. It is to Father Gutiérrez that King Ferdinand turns to for real spiritual guidance.

Father Gutiérrez stops and places his first finger on his lips. He swings the torch down and then slowly up to show Isaac the five steps that lead to a small wooden door. The priest ascends, takes out a key from his surplice and places it in the lock. Isaac expects to hear a creak as the lock turns but there is no sound. The priest pushes the door open. Isaac feels a gentle breeze and takes a deep breath of fresher air.

Stooping through the doorway, he gratefully raises his head to be greeted by a row of moulded angel faces. They are in the King's private chapel. Beneath the angels he sees the painting of Mary and the baby Jesus which forms the centrepiece of the altar. They, in turn, are looking down on King Ferdinand who is on his knees, head bowed, hands clasped in prayer. Father Gutiérrez makes the sign of the cross; Isaac bows his head.

The King finishes his whispered prayers, rises and turns to face them. If he is surprised to see Isaac, he does not show it. Father Gutiérrez advances, holds a hushed conversation with the monarch and leaves the chapel. Ferdinand folds his arms and stares, expressionless, at Isaac.

He does not know how to begin, cannot find the right words to request what he has come for. He remembers the last occasion he had been in a church and feels ashamed again of how badly he behaved. He looks at the painting of the Madonna and the child. Mary's face lit by a beautiful smile as she looks down at the baby she cradles so carefully. Isaac lets his head sink towards his chest and sobs.

The King strides the five paces between them, takes

Isaac gently by the forearm and leads him to sit down on the wooden bench in front of the altar. He waits for Isaac to compose himself before speaking. 'I think I know most of what has gone on, there is no need to tell me the story. I am sorry you have lost Maria, I really am ... but Isaac, what do you expect me to do? I'm merely a King.'

Isaac takes a deep breath, raises his head, being careful not to look at the face of the Madonna, and says with as confident a voice as he can manage, 'Your majesty, this madness all started with Fernan's murder. I believe Torquemada used his murder and the claim of Jewish pagan practice as a pretext to bring the Holy Office to Seville, against your wishes. I think I know who committed the murder, and if I can bring you the proof, we can stop this madness.'

He pauses and looks for some sign of acknowledgement in the King's face, but he remains impassive. Isaac takes another deep breath and continues, 'I only need a few days to prove, beyond any doubt, that what I believe is the truth. That's all I need your protection for, Your Majesty.'

Ferdinand reaches out a hand and places it on Isaac's right shoulder. 'It's taken you a long time to accept that this is the only solution.'

Isaac bows his head.

'I do not think anything can stop this madness. Torquemada's malice has stained my beloved Seville so very deeply,' the King says, his voice almost breaking.

Isaac briefly places his palm over Ferdinand's hand.

'But if there is a small chance that we can tip the scales towards some sort of greater sanity, then I am willing to take it,' the King says, 'but I can only give you my protection until the Queen returns from Cadiz. In two days.'

'It will be enough, I will make sure of it, I promise,' Isaac says looking directly into the King's eyes.

BOOK III

April, 1495

CHAPTER
THIRTY-NINE

S *eville*

AFTER THE MEETING with His Majesty, Isaac and Father Gutiérrez trudge back through the underground passageway. Isaac clutches the King's warrant. He handles documents every day, whether prosaic contracts or the sacred texts of his true faith. But he believes these scrolls are the most precious he has ever held. The signed warrant grants, "Señor Isaac Camarino Alvarez and his family the full protection of King Ferdinand II of Aragon." It further states that, "Any person who prevents Isaac Camarino Alvarez, or his associates, from conducting their lawful business will be answerable to King Ferdinand II of Aragon."

They have the time Isaac requested, now they must make the most of it. He needs to find out exactly what happened to Fernan on the night he was murdered. The Inquisition has not bothered to investigate the events properly. Torquemada and Alonso do not appear concerned about the facts, only how the murder serves their purposes. If he is to convince the King, and especially the Queen, he knows that he will need hard proof. Preferably a confession.

To enforce the warrant, the King has assigned, Paco, his chief of guards to them. He is short, surly and uncommunicative. Isaac believes that he does not relish the task, probably considering it beneath him. It is clear His Majesty regards Paco highly. Isaac is grateful to the King for assigning one of the most well regarded of his retinue. However, he does not look particularly strong and Isaac cannot judge how intelligent he might be. But no matter, it is not his brain or his strength they need, mainly his presence.

When the three of them arrive at the cathedral, Isaac tells Rodrigo, Alejandro and the children the result of his conversation with the King. Gabriel's face shines with excitement when he sees Paco. Isabel listens intently. Isaac sends Alejandro and Paco to fetch Señora Beatriz from her home and bring her to the safety of the cathedral. He wants to question her about the last night of Fernan's life. At their first meeting she was too upset to provide any information and Isaac had been too embarrassed to ask.

Isaac believes that Alejandro is safe with Paco, especially as they have the second copy of the warrant Isaac had the foresight to ask the King to sign. As they leave for Triana Isabel asks, 'What can I do, Papa?' She is anxious to be of use.

'My dear, if you could look after Gabriel in Father Gutiérrez' chambers,' Isaac replies.

She answers by narrowing her eyes at him. But then she takes Gabriel by the hand and leaves. Isaac hopes this is a sign of her increasing maturity. *But really what else did she think she was going to do?*

Isaac asks Rodrigo to accompany him to the sacristy, and places two high-backed chairs directly across from one other. He sits and indicates with his outstretched palm for Rodrigo to take the other. Rodrigo hesitates, Isaac assumes out of a sense of propriety. Isaac smiles up at him and Rodrigo sits down.

'Time presses in on us Rodrigo. I have to ask you about the night your son died.'

'He was murdered.'

Isaac bows his head, waiting for permission.

'Go on, señor. I know you must.'

'Just tell me what you can remember, please, Rodrigo. Not just about the night itself but all the events leading up to it. Spare no detail, even if you think it's not important.'

Rodrigo clasps his hands together, takes a deep breath, and begins, 'Fernan had a beautiful voice, loved to sing. He heard the sugar sellers cryin' out and copied 'em. And he used to sing with his mother. She loved it.'

Isaac counsels himself to remain patient; the man needs to tell the story in his own time, and in his own way.

'One day, must've been shortly after Christmas, one of the fine señoras from Seville that come to Triana sometimes from the Church to bring food and clothes hears Fernan singing in the street. It might've even been your wife?' Rodrigo's voice lifts, as though happy at the possibility.

Isaac forces a smile, nodding encouragingly.

'Anyways, she says to my Beatriz that the boy has a fine voice and should join the choir at the cathedral. We was so pleased, 'specially Beatriz.'

Isaac smiles again, this time with more sincerity.

'So, he went every Wednesday evening after dinner.

Normally, Beatriz would take him, listen to the choir and bring him home. She loved it, but it did keep her from the laundry work. She bent my ear something awful with how beautiful it all was and how I should come at least one time. I always said yes. But I never did.'

Isaac forces himself to be still and quiet.

'The last few times Beatriz told me that one of the men at the cathedral took a real shine to Fernan. Kept on at her about how beautiful his voice was. Fernan seemed to like him too. A few weeks ago he said he'd be happy to walk Fernan home after practice so Beatriz didn't need to wait. She was torn, we need the few *maravedies* that doing the laundry work brought in. And with me being away so much Beatriz thought it wouldn't do any harm for the boy to have a bit of male company once in a while. And he was a part of the church, after all.'

Isaac's dry cough fills the silence.

'So,' continues Rodrigo, 'the bloke did it for a couple of weeks with no problem. But then the third week, that was the night ...' He rubs his palms together.

'But,' Isaac hesitates, 'but, why didn't you tell anyone about this? Why didn't you tell anyone the name of this person?'

'But we did!'

'Who?'

'Those *inquisidores* from the Holy Office who came to question us. We did tell 'em, we did, 'onest to God we did. We thought they would take care of it, investigate and like. They told us, on pain of death, not to tell anyone else. We trusted 'em to find out the truth, but that man is still free. We don't want to cause any trouble in case we end up in the *castillo*, ... like your lady wife, señor.' He hangs his head.

Isaac pats Rodrigo's knee. 'I believe you Rodrigo. But

the time to be too afraid to act is over. God knows that I've taken time to find my courage. Now you must tell me the name of the person from the Holy Office that you spoke to.'

Rodrigo looks up, digs his teeth into his upper lip and heaves a deep sigh.

CHAPTER
FORTY

*S*eville

ISAAC KNOWS the man Rodrigo names. He remembers the part he played in Juan's capture. He thinks he can recall what he looks like. He knows the most likely place to find him.

Bar Averno has not changed since his last visit with Alejandro. This surprises Isaac, so much else in his life has. Still dimly lit, even at midday on a bright spring morning. Black wooden beams overhang the dark corners, tendrils of pipe smoke curl into the air. It is unbearably noisy, full of braying male voices. Excitement is in the air as Semana Santa will be celebrated this week, and much of the talk is of preparing the *pasos* for the processions.

He takes a seat in the corner next to the grubby front window. This gives him as good as view as is possible over both the entire room and the front entrance. He beckons the barmaid, who recognises him with a smile.

'Nice to see you back, señor. Been a few weeks. You was last in here with that handsome gentleman, Señor Alejandro?' She beams at him, inviting conversation.

Ordinarily, Isaac would dismiss her with a grunt and an order for a mug of wine. He gives her his biggest smile and replies, 'I've been busy with one thing and another. I'm glad to be back now.'

She looks around the bar and gives him a quizzical look.

Isaac realises his clumsiness. 'Yes,' he continues, 'bring me a mug of red wine. And tell me,' he pauses, 'do you know the nightwatchman at the cathedral?'

'What if I do?'

Isaac fishes in his pocket and pushes twenty *maravedies* across the table. The barmaid looks down at the coins and then out of the window, fists on hips. He adds another twenty and she quickly scoops them up.

'What do you want to know?'

'What time of day does Cristobal Arias normally come in?'

ISAAC'S HEAD jerks back at the sound of church bells. He wipes away a thin stream of drool from his chin. He rubs his eyes and tries to look out of the window which is even dirtier than he thought. He realises it is not just dirt. The sun is setting, and the bells are ringing for Vespers. He has been asleep for most of the afternoon. He catches the eye of the barmaid and asks her whether Cristobal has been in whilst he was asleep. She says he has not. He tells her to bring him wine and bread, he is suddenly very hungry.

As the barmaid returns with the food, the door is flung

open and a large man blocks out most of the remaining twilight. He waits, as if expecting recognition of his presence. Receiving none he slams the door closed and advances towards the bar. The barmaid sets Isaac's wine and bread down and then looks over at the large man. She palms the fifty *maravedies* Isaac has left on the table.

Now what? Isaac has not planned further ahead than this moment. He chews the salty, crusty bread with a grunt of appreciation, takes a swallow of wine, and stands up. He goes over to the bar and places himself next to Cristobal Arias who stands alone, waiting for his mug of wine.

'Good evening to you, sir. Do I have the pleasure of speaking with Cristobal Arias?' Isaac thinks his excessively polite tone a clever ploy to put the nightwatchman at ease.

Cristobal turns his head and looks into Isaac's eyes. This is unusual for Isaac as there are few men in Seville as tall as him. But this fellow is also broad, and powerfully built. *Perhaps I should have thought this through a little more carefully.*

'If you are, what of it?' Cristobal grunts.

'I need to have a word with you about certain ... certain recent events.'

The nightwatchman turns his entire body to face Isaac and looks him up and down. He studies his face intently, expectantly.

Isaac, unnerved, realises what is expected. 'I am Señor Isaac Camarino Alvarez,' he declares loudly with an assertiveness he does not feel. And then, as if waking from his stupor, he remembers his advantage. He leans forward and says quietly, 'and I am here on King Ferdinand's business.'

The nightwatchman's eyes widen and he leans one arm on the bar, as if for support. The whole of Bar Averno is silent, and Isaac feels as though everyone is watching them. With one motion, Cristobal levers himself up from the bar and with his other arm shoves Isaac backwards onto the sawdust strewn floor. He bolts through the door, slamming it closed behind him.

Isaac pulls himself up and makes to follow but finds himself once again sprawled on the floor. He accepts the hand that reaches down to help him up and hears a polite apology and stifled laugher. He turns to look at them all, as deliberately and as calmly as he can manage. A loud cough breaks the silence. Conversations restart, wine mugs clink and laughter fills the room. But nobody meets his eye. He makes to leave, knowing Cristobal will be long gone. As he puts out a hand to push open the heavy wooden door the image of Juan careering towards him threatens to unravel his calmness. Isaac walks out into the night.

CHAPTER
FORTY-ONE

saac watches as Alejandro clasps Rodrigo's shoulder. It is nearing midnight at the end of the first day of the King's protection. Rodrigo's knees give way and Alejandro helps him sit in a pew. They are in the main body of the cathedral. Alejandro is telling Rodrigo the news he has already hurriedly given to Isaac after his return from Bar Averno – Beatriz is dead. Rodrigo pushes Alejandro gently away and kneels down to pray.

'Thank you, Alejandro; I don't think I could have managed it,' says Isaac.

'I know, I know,' Alejandro pauses, and then says hesitantly, 'A neighbour told me it happened whilst Beatriz was being questioned by "Tomás Torquemada himself." As though such notoriety should make it easier to bear.'

'Questioning?' sneers Isaac. 'Is that how we hide evil now? In semantics? 'We have no time to dwell on these matters. Grief will have to wait its turn.'

Alejandro nods.

'Let me tell you what happened to me today.' As Isaac

recounts the tale of his meeting with Cristobal Arias he notes Alejandro battling to stop himself from smiling. 'And then the bastards just laughed,' concludes Isaac.

Alejandro put a finger to his lips and glances at Rodrigo. Then he muffles a laugh with his palm.

Isaac shakes his head but allows himself a small smile. 'Listen very carefully, this is what we have to do now.'

THE CHAMBER's stone floor is pooled with fetid water and the air is so still Isaac struggles to catch his breath. Arias is tied to a chair in the centre of the room, the light from the torches in the sconces flickering across his impassive features. His cries are muffled by a dirty muslin cloth that stops his mouth. Isaac stands in front of him, flanked by Rodrigo to his left and Alejandro to the right. Isaac glances behind Arias to the wooden table laden with eight earthenware jugs of water. Paco stands guard at the door.

Thank God for Paco. Without him they would not have been able to subdue Arias. Father Gutiérrez told them where he thought the nightwatchman lived. Isaac decided to accost Arias at his house after the embarrassment at the bar. He'd believed he could discuss matters with Arias in a civilised manner. He would not make that mistake again, there was too much at stake. Paco and Alejandro found the fool and used the cover of night to bring him through the *calles* to a chamber in the catacombs under the cathedral. Isaac wonders why Arias had not left Seville after the incident at the bar. Stupidity? Or was he arrogant enough to believe he was protected? If so, exactly who was protecting him?

'Cristobal, shall we continue our conversation?' Isaac

says, pulling the dirty rag out of the nightwatchman's mouth. 'As I told you before we are on the King's business. All we need is your account of what happened on the night that this man's son, Fernan, was murdered,' Isaac indicates Rodrigo.

'King's business? Devil's more like,' Arias says.

'We have a warrant, signed by His Majesty,' Isaac responds.

Arias snorts and spits at Isaac's feet. 'If it's really King Ferdinand's business why do it at night in the catacombs?'

'Enough of this,' Rodrigo mutters, taking a pace forward and backhanding Arias across the right side of his face. The force of it swings his head to the left where it meets Alejandro's fist with a crack. The blows echo off the walls of the chamber. Arias winces and bows his head. Rodrigo growls and draws back his fist.

'Stop,' shouts Isaac, 'there is no need for this. Is there, Cristobal?'

Rodrigo grabs Arias' shirt, but stays his fist, poised to strike.

The nightwatchman looks up, livid red marks on both cheeks, a deep cut appearing on the left, 'You'll all be in hell before I tell you anything.'

Rodrigo smashes his fist down on the bridge of Arias' nose. Blood erupts, spattering Isaac's shirt. Arias' head sinks to his chest. Isaac steps forward, and pulls Rodrigo away, pushing him towards Paco, who restrains him firmly.

Isaac bends over, his face level with Arias' and whispers, 'There really is no need for this, please, we need not do it this way,' glancing once more at the water jugs.

Arias raises his head, growls and spits into Isaac's face. Isaac punches him as hard as he can in the stomach. He turns and walks over to Rodrigo, nodding at him as he leaves the chamber. Isaac hears the splintering of wood as the chair crashes back onto the floor. Then Arias' muffled screams as the muslin cloth is replaced in his mouth, and next the scraping of earthenware on wood as a heavy water jug is lifted off the table. Isaac is completely calm.

FORTY-TWO

Night has begun to take hold as they leave the cathedral. Isaac leads the way, lantern aloft, Alejandro, Isabel and Paco struggling to keep pace. The bright crescent moon bathes the plaza in a soft, silvery shimmer. Their footsteps percuss the cobbles, echoes reverberate around the unnaturally empty plaza. Isaac hopes it was the right decision to leave Gabriel in Rodrigo's care. He consoles himself with the thought that who could be more trusted to look after Gabriel than one who knew the deep anguish of losing their own son?

'It won't remain this quiet for very long,' Alejandro calls out.

Isaac does not respond, does not break stride. They are heading for the Inquisitions' headquarters at the Castillo de San Jorge; a walk that would have normally been completed easily before the lantern was extinguished. But tonight was Jueves Santo, and the processions are making their way from the neighbourhood churches to congregate at the cathedral. Isaac knows they have to make it to the Puente de Barcas quickly, or the crowds of penitents following the *pasos* will trap them.

A few years ago, Isaac had been one of the *nazareno*. He had taken part shortly after his decision to convert to Catholicism. Dressed in a long purple robe, wearing a tall pointed black, satin hat, he held a candle aloft and walked alongside a float bearing an elaborately decorated statue of the crucified Christ. He found himself almost overwhelmed by the noise, the sickly smell of the incense and the proximity of so many people. He had never repeated the experience.

As the candle in Isaac's lantern begins to sputter, the breeze carries a steady drumbeat and the faint phrases of the beautifully wrought *saetas* sung as the *pasos* pass by. Just a few *calles* away. 'Hurry, we must hurry,' Isaac says breaking into a run. He takes a left turn, believing it to be a short cut to the bridge across the Guadalquivir. They are confronted by the dying form of Jesus Christ, his prostrate body covered in scarlet blood, cradled by the figures of his mother, Mary Magdalene, and Joanna and Susanna. The *pasos* move agonisingly slowly towards them, borne aloft on the necks of the *costaleros,* shuffling along, hidden from view under the curtain surrounding the platform. Isaac turns back on himself, so sharply that he almost runs into Isabel, Alejandro and Paco. He pushes past them trying to return the way they have come, only to be confronted by the Virgin Mary. They are trapped.

Paco finds his voice, 'Out of the way please, business of the King,' he booms. The phantom like *nazarenos* slowly move to one side, muttering indignantly as Isaac, Alejandro and lastly Isabel, push their way through in Paco's wake. Isaac feels the heat from the torches that the penitents grudgingly hold aloft. Finally, they emerge at the river crossing to Triana. Isaac turns around, exchanging grim smiles with Alejandro, and calls out for Isabel. She is not there.

Isaac frets about the decision to send Alejandro and Paco on to the *castillo*, leaving him to search for Isabel alone. But without Paco to enforce the warrant they would not be admitted to the Inquisition's headquarters and could not detain the person they needed to. In any case it is too late now.

Isaac presses on through the crowds as they close back in, absorbing and swallowing him. He calls Isabel's name as loudly as he can but the pulse of the drums, the keening *saeta's* and the chanted prayers all muffle his increasingly desperate cries. He is swept along by the crowd pushing him ever nearer to the cathedral. Isaac feels as though he has been drawn out by the tide but is now being washed back in. The *nazareno's* torches bathe the walls in shades of fiery orange, distorting and elongating the shadows of their hooded figures.

Isaac senses a movement ahead of him that is out of keeping with the natural rhythm of the crowd. He strains to see what he believes he felt. He thinks he sees one of the hooded *nazarenos* turn back to look at him, whilst all the rest face forward. The penitent seems to be dragging something, or someone behind him. Isaac pushes harder against the bodies surrounding him, forcing a path through them, barking, 'King's business, stand aside, King's business.'

The procession bursts out of the *calle* and Isaac is spewed out of the crowd and into the wide plaza in front of the cathedral. He is disoriented by the dull chorus of thudding drums and the sweet smell of incense as the processions spill out from the *calles* funneling them towards the cathedral. The walls of the plaza take on the blazing orange glow from the penitents' torches.

He sees the lone *nazareno* pulling Isabel along behind him as she screams for help. He is dragging her across the plaza, heading for the entrance to La Giralda. The other penitents ignore them, entirely focused on reciting their prayers, reaching the cathedral and making the return journey to their church. Isaac draws his rapier and runs.

RODRIGO WATCHED Gabriel's chest rise and fall, rise and fall. The hypnotic quality reminded him of the swinging of the *incensario* in the cathedral. It brought a measure of calmness. He sits on the bed in Father Gutiérrez' chambers watching the boy sleep. He feels no guilt for what he had done to Arias, his only thought being, 'the bastard deserved it'.

He was glad that the nightwatchman would never be able to harm another child. Rodrigo had no sympathy for his excuse that, 'somebody else made me do it.' He believed in, "an eye for an eye," no matter what Jesus said about turning the other cheek. He felt he could walk the world with less shame now that he had avenged Fernan's death. But no measure of justice would bring his son back. This thought was accompanied by a loud groan as grief threatened to overwhelm him.

Gabriel stirred at the sound and mumbled, 'Papa?'

Rodrigo bent over and stroked the boy's hair, the touch causing him to awake fully. He sat up and rubbed a palm against his eyes. 'It's me, Señor Rodrigo. Remember, your Papa's gone out on business.'

'On the King's business?' Gabriel yawned.

Rodrigo couldn't help laughing as he said, 'Yes, that's right young master, on His Majesty's business.'

Gabriel turned to look at him and said, 'Do I remind you of him?'

Rodrigo looked away and stared at the floor. The boy reached over, put his hand of top of Rodrigo's and patted it. 'I liked the soldiers I played with at your house. Did you make them for Fernan? Will you make some for me? Will you, please?'

Rodrigo raised his eyes and said, 'Yes my boy, I will.'

Gabriel rewarded him with a grin and Rodrigo felt his heart warm.

'WOAH, not so fast there, Señor Camarino Alvarez,' says a tall man who suddenly steps in front of Isaac as he runs across the plaza. He is momentarily stunned, the man seeming to materialise out of the very air. Over the man's left shoulder he sees Isabel disappearing as the *nazareno* approaches the door to La Giralda. He makes to move around the apparition. But the man draws his rapier and bars Isaac's way. He sees the long, jagged scar that runs down the right side of his face. Isaac has seen that scar before.

The man sees Isaac staring at his scar and smiles. 'Think you know me?' He pauses, delighting in Isaac's confusion. 'I wonder where it could have been? Perhaps at court, as you're so fond of telling everyone you're on the King's business.' He laughs. 'No? Then where else might it have been?'

As the man mockingly strokes his chin, Isaac takes a step forward, draws his rapier and slashes it with all his strength at the man's sword hand. He screams as his sword clatters to the ground. His severed right-hand dangles at the wrist, blood spews and collects between the cobbles at his feet. He sinks to his knees, the screams now howls.

Isaac takes a handful of the man's hair and wrenches his head back, exposing the neck. 'I know who you are now. You're the dead man who gave Juan de Mota to the Inquisition,' he whispers, as he draws the blade of the rapier across the man's throat.

CHAPTER
FORTY-THREE

I sabel tried to focus on the cold stone wall at her back and the cool breeze on her face. She tried to block out the pain in her arm caused by the *nazareno* dragging her up to the bell tower. After ascending a set of stone steps to arrive at the balcony atop La Giralda Isabel ran to the furthest corner. Opposite stood the *nazareno*, blocking any opportunity for her to escape.

A crescent moon hung low in the sky, its light suffusing the platform with a pale, silver glow. The sound of slowly receding drumbeats drifting up on the breeze returned her to the present. She risked a quick glance over the edge of the balustrade, down into the darkening plaza, and could just make out the *pasos* returning to their neighbourhood churches. Isabel looked for her father. She thought she had heard him shouting her name as she was pulled through the crowds and across the plaza.

She glanced back to see the *nazareno*, purple cloak glistening softly in the moonlight, his palms turned upwards, stretched out towards her as though trying to soothe her. He slowly reached up with his right hand and pulled off the tall, satin hood by its pointed end. Isabel gasped and put her hands to her mouth. She wanted to scream, to say something, anything, but felt as though she were choking.

Alonso dropped the hood to the wooden floor and walked slowly towards her, palms still outstretched. Isabel tried to shrink further into the corner. She wanted to close her eyes and make it all go away. A fragment of the song her mother used to sing to lull Gabriel to sleep returned to haunt her, 'Mama loves you, Papa loves you, we both love you very much.' She looked again over the edge, into the chasm of the now completely dark plaza.

Isaac's fists are sore from pounding on the door at the base of La Giralda. The *nazareno* must have dropped the wooden beam across the door, locking it from the inside. Isaac takes a few steps back, looks up and listens. He hears only the diminishing sound of the drumbeats as the *pasos* leave the plaza. Hurrying around to the side of the tower that faces the Guadalquivir, he strains his eyes for footholds in its sheer walls. He notices a small opening at about twice his height; it is just big enough to fit through. Then he realises the foolishness of attempting to climb up to even that point. Had he been twenty years younger, it would still have been futile. *Sometimes desperation makes fools of us all.*

He turns at the sound of his name being called across the plaza. Paco and Alejandro are trotting towards him. 'Where is the suspect?' Isaac calls out. Receiving no response, he strides towards them. 'What happened?'

Alejandro explains that the warrant had gained them access to the *castillo* but the person they had gone to arrest was not there. Nobody could, or would, tell them where he was; even the royal warrant was not sufficient inducement.

Isaac explains the predicament and his foolish idea to climb up to the opening. Paco looks around the plaza and says, 'Wait for me.'

'I NEED YOU TO UNDERSTAND,' Alonso said, 'you of all people, my child.'

Isabel stared at him and shook her head.

'You have lost so much, been so mistreated. You have lost your mother and suffered the unwanted attentions of one who should have known better.'

Isabel gasped and said, 'Why have you brought me here?'

'I did not intend to. I joined the *nazarenos* to take part in their act of penitence. And then quite by chance I saw you. You have such a kind face, the face of an angel. I just wanted to explain myself to you. I thought that if we had time alone, together, I could make you understand.'

Isabel did not know how to respond, so she waited. Something she had learnt from her father; patience can lead to revelation.

'I did not intend for innocents to be hurt. I am truly sorry.' He dropped to his knees, interlaced his fingers and gently shook his hands at her, begging forgiveness. 'The Moors had a saying from their holy book that the murderer of one innocent will be judged by The Almighty as though he had murdered all of mankind. I fear that to be the truth.'

'Why do you claim so much guilt, so much responsibility for all of this?' Isabel found her voice, emboldened by the prelate's contrition. 'You are merely the Grand Inquisitor's deputy.'

At this characterisation Alonso flashed his eyes at her and Isabel saw a glint of steel in them. Then his shoulders sagged. 'I may be just Brother Tomás' deputy but this is all my fault; it is my responsibility. If I had been less arrogant, only the guilty, only the heretics, would have received their due punishment.' He bowed his head. 'I should have prayed harder and listened more attentively to The Almighty's guidance.' He slapped each side of his face rhythmically, muttering, 'Mea culpa, mea culpa, mea culpa.'

Isabel took a pace forward and drew herself to her full height. 'Stop that and tell me everything,' she said.

'Will you hear my confession?' Alonso asked.

What blasphemy is this? But she was intrigued, and she agreed. If this was a way to find out the truth, then so be it.

In faltering tones he told her. As he finished unburdening himself Isabel became aware of movement from the stairs.

ISAAC AND ALEJANDRO push the now unbarred door wide open. Paco stands the other side, grinning. 'I used one of the stone mason's wooden ladders they leave lying around so carelessly,' he says. 'I climbed and then pulled it up behind me.'

Isaac clasps Paco's shoulder, 'Thank God that one of us is still thinking clearly.' The three of them draw their swords and begin a rapid ascent. Alejandro striding ahead, Paco following easily and Isaac doing his best to keep up. They quickly pass the point where Paco had gained entrance to the tower, the wooden steps still angled against the wall.

Isaac resists the temptation to call out for Isabel, to tell her they are coming. The element of surprise is their only advantage. They slow as they ascend the steep, stone steps at the height of the tower and Isaac takes the lead. He reaches the top and cautiously raises his head over the edge of the final stair. He is so astonished by what he sees that he can do no more than watch, as though it were a vision.

Isabel is standing in front of the kneeling Alonso, his head bowed in concentration. Isaac hears him say, 'I am sorry for these and all the sins of my past life.'

ISABEL WAS CONFOUNDED by what she heard. Torquemada's right-hand man was confessing to her. It must be blasphemy. Then she remembered her mother and all the other poor souls who had unjustly died. *Was that not ungodly too?* At that thought she felt a powerful surge run through her. She made the sign of the cross and intoned, 'I absolve you and declare you absolved of thy sins in the name of the Father, and of the Son and of The Holy Ghost.'

He looked up at her, palms touching, fingers pointing upwards, praying. Isabel moved to one side barring Alonso's view of her father. She looked over him, shook her head and put a finger to her lips. She bent down, put a hand on Alonso's shoulder and whispered in his ear.

Alonso made the sign of the cross. He stood up, looked at Isabel and muttered, 'Bless you my child.' Alonso appeared to notice a noise, glanced behind him and saw Isaac advancing, rapier drawn. His eyes darted around, searching for an escape. Isaac and Paco spread out, Alejandro behind them. Alonso glanced at Isabel, turned and began to run towards the balustrade. Isaac saw him as a blur of silvery purple, luminous by the light of the moon. He felt something pass closely by his ear, and then watched as Alonso fell heavily, clutching at the back of his thigh as dark, crimson blood pooled in rivulets on the floor.

FORTY-FOUR

'How are you feeling now?' Isaac asks as Isabel enters the roof terrace at Casa de la Felicidad. Gabriel has just been to kiss him goodnight and Catalina is putting him to bed. She is still weak from interrogation but has insisted that she return to work. Isaac has been enjoying his first few moments of solitude since yesterday's events at La Giralda.

Isabel grips the iron railing edging the terrace and peers over. Isaac is reminded of the image of Alonso making for the balustrade of La Giralda. What would have happened if Alejandro had not stopped him with such an accurate throw of his dagger? Isaac, Paco and Alejandro carried Alonso back to the Torre and Torquemada's safe keeping. But not before Torquemada had agreed to Isaac's demand that Catalina be released. The royal warrant seemed to sway Torquemada to clemency. Isaac did not inform the Grand Inquisitor of Alonso's confession. This was valuable information and he doubted Alonso would readily tell Torquemada. It had been a dangerous gamble, but with one of the King's personal bodyguards at his side, it was a risk Isaac felt worth taking.

Isabel looks at the sun setting over the Guadalquivir. Isaac can just make out the fading outline of the *castillo* behind her. The sky's last traces of azure are shading into the black of night, and moonlight is already glistening over the river's surface. The swallows swoop and chatter, enjoying the last of the daylight. It is a calm, peaceful transition from day to night. Qualities Isaac hopes they will all feel again.

Isabel turns and says, 'I wish I knew Papa.'

'Come and sit with me, drink a glass of sherry, just a very small one, and enjoy the last of the sunset. We don't have to talk.'

'I want to talk, but I don't know how to begin.'

Isaac looks at her over steepled fingers. 'You can begin by sitting down, drinking some of this fine manzanilla, and perhaps the words will come.'

Isabel does as she is asked. After the first tentative, warming sip she takes a deep breath. 'You haven't asked me anything about yesterday.'

'I knew you would tell me in your own time. And that you would have questions for me too. Let *me* begin then.' Isaac tells her how he had found out about Arias and what the nightwatchman had told them of Alonso. He spares her the details of exactly how they made him talk. Isaac notes that she does not appear surprised when he tells her that Alonso had commissioned Arias to murder Fernan. At the point in his story where he, Paco and Alejandro are standing at the top of La Giralda he says, 'That is just about everything I know, my dear.' He refills his glass and looks away, out into the night. 'What I can't quite work out is why Arias agreed to murder a child. I suspect we will never know.'

Isabel puts her sherry glass down on the table. 'Father Alonso ... he told me that he was sorry he grabbed me, that he had not planned it. He felt an overwhelming sense of guilt he thought could be assuaged by taking part in the *paso* as a *nazareno*,' she says. 'He said that when he saw me he was possessed by a sudden compulsion to confess to somebody who would understand.' She closed her eyes and pursed her lips. 'Why did he think *I* would understand him?'

Isaac remains silent, knowing that now Isabel has begun, she must be allowed to continue in her own way.

'He told me he was sorry for what happened to Mama and for ... the other things that had happened to me. Begging for my forgiveness, he said that absolution from an innocent would help him in the afterlife.'

'I suppose that makes some kind of sense. But I'm not sure that it is worthwhile trying to understand the actions of a madman.'

'Do you really think that's what he is?'

'I think the whole Kingdom is gripped by some form of insanity. But there's a peculiar quality to Alonso's actions that I cannot fathom. We know little of him, of his past, of what events may have made him. And I don't really think we should waste our time trying to understand; we have other priorities.'

Isabel looks out across the river and seems to consider this. She stands, smooths her dress and turns to leave.

'I do have one question,' Isaac says softly.

She stops but does not turn to look at him.

'What did you whisper to Alonso?'

She returns to the railing, places both hands on the

cooling metal and says into the night, 'He asked for my forgiveness. I gave it to him. I suggested to him that if he was really sorry, there was only one course of action he could take to show just how penitent he was.'

Isaac struggles to keep his voice even as he asks, 'And do you believe he was about to carry out what you advised him to?'

Isabel turns, crosses over to him, kisses him lightly on the cheek and says, 'Goodnight Papa.'

THE NEXT MORNING Isaac awakes long before the children, the sun only just reappearing. He wants to walk before attending the summons he has received to meet with the Their Majesties. Hurriedly eating a crust of rye bread he leaves Casa de la Felicidad.

There is enough time to take the long route to the Alcazar. He will walk to the Torre del Orro then along the river and wind back up through the *calles* of Barrio Santa Cruz. It will give him time to think, to try and make sense of the last few days and prepare himself for an audience with Their Majesties. He has to decide how much of the story they need to know, how much he really knows himself and what he can prove. It all might depend on who is present at the audience.

Summer is most certainly close now. Reaching the Torre he begins to feel uncomfortably warm. The sun rises very quickly at this time of the year. It is already above the houses in Triana, on the opposite side of the river. He turns to his right and follows the dusty path. The shallow river is on his left, bright sunlight already shimmering on its still, glassy surface. That stillness will not last for very much longer. By the time he reaches the crossing to Triana, the tide will be coming in rapidly and the river beginning to fill with barques and large ships setting sail and returning from long voyages. He wonders which one he most resembles? Is he just setting out on a long journey or is he about to complete one?

This thought reminds him that he should ask the King whether he still has an official position at the Real Alcazar. Though he is not sure he really wants one. But what else would he do with his time? He cannot stay at home with Isabel and Gabriel all day. Maria managed the house and the children's education admirably. He is not well suited to either; he does not have the patience.

Isabel. *What on earth is he going to do about Isabel?* He thinks about last night's conversation. What had she meant when she said that Alonso had apologised for, 'the other things,' that had happened to her? He could, of course, simply ask her, but he fears the answer. Was Alonso referring to the time they spent with Torquemada? Did Catalina know? Should he ask her? Too many questions, and the one person he could rely on for guidance is gone. Feeling a pain in his chest, he stops to rest.

He turns into the Barrio Santa Cruz and finds his way to the disused synagogue. The sun has not yet found the dark *calle* in which it is situated. He touches the still cool walls and whispers, 'May His great name be exalted and sanctified in the world in which he created according to His Will. May He establish His Kingdom and may His salvation blossom and His anointed be near.' Maria had been his real salvation.

FORTY-FIVE

Isaac taps his foot impatiently on the mosaic floor as he waits in the anteroom for admittance to the King's chambers. Finally, a courtier approaches and beckons him. Isaac follows and enters the throne room. He has never seen it before; his previous meetings with His Majesty were usually in more informal settings.

The Queen and the King sit on golden thrones, raised on a dais reached by five steps covered in thick red carpet. On the wall behind them are two full-figure portraits of Their Majesties. The Queen's is centrally positioned and almost twice the size of her husband's. Beside the portraits, to their right, stands a large wooden crucifix with a full figure of Christ. His head hangs to one side, blood dripping from his crown of thorns. The sculptor has given him an angry look, and Isaac wonders whether that is appropriate.

Torquemada stands on the dais to the Queen's left, arms folded beneath his cassock. Behind them stands a courtier guarding a closed door. Paco stands to attention on the King's right. Isaac glances at him. Paco's nod is almost imperceptible. Torquemada's thin lips part in the feint impression of a smile. Isaac ignores it, approaches the dais, bows and says, 'Good morning Your Majesties.'

'Señor Alvarez,' replies the King. The Queen inclines her head in his direction.

'What you have now discovered in the course of your investigation into the boy's murder' the King enquires.

Isaac looks down, in an effort to compose himself. He had hoped Torquemada would not be present. How much of the truth should he tell? He hears the Queen cough. Torquemada bends down and whispers in her ear. There is only one choice.

'Your Majesties.' He glances at Torquemada. 'I know who commissioned the murder of the boy, Fernan, and who carried out the heinous deed. What I am unsure of is exactly why it occurred, though I am able to speculate with sufficient confidence.'

'Ask him to get on with it, for pity's sake,' the Queen hisses at her husband.

'Apprise us of the facts, Señor Alvarez,' the King says.

'Friar Alonso de Hojeda suborned Cristobal Arias, the nightwatchman at the cathedral, to murder Fernan. I am unclear what inducements or promises were offered,' he says, peering at Torquemada. 'Friar Alonso then propagated the lie that a gang of Jews committed the murder. The blood libel.'

The silence that follows seems interminable to Isaac. He holds Torquemada's gaze.

'Why do you believe Friar Alonso did this?' the King finally asks.

Isaac glances at the Queen, who is impassive, and continues, 'I believe Friar Alonso thought that by doing so, he could persuade Your Majesties to open a Holy Office for the Propagation of the Faith in Seville.'

The Queen beckons Torquemada with a forefinger. He bends to listen. Isaac cannot not hear what is said. Torquemada straightens. Is that sweat on his forehead?

'And exactly what proof do you have of this tale?' The Queen enquires.

'Your Majesty, we have the testimony of Cristobal Arias and Father Alonso's confession. And you have my word.'

The Queen snorts. 'How was this nightwatchman's testimony obtained?' she demands. 'And who heard Father Alonso's confession?'

'Cristobal Arias' testimony was obtained during questioning by myself and my associates. A member of the King's Guard,' he gestures towards Paco, 'was also there, as you are aware, Your Majesty,' he nods towards the King.

'And these *associates* are?' the Queen asks, her left eyebrow raised.

'My trusted deputy, Señor Alejandro de Cervantes, and Señor Rodrigo Duarte.'

Isaac watches as Torquemada whispers once more into the Queen's ear. 'This Rodrigo is Fernan's father?' she asks.

Isaac nods.

'And who heard Father Alonso's confession?'

'Isabel, my daughter.'

The Queen struggles to suppress her laughter. She looks over at her husband who glares grimly down at Isaac.

'The boys' father and your deputy will swear an oath, before the Almighty, that what you say is the truth?' The King asks.

'Yes, Your Majesty.'

'And your daughter, who has so recently suffered the regrettable loss of her mother, has ... all of her faculties?'

'Yes, Your Majesty. I have no doubt she is telling the truth. I witnessed Friar Alonso's confession. Though I could not hear everything, it was undoubtedly a confession. And I believe my daughter absolutely.'

'Why on earth would a Friar confess to a mere girl?' The Queen asks.

'I have thought about that too. It is, after all, blasphemous. But my speculations got me no nearer the truth. Perhaps it would be best to ask Friar Alonso himself, Your Majesty?'

'Bring him in,' the Queen indicates with an upturned palm to the courtier standing outside the door behind Torquemada. The courtier exits and returns, leading a limping figure. Alonso shambles across the dais and stands beside Torquemada, who moves one pace to his left, staring resolutely at the back wall of the chamber. Alonso looks around but does not meet Isaac's eye. The courtier gently pushes him towards the centre of the chamber. He drags himself down the five steps and stands beside Isaac, facing the King and the Queen.

'Father Alonso,' the Queen begins, 'you have been listening to Señor Alvarez's ... *story*.' She waits until Alonso agrees. 'Are we to believe that this preposterous tale could possibly be the truth?'

Alonso looks up at the Queen, then to the King, and then over at Torquemada, who glares back. Then his eyes alight upon the figure of Jesus on the crucifix. He stares, as if transfixed. The silence extends for so long that Isaac is about to say something to Alonso when the Queen barks, 'Well?'

'Your Majesty ... I mean Your Majesties ... Brother Tomás ...' He sinks to his knees, palms together, and rocks back and forth, muttering something. Isaac leans forward and hears Alonso repeat, 'Mea culpa, mea culpa, mea culpa.' He falls forward, prostrating himself, and Isaac hears the Pater

Noster prayer, 'Forgive us our trespasses, as we forgive those who trespass against us. And lead us not into temptation; but deliver us from evil. For thine is the Kingdom, the power and the glory, for ever and ever. Amen. Amen. Amen.' Isaac joins in sotto voce with the final, 'Amen.'

Queen Isabella inclines her head at the courtier who helps Alonso to his feet and leads him out of the chamber. She waves Isaac away with the back of her hand and another courtier escorts him to the rear of the chamber. The royal couple turn to each other and confer animatedly. Torquemada tries to join the conversation but is signalled to move away by the King. He steps down from the dais and stares at Isaac. The royal conversation becomes heated, both voices are raised. The King turns to Paco and he approaches. It appears to Isaac that the Queen is questioning him in detail. She tightens her lips and narrows her eyes.

'You may approach,' the Queen barks at Isaac. When he once more stands before them, she begins, 'We,' she glances at her husband, 'have decided that your report is most probably the truth.'

Isaac exhales.

'Friar Alonso was not in possession of all his faculties. The murder was the result of his diseased mind, and it was his responsibility alone.'

She turns and gives a faint smile in Torquemada's direction.

'The purported murderer of the boy is dead. The boy's father will receive five-hundred ducats of blood money in full compensation for his loss. But, Señor Alvarez, your version of the story will not leave this chamber. The Jews killed the boy,' she pauses, continuing to stare at Isaac.

He bows his head slightly, and she continues, 'Father

Tomás, this matter is now closed. You will not propagate or pursue the matter any further, is that understood?'

Torquemada hesitates, opens his mouth as though to speak, but then thinks better of it. He bows and whispers, 'Yes, Your Majesty.'

'Father Tomás, as for Alonso, we will talk privately of his future,' she raises an expectant eyebrow and Torquemada bows again. The Queen, her features immobile, rises and leaves the chamber through the door behind the dais.

An expectant hush follows the Queen's departure; it creates a void that they all wait to be filled.

The King draws himself up to sit squarely on his throne. 'Isaac, I have need of an adviser to join my court. I wish to keep a close eye on the trade with the Indies, and your knowledge of this will, I am sure, prove invaluable. You will begin almost immediately in that position. However, I expect you to take a day or two to spend time with your family and settle your affairs. I also expect you to ensure that from this point onwards your domestic situation will not interfere with the conduct of your duties. This may require a period of reflection on your part.'

Isaac is motionless until he remembers what to do. He bows deeply and mumbles, 'Of course, Your Majesty. Thank you. I would, of course, be delighted.'

'I will expect you to work with Father Tomás and his four new associates closely,' the King continues. At the mention of his name Torquemada turns to look at the monarch, who does not meet his eyes. 'Her Majesty and I have exchanged correspondence with His Holiness Pope Sixtus,' Torquemada's eyes widen, 'regarding the work of the Inquisition.'

The King pauses, Torquemada continues to stare.

'He shares our ... concerns about the recent work of the

Holy Office in Spain. He has appointed four new deputy Inquisitors to help the Grand Inquisitor with his work. I am sure that is very good news for you Father Tomás? It will lighten your load, especially with the loss of Friar Alonso.'

Torquemada hesitates and is about to say something, but appears to think better of it and bows his head towards the King.

Isaac wonders about the King's use of the word "loss". He feels some pity for Alonso. But it is only fleeting. He stands tall, looks at the King and bows once more. As he raises his head Paco smiles at him. He turns and leaves the chamber.

CHAPTER
FORTY-SIX

T*he family estate, Pozzoblanco, May 1495*

ISAAC FEELS the back of his shirt becoming damp with sweat as he sits on the porch in Pozzoblanco. Thankfully, the sun is almost hidden behind the distant hills, outlining the summits in a deep red. Isaac is relieved as the heat begins to go out of the day. This feeling will be short lived as he knows the insects will soon be bothersome.

They had arrived the evening before, completing the two-hour ride from Seville in the cool of the early evening. Rodrigo, Catalina and Gabriel had ridden ahead in one carriage and Isaac, Isabel and Alejandro behind in another. It had been a dusty, exhausting journey as the carriages rattled over the rutted track. Isaac was surprised when Gabriel wanted to ride ahead. He knew that his son had grown close to Rodrigo since the night he had taken care of him at the cathedral. It was hardly a surprise that Rodrigo would reciprocate. Isaac was thankful for both their sakes.

He can just make out Catalina's rough tones, no doubt telling Rodrigo what to do. They are inside the house preparing dinner. Rodrigo is attempting to help her, but it sounds like he is mainly getting in her way. He thinks he hears her call him, 'An old fool.' Catalina's way of showing affection can be a little opaque. Alejandro and Gabriel are at the river where Isaac and Juan used to swim. They had asked Isaac to join them, but he prefers to enjoy a quiet sunset. And he is not sure he is ready to return to the river just yet. He is afraid that he will be overwhelmed by memory.

A warm breeze stirs and brings with it the faint tones of chanting voices. Isaac leans forward in his chair and strains to discern the words. He makes out his son's still high-pitched voice – that will change soon enough. The breeze drifts away, bearing the chant with it. Then a file of three figures emerges from behind the bank of earth that hides the path leading to the river. The sun dips below the hills behind them and, for a moment, Gabriel, Isabel and Alejandro are etched as dark silhouettes.

Gabriel runs towards him shouting, 'Papa, Papa, Papa.'

Isaac stands up, wondering what is wrong. Gabriel runs into his arms and Isaac asks, 'What is it, what is it?'

'Nothing Papa.' He looks up at his father quizzically. 'I'm just happy to see you!'

Isaac exhales and hugs his boy tightly. 'What was that I could hear you chanting just now?'

Gabriel grins and says, 'Hotter than hell, hotter than hell.'

How long has it been since he heard that phrase? So

much has happened, so much has been lost. Gabriel chants it louder and louder until Isabel arrives and tells him to stop. Alejandro is just behind and slumps onto the wooden bench next to her. Isaac smiles at Isabel, who returns a weary grimace. 'Catalina,' he calls out, 'jugs of water please.'

'I hope we will be celebrating with more than just jugs of water,' Alejandro says.

Isabel flashes Isaac a small smile. Alejandro begins to say something, but Isaac cuts across him, 'No, you are right Alejandro. We do have much to celebrate.'

Catalina arrives and sets the earthenware jugs on the table with four mugs. 'Dinner will be ready by sundown so will you all please wash up.'

ISAAC STANDS on the porch savouring a small glass of *manzanilla*. Dinner was highly satisfactory. Catalina roasted the hare Rodrigo caught that morning to perfection. Isaac looks up at the full moon, its silver glow tinged with feint hues of orange from the recently departed sun. The image sparks the memory of the night at La Giralda when he thought he had lost Isabel too. He feels her hand on his shoulder and moves his palm to cover it, stroking it fondly. She moves round to stand beside him.

'It's so beautiful here,' Isabel says. 'So still and calm and simple.'

Isaac lets the moment linger, feeling its balm.

'But I couldn't live here, it would drive me quite insane.'

'Of course not, my dear. That realisation is entirely the point of enjoying a restful time in such a place.'

She places her head on his shoulder.

He takes a sip of sherry. 'I can see that you are enjoying Alejandro's company.'

'Papa, please, don't spoil it.'

'He's a fine young man who has shown his true worth to us. I value him very highly.'

Isabel lifts her head. 'Papa, there is something I need to say to you. Something that perhaps I should have told you before, but I wanted to wait for the right moment.'

Isaac continues to look up at the moon and takes another sip of sherry.

'When I tell you, I hope you realise why I waited until some time had passed.'

Isaac is curious and nods encouragingly.

'Just before she passed away, when we were with Torquemada, Mama wrote a letter to me. It explained why she felt we must escape and leave her alone. She believed it was the only way to take Torquemada's power from him.'

'Power over what, over who?'

Isabel stares out into the night. 'Over me.'

Isaac is not entirely surprised. He has thought of the possibility over the last few weeks, whilst trying to understand why Maria sacrificed herself. He puts an arm around his daughter's waist, pulling him to her and kissing the top of her head.

Isabel wipes the tears from her eyes, takes a deep breath and says, 'But that's not the most important thing Mama wrote in her letter. She asked me to tell you something.'

Isabel moves away from him, takes both his hands in hers and gently pulls him round to face her.

She closes her eyes in concentration and begins. 'Isaac, I love you very, very much but I don't believe I have any other choice. The children are most important, they are the best of us. I will wait patiently for you to join me. There is no need to hurry, my love, you have work to finish and Gabriel and Isabel need you. We will have all of eternity together.'

Isabel opens her eyes and brushes away her father's tears.

EPILOGUE

THE TESTIMONY OF ALONSO DE HOJEDA

A board the *Santa Maria de Guia,*
somewhere in the Atlantic,
June 1495

AFTER THE FIRST WEEK, when I couldn't eat a thing and vomited several times a day, I've begun to quite enjoy being on board a ship. The tang of the salty sea air in your nostrils can be rather bracing, and when the sea is calm, the gentle swaying of the ship is quite soothing. There is a routine to my days that acts as a balm for my troubled soul. Between receiving the confessions of the sailors (and hearing some quite shocking admissions, which I am certainly not going to set down here) I have adequate time for prayer, study and reflection. I now realise how difficult it was to carry out all my duties in Seville and meet Father Tomás' high standards. Cristoforo Colombo has yet to attend confession, but I am sure he will find the time, sooner or later.

Sufficient time for prayer and deep reflection make it easier for me to understand that I must record my deeds unequivocally. What I did cannot be easily forgiven, and I need to make my full confession available after my death, through these pages. It was fortunate that Brother Tomás did not think it necessary to search my cell and allowed me to bring all my belongings. He seemed to be in quite a hurry to be rid of me. I don't blame him for that. I only regret that my actions caused so much harm to so many innocents. I could not be expected to foresee that. I do not possess the powers of The Almighty after all.

And so, I confess that I suborned Cristobal Arias to commit the murder of a child, of Fernan. I told Cristobal that if he did not agree I could not be responsible for what might happen to him, and his family, once the Holy Office began its operation in Seville. As it surely would. At first, he resisted, but I told him that I had proof he was one of them, a *crypto* and that I would ensure the Holy Office would investigate him. And then I sweetened the pot by promising him, and his family, the full protection of the Holy Office. I ensured Fernan's murder was interpreted by Brother Tomás, and by Her Majesty, as having been committed by the Jews, and that it was propagated as such. The so called "blood libel".

That is the full horror of my sinful actions. I would like to think you are surprised, that you would not believe me capable of this. My actions were not evil. I had the absolute best of intentions. I am not a murderer. It was imperative that Seville, of all places, was cleansed by the Inquisition. We could no longer tolerate the King's protection of the city. We must remember we are bound by a higher duty. We could not let Seville harbour the *marranos* and *cryptos* any longer. It was shameful, and an affront to The Almighty.

I took it upon myself to act, as I knew Brother Tomás would not approve. I wanted him to be able to deny it, if it ever came to light. He might have deemed it an unworthy act of treachery. He has such an admirable purity of vision. And when I think of the greater good, the hundreds, perhaps thousands, of souls we saved that are now ensured a place in heaven then I believe the sacrifice of Fernan was worth that. I would like to believe his parents would agree with me, their grief having diminished with the passing of time, that they would be able to see that the death of their son was truly meaningful. They should believe that his sacrifice was worthwhile. They could find comfort in that.

Perhaps in the fullness of time, if The Almighty should permit me to return to Seville, I will seek them out and discuss it with them. I suppose that I will still need to seek their forgiveness.

And one other person has occupied my thoughts. Andreas keeps returning to me. In my dreams we are once more young noviciates, carrying out our duties. I can still picture him that first day and hear his mockingly deep voice crying out, 'Brother are you here to save me?' The way he imitated Father Bartolome's manner still makes me smile. I know that it shouldn't. I'll never know what happened to Andreas, but I know my love for him still exists. With his good nature and open heart, he will have found satisfaction in whatever the Good Lord chose to provide for him. I miss him every day, and that feeling grows stronger the further from Spain we travel.

Once I have fully atoned and felt the cleansing balm of The Almighty's forgiveness, I will return to the business of saving more souls. After all, Brother Tomás and I were very efficient at it. And now I can look forward to the splendid opportunity to save the souls of the savages in the Indies. This must have been The Almighty's purpose for me all along. Though, I trust that some of the crasser methods

Brother Tomás employed in Seville will not be as necessary in the Indies. I'm sure the natives possess an innocence that will make them more immediately receptive to the word of the Lord.

Despite what I may fervently wish, I shall have to accept that I may never see Seville again. But what an adventure awaits me! The Almighty's plans are a great mystery to us all, but his wisdom and knowledge are infinite and indisputable. Of this, I have no doubt. Absolutely no doubt.

Thank you for reading *Blood Libel*. If you enjoyed it you can:

* Read on for an exclusive extract from Isaac's next adventure, *The Heretic's Daughter*.

* Leave a review: Amazon US Amazon UK

* Write to me. I'd be delighted to hear from you at: michael@michaellynes.com

* Download a free short story:
   www.michaellynes.com

THE HERETIC'S DAUGHTER - AN EXCLUSIVE EXTRACT

P rologue
Seville, Andalusia, 1498

ISAAC YEARNS for a place that no longer exists — Seville before the Inquisition. A place where Torquemada did not call out the names of the heretics to be punished. Where Queen Isabella and King Ferdinand did not watch impassively as executioners smeared a blonde-haired girl's tunic with sulphur — to quicken the journey of the flames from the crackling pyre at her feet. A twisted mercy. Where Isaac did not see white tendrils of smoke, hear shrill screams or smell the bitter stink of charred flesh. Where he did not witness Juan's body melt into the inferno.

The Seville of his dreams is a blur of memory. Sunny afternoons with Juan swimming in the river, sword fighting, and wrestling. Sometimes Maria comes to him and those are the sweetest memories. Overwhelmed by the vision of his wife he pushes her away, returning to play with Juan.

Joy is fleeting and turns to guilt. Why should he be rewarded with visions of the good times? He had not saved his wife, had not defended his best friend. His penance is the sharp thrusts of pain in his chest as the horrors of Juan's execution and Maria's murder flash through his imagination. Each stab reminding him of his oath — *I will make you pay, Torquemada, no matter how long it takes.*

CHAPTER **One**

Abu Ali Sina, the apothecary, began his morning ritual by kneeling to light the nuggets of oud on the incense burner. Crackling and sparking, they released their heavy, woody fragrance. Inhaling the smoke, he stood and stretched his tall, slender frame. The scent always brought Khadijah to mind, and he whispered a prayer for his wife's soul.

He kept the incense burner behind the counter; the Catholics did not appreciate the *Mudéjar's* perfume. He would have ten running all day, but that would be provocative. He could not afford to lose Catholic patrons; there were not enough *Mudéjars* left in Seville to keep his business alive. And there were no Jews left at all. He didn't want to run away to Granada, as so many of his friends had. It was easier to worship Allah there. But he would have to close the shop that had been in his family for five generations. He did not want that guilt.

Surveying the rows of orange and blue earthenware jars filling the tall mahogany shelves behind the counter, he took a mental stocktake. Enough cumin, anise and horehound, but mandrake root was very low. He normally prescribed it to ease stomach-ache, but perhaps its other use as an aphrodisiac was causing the high demand? The large glass jar on the counter was still full of slippery, copper-coloured leeches. Was blood-letting falling out of fashion?

The rasp of the shop door announced the day's first customer. A tall, cloaked figure moved through the deep shadows, disturbing motes of dust. Ali Sina had only lit a few candles; he had to save what little money remained. Besides, nobody usually came in this early.

'Good morning, apothecary,' came a deep growl from the half-light.

'Good morning. You're most welcome, señor.'

The man's wide-brimmed hat hid most of his face. Ali Sina could make out a beard and the glint of perhaps blue eyes. He looked familiar, but the apothecary didn't think he had visited the shop before.

The man wrinkled his nose. 'Couldn't you burn some orange or lavender? Can't stand that Moorish smell.'

'I'm sorry, señor. I rarely have customers this early.'

The man ignored the apology and looked up at the jars. Ali Sina followed his eyes, trying to guess what he was looking for. Perhaps some sage or chamomile to ease his digestion? The man coughed. Ah, a cold?

'I need something for my chest, it's very heavy.' He coughed again, louder this time, as if to emphasise the point.

The apothecary reached for an orange jar decorated with a complex geometric pattern. Setting it down next to the pestle and mortar, he measured a precise quantity of white powder on a brass weighing pan, tipped it into a square of cloth, twisting it closed with twine.

'Put a pinch of this hyssop into a glass of wine twice a day. You will feel better within two or three days.' The apothecary placed the small parcel on the counter.

The man rummaged in the leather pouch hanging from his belt, put twenty *maravedies* on the counter, pocketed the cure, but did not leave.

'Can I help the señor with another remedy?'

'Yes, I would like some arsenic.'

'Some arsenic?'

The man gave a curt nod.

The apothecary hesitated. 'Señor, I'm required by the authorities to enquire for what purpose?'

'Of course, it would be remiss of you not to ask. I need it for vermin.'

Ali Sina held the man's eyes for a few moments. The sun had crept into the shop and he could now definitely see glints of blue glimmer in the man's unblinking, pale eyes.

'We have a problem with rats. It's the only thing that keeps them at bay.' He moved his right hand to cover the grip of the rapier sheathed at his side.

The apothecary pushed a set of wooden steps that ran on wheels to the end of the counter. Climbing to the top, he reached for one of the highest jars. It was covered in a blue leaf design, a beautiful container for such a vile substance. Placing it on the counter, he cautiously removed the stopper. There was no scent – arsenic was both odourless and taste-less. The ideal poison. He tipped out a small pyramid of the shiny, silver-grey crystal into the weighing pan. He glanced at the man, who raised his index finger to signal a larger quan-tity. The apothecary doubled the amount; the man nodded. He poured the crystals into a glass vial and stoppered it with wax. The man reached into his leather pouch and placed one hundred *maravedies* on the counter, double what the apothe-cary would have charged. Ali Sina took half of the money and pushed the rest back. The man gave a sardonic grin as he scooped up the coins and returned them to his pouch.

Ali Sina kept hold of the vial.

The man stared at him.

'I will have to insist you sign the register for the arsenic, señor. It is a requirement of the authorities.'

'The authorities?' The man rolled his eyes.

He moved the vial down to his side. With his right hand

he opened a large book, took a quill pen, and wrote the date and the amount of arsenic provided. He held out the pen. The man grabbed it, scrawled a signature, and slammed the register shut. Ali Sina placed the vial in the man's outstretched hand.

'Thank you, apothecary. If the rats prove stubborn, I trust you have plenty more?'

The apothecary narrowed his eyes. 'You already have enough arsenic to kill a hundred rats, señor.'

'Seville is teeming with vermin of all varieties. Some larger than others.' He arched an eyebrow and grinned.

'I have already given you the maximum quantity regulations allow. Señor.'

'Damn the regulations,' said the man as he again touched the grip of his rapier.

'As an apothecary, I have to abide by them. I'm sure you can understand.'

'How is business?' the man said, turning to survey the empty shop.

Ali Sina did not respond.

'You must be the last of your kind left in Seville?'

'If you mean the last apothecary, then yes, I am.'

'All the other Moors have run off to Granada.' He scowled. 'You're very brave to stay.'

'Thank you, señor.'

'Or perhaps, stupid.'

He forced himself to remain silent.

'That front door of yours is not secure. It would be a great shame were anyone to enter while you were asleep and vandalise your fine establishment. Or perhaps even harm your good self.'

Ali Sina tapped the stopper of the jar of arsenic and held

the man's gaze. 'It's been a pleasure to help you this morning, señor. I look forward to your return.'

The man grunted in apparent satisfaction and turned to leave. He ducked under the lintel and left the door ajar behind him. Ali Sina opened the register of poisonous substances. The signature would have been difficult to decipher, even without the ink being smeared by the man closing the book so violently. Was that an A? But why write his real name? At least there was a record of the date and a description of the man in his mind. That might prove useful should a poisoning occur that the authorities investigated. He was sure it was not the last he would see of the stranger. He would need to be prepared. Perhaps Isaac knew the man and could advise the best way to handle the situation. He had many contacts in his position as adviser to King Ferdinand. His old friend would know what to do.

READ on to find out what happens to Isaac and Isabel

Amazon US Amazon UK

AUTHOR'S HISTORICAL NOTE

In the Catholic Kingdoms of late medieval Spain oppressive policies and attitudes forced many Jews to embrace Christianity. These *conversos* were suspected of continuing to practice Judaism in secret. They were labelled 'crypto-Jews', or even worse *marranos*, meaning swine. The religious establishment sought to save the souls of these heretics by persuading them to return to the right path.

Friar Alonso de Hojeda, a Dominican Friar from Seville, convinced Ferdinand II of Aragon and Isabella I of Castile Queen Isabella of the existence of crypto-Judaism in 1478. As a direct consequence the Spanish Inquisition was instituted in 1481 and a royal decree in 1483 expelled the Jews from Spain. Tomás de Torquemada, Queen Isabella's confessor, was appointed as 'Grand Inquisitor of All Spain'. Pope Sixtus assented to the formation of 'The Holy Office of the Propagation of the Faith' as he required continued Spanish military support to defeat the Ottoman Empire.

The Inquisition used torture to elicit confessions and delivered judgment at public ceremonies known as *autos da fe*, 'acts of faith', before they gave their victims over to the

270

secular authorities for punishment. The first *auto da fe* was held in 1481, and in total some thirty-thousand men, women, and children, were condemned to death and burnt alive. Their gruesome fate was intended to set an example to others.

After fifteen years as Spain's Grand Inquisitor, Torquemada died at the monastery of St. Thomas Aquinas in Ávila in 1498. His tomb was allegedly ransacked in 1832, his bones stolen and ritually incinerated in the same manner as at an *auto-da-fé*.[1] The Spanish Inquisition was not finally abolished until 1834. The decree expelling the Jews from Spain was only formally rescinded by the Spanish government in 1968.

This is a work of fiction. Although the narrative has an historical foundation some dates and events have been conflated or amended to fit the dictates of the story. For example, the Inquisition was operating in Seville much earlier than I've indicated and Friar Alonso's early life has been fictionalised. If the book inspires you to research the period, I found the following texts to be useful starting points:

- Fletcher, Richard. *Moorish Spain*, Phoenix, 2001
- Green, Toby. *Inquisition: The Reign of Fear*, Pan Books, 2008.
- Karabell, Zachary. *People of the Book*, John Murray, 2007.
- Lowney, Chris. *A Vanished World*, OUP, 2005.
- Menocal, Maria Rosa. *Ornament of the World*, Little Brown and Company, 2002
- Rubin, Nancy. *Isabella of Castile*, St Martins, 1991.
- Ruiz, Teofilo Z. *Spanish Society 1400-1600*, Routledge, 2001.

- Schama, Simon. *Belonging: The Story of the Jews, 1492 – 1900*, Bodley Head, 2017.
- Thompson, Augustine, O.P. *Dominican Brothers, Conversi, Lay and Cooperator Friars,* New Priory Press, 2017

1.Murphy, Cullen (17 January 2012). God's Jury: The Inquisition and the Making of the Modern World. Houghton Mifflin Harcourt. p. 352

ACKNOWLEDGMENTS

This series was inspired by a trip to Seville in 2013; in particular, the passion and expertise of Moisés Hassán-Amsélem. He also very kindly read the manuscript and provided expert commentary on the historical aspects. Any mistakes are entirely my responsibility, as are any deviations from historical fact.

It took much longer to write *Blood Libel* than I envisaged. It would have taken even longer without the help, advice and support of fellow writers and my family. In particular, Paul Kingsnorth's forensic insight on the early manuscript was crucial. Louise Walters provided expert editing. Purnia Shah, Gillian Duff and Sarah Clayton gave feedback and encouragement that made this a better book. All self-published authors need someone like my son, Adam, to give invaluable technical advice and support.

Thank you to all of you.

ABOUT THE AUTHOR

Blood Libel is Michael's prize-winning debut and the first full-length Isaac Alvarez mystery. He is originally from London, but currently lives with his family in Dubai.

www.michaellynes.com